Sandy Black
and the
7 Giants

JULIAN MIMS

www.TrueVinePublishing.org

Sandy Black and the 7 Giants
Julian Mims

Published by True Vine Publishing Co. LLC
810 Dominican Dr. Ste. 103
Nashville, TN 37228
www.TrueVinePublishing.org

ISBN: 978-1-956469-51-6 Paperback
ISBN: 978-1-956469-52-3 eBook

Copyright © 2022 by Julian Mims

Printed in the United States of America—First Printing

Acknowledgments

This adventure would not have been possible without the love and support of family and friends. To Pastor Tony Good, I thank you for your consistent direction and friendship. You, indeed, are my brother-in-arms. To my great friends Vernon and Jill Lynch, I thank you for giving me confidence that this journey was worth finishing. To my Sister Sylvia Mims Goncalves, I thank you for staying the course with your album, which motivated me to finish this book.

Finally, to my brothers Aaron Mims and Anthony Mims, I thank you for your support and listening ear all these years. I would ask what you think of an idea I would have for the story, and you are always there. Finally, to my virtuous wife, Tina Mims, I thank you for encouraging me to finish this race. Being my cheerleader and expressing my excitement outwardly, I felt inward about my story and ideas.

Last but not least to my parents, Ron and Virginia Mims, I am thankful to God that he chose you to be my parents. I would not be who I am today without you. What has made this story possible is what I have gotten from you both. I love you so very much and hope this story represents how you raised us with the ability to dream and the will to fight for those dreams, above all else, the responsibility to take action. Finally, I thank anyone else, friends or family, that has been in my corner. This has been a journey that started December 25th, 2009, and guess what?...We made it, and I hope you enjoy the story.

Table of Contents

Chapter 1
SANDY & MOM

It never dawned on Sandy that the end would come so soon. The monitors beeped eerily in the small Westlake Memorial Hospital room where Sandy sat at her mother's bedside. Lena Goudeau was a stately, attractive woman with long, luxurious black hair, but after several rounds of chemo she was a shell of her former self. Her once curvaceous body now frail and emaciated, her beautiful copper skin now pale and sullen. Every day she wore her favorite black floral silk scarf to hide her hair loss. Even so, one could not deny her beauty with her dazzling hazel eyes, high cheekbones, and radiant smile. Everyone who knew her loved her.

Difficult as it was to watch her mother wasting away before her, Sandy was determined to be her rock as she had been hers, right until the very end. The doctor had said that she had another few years to live, but things suddenly took a turn for the worse and a month later was woefully short of that. While Sandy was lost in thought, Lena woke from her sleep in a fit of coughing, looked at her daughter and smiled weakly. Upon seeing her wake,

Sandy reached out for her mother.

"Mom, please don't go!" seventeen-year-old Sandy cried as she held her mom's skinny hands. "I can't live without you."

Lena's eyes filled with tears as she beamed with pride looking at her daughter, all grown up. It was a difficult road raising her daughter alone, but she had become a fine young woman indeed. She had no doubt that she'd raised her well and that she had taught her everything she needed to survive in this world.

She smiled and spoke slowly, "Sandy, we've always known this day would come. You have a bright future ahead of you, my love. You have always been and will always be a beautiful princess; remember that. And one day, a handsome prince will come and sweep you off your feet. You'll be married and happy."

Sandy sobbed, "But Mom, I want you to be there when I get married. I want to see your smile as I walk down the aisle in my white wedding gown. Please don't leave me!"

With trembling hands Lena reached for Sandy's long black curly hair and stroked it gently. *Such a beautiful child*, she thought. Even with tears streaming down her face, Sandy was an exceptional beauty. Her complexion the smooth, tawny hue of the finest sand, her lips plump and rosy and eyes the color of honey. "Don't cry, baby. I'll always be with you." She looked straight into Sandy's eyes. "I have sent word to your father. He will come to take care of you."

Sandy sniffed and wiped the tears that clouded her eyes. Confused, Sandy asked, "But-but didn't you say my father left us after I was born?"

Her mom paused for a moment then with a deep breath continued, "Sandy, everything I have told you about your father isn't true."

"Mom, what are you saying? I'm lost here!"

"Baby, I lied because I didn't want you to blame me. It's a bit more complicated than it seems."

"How? Tell me, Mom!"

"Your fa—" Ms. Goudeau grabbed Sandy's hand, gasping for air.

"Mom! "Sandy cried in horror.

"He's a... a King," Ms. Goudeau said and went still.

Sandy shook her mother's frail body and erupted in tears. "Mom! Mommy, no!"

Suddenly the alarms went off. Nurses and doctors rushed into the room. Two nurses had to pry Sandy off as she wailed on her mother's chest. This was a nightmare she wished she could wake up from.

That night, Sandy lay sprawled on her bed. Her pillows were soaked, and her throat was raw from crying. The words, "He's a...a King," floated in the air as if a spirit was whispering a song. *Mom's mind must have been messed up. Why did she use "King?" Maybe she wanted to use some other word to describe my father. But who is he?* So many questions raced through her mind but now, there was no one to answer them.

The following week, there was a memorial service for her mother. Sandy greeted her guests on autopilot; it took all her energy to thank them all for their well wishes and listen to them regale her with stories about how amazing her mom was. Sandy held her head high, knowing her mother would expect her to be strong and to remember her as the spirited woman she was.

The following day Sandy sat in her mom's lawyer's office, trying hard to focus as they went through her will. Her eyes were groggy as she hadn't slept well in days.

"Ms. Black?" Mr. Stein called.

Sandy looked up at the small lawyer with the tiny glasses.

"I'm sorry Sir. You were saying?"

"Your mother, Ms. Goudeau, has made all of the arrangements for ownership of her home and all of her assets to be passed to you."

As Mr. Stein droned on, Sandy's mind exited the office and rewound the film of her mother's life.

She saw herself at five-years-old walking back from school with her mom. She saw her mom sitting on the grass in the park while she played hopscotch with other kids squealing with delight as her mom pushed her high on the swing that hung from the large old tree in the front of the house. The same tree she loved to climb and tell all her secrets to, as if it were her best friend.

She fast forwarded to age 14, when she found her mom sitting in the kitchen with tears flowing from her eyes. That was the day her mom told her about the breast cancer. She saw herself dumping her books in her school bag and racing home when the school bell rang to take care of her mom, who she met on the bathroom floor too weak to get up on her own. She saw her mom pushed in a wheelchair by a nurse on her graduation day. She struggled to take pictures that day with her mom without shedding tears. Finally, she saw her mom in the hospital bed, gasping for breath and uttering her final words; "He's a...a King."

"Ms. Black! Is everything ok?"

Sandy snapped back from her memories into the present.

"I'm sorry, Mr. Stein, you were saying my mother took care of everything and the house is mine now."

Mr. Stein looked at Sandy, concerned. "We don't have to do this today, Ms. Black. There is no need to rush - everything is well laid out, and you can take a moment if you need to. I am sorry about your loss. This has got to be a lot to understand and take in."

"It's OK, Mr. Stein. My mother told me she had put things in place for me, we can proceed. What is left for me to do to conclude our business?"

Mr. Stein smiled.

"All that is needed of you now, Ms. Black, is to sign these documents, and I will take care of the rest."

Sandy took the pen Mr. Stein offered her and signed the documents. She placed the pen down and rose to her feet, extending her hand to the lawyer.

"Thank you, Mr. Stein. My mother trusted you to handle her affairs. I thank you so much for all your help."

Mr. Stein rose to his feet and shook her hand.

"It has been my pleasure. Your mother was a wonderful woman; she did everything she could to ensure you were taken care of. Please call me if you need anything."

Sandy felt completely numb, yet she still attempted a smile as she left the office and drove home in her small silver car Prius.

***

A few days later, Sandy sat at home in her mother's favorite chair near the fireplace. She couldn't sleep so she had lain awake all night, dressed in her mother's robe and pearl earrings. Thoughts of recent happenings filled her head. She got up and pulled out a big box that had been kept under her mother's bed, and carried the box to the kitchen. Making herself a cup of coffee, she opened the box which contained photo albums and opened one of them which contained pictures of her when she was two years old. Seeing her mother in the pictures brought tears to her eyes. Suddenly Sandy felt so alone. She had no real friends and no other family, and there was no one she could turn to in her grief. As she picked out another album, someone knocked on the door. She put down her cup of coffee and glanced at the clock. It was 2 a.m. Cautiously, Sandy asked who was at the door.

"I am looking for a Ms. Sandy Black!" an unfamiliar voice said.

Sandy searched for a weapon.

"Who are you and why are you looking for me?"

The man behind the door cleared his throat before speaking again. "I have come on behalf of his majesty, King Enoch Black, to escort you to his palace. He awaits your arrival," the man behind the door said.

Sandy grabbed a bat, and held up her phone while recording. She opened the door, thinking it was a neighbor playing some stupid trick. She then saw a plump man in very strange attire. The man had a long black cape with blue lining, black shiny boots, and brown leather pants. On his pinkie finger was a platinum ring with some sort of symbol.

"Hello; my name is David, and I will accompany you to your father's castle." He bowed.

"You know my father?" Sandy asked, stunned, the bat falling from her hand.

The man's eyes lit up. "Yes, of course I do. He is the King of our land. Everyone knows who he is. And I am David, his chief of servants."

Sandy remembered what her mother said. Why would she say that and why had this random guy David showed up to say the same thing?

"You must mean he owns a company or something like that," Sandy said. David tilted his head, obviously confused.

"I don't know of this company, but your father, the King, is the ruler over everything in his kingdom. We must go soon, my lady, for our window to leave will not be open much longer."

David reached for her hand, but Sandy pulled it away.

"Wait! Wait, I'm not going anywhere with you! For all I know, you could be some crazy person just trying to get me to go away with you."

David appeared shocked. "My lady, I am at a loss for your perception of me; however, I do understand your hesitation. Your father told me you might be a bit resistant. Maybe I will tell you a truth only few would know. Might I tell you that you are a royal princess, and you have a birth mark on the back of your neck shaped like a flower. A rose to be exact; a black rose that looks like this." He held up the ring on his finger with the same rose that was her birthmark.

Sandy knew something was peculiar about this David. The way he had come for her after her mother said her father would come - the timing, everything - seemed uncanny, as if this was supposed to happen. He also knew about the birthmark she always kept covered with her long black hair. She hadn't told anyone about that. Though she should have closed the door and called the police, something felt safe about this David. The more she listened, the more inquisitive she became.

"So how do you know about my birthmark; what is it you really want from me? And what happens if I don't go with you?" Sandy challenged while looking out the door, searching for some form of transportation. She turned off the video on her phone and placed it on the table near the door.

"I don't see a car. How did you get here and how are you taking me anywhere? Are we going to just magically fly away?"

And incredulous Sandy laughed at the idea. David frowned, visibly becoming a little bit frustrated trying to convince Sandy.

"My lady, all who are of the royal bloodline have this mark.

And we must leave soon while it is still night and children are dreaming," David urged, "for once they awake the portal to the kingdom will be closed."

"OK, this is weird. A portal to a different world is only open when little children dream. And my father is the King of this land, right? You must think I'm five!"

Sandy decided that she had heard enough and went back inside. As she attempted to shut the door, David stepped on the threshold and wedged his boot between the door and frame.

"Wait, I can prove this to you!"

Sandy put her hand on her hip and cocked her head to the side. "You have five seconds."

David stepped back and looked up at the sky. He pulled a small golden whistle out and blew it once. Sandy heard a loud flapping of wings and then a whoosh! The rush of wind blew dust in her face but when she wiped the dust away, she gasped when she saw a brilliant blue dragon land in front of her house. Sandy screamed and jumped behind her door.

"Ooh my goodness!" Sandy was floored. In her driveway was the most beautiful and terrifying creature she had ever seen! The dragon stood majestic, taller than all the trees in the neighborhood, its massive wings perched at its side as it waited attuned to its master's command. Its scales, a brilliant iridescent blue, gleamed in the moonlight.

David turned to her and chuckled. He took the hand of a mesmerized Sandy and led her towards the dragon. "This is Ballah, my dragon! Ballah, meet the Princess Royale, Lady Sandy!"

h focused his gaze on Sandy, snorted in approval and gave a noble bow. Curiously, Sandy reached out her hand to the dragon, who leaned into her touch and nuzzled against her hand.

A laugh escaped her lips when she saw how sweet the dragon

14

was! "Hello Ballah! Aren't you handsome?" The dragon closed its eyes and gave a deep rumble, almost a purr in response.

David interjected, "I am sorry to have to speed this along, but like I said, my lady, this should be proof enough. We have to leave… now!"

Sandy nodded in agreement and David took her by the arm and pulled her up onto the saddle. Within seconds the two lifted off into the air to a land unknown.

Chapter 2
A New Beginning

Sandy and David looked down over the city as they flew through the air.

Still amazed over the recent events, Sandy took a deep breath as she gripped David's waistcoat. *I might just be dreaming*! She thought. "Wow," Sandy exclaimed as the wind whipped through her hair. "I feel like Superman!"

David, with his hands on the reins and eyes focused on the journey, leaned back and asked, "Who is this Superman?"

Sandy, remembering that David wasn't from her world, replied, "Ooh, never mind."

They climbed higher and higher when David decided to give Sandy instructions.

"Hold on tight, Princess! And close your eyes."

To Sandy's horror, the dragon abruptly began his descent with a nosedive at almost the speed of light.

Sandy screamed as they fell faster and faster towards the park she used to visit with her mom when she was a kid. Then, right before they could hit the ground, a shining gateway opened pushing them into another world. Sandy glanced back just in time to see the fabric of her world close behind them and the darkness disappear.

It was daytime in the strange world. The blue sky was calm and cloudless. Trees sang and birds talked as they sat on the branches. The air was pure and clean. Sandy suddenly felt light-headed. "David, where are we?"

David smiled. "We are in the land of Moria, Princess, where dreams are real."

"I've seen this in my dreams."

"Of course you have. You were born here."

Sandy chuckled. "That's impossible. I was born in L.A." The words had barely left her lips when a dragon flew by, its scales shimmering brilliantly as it spiraled down to a nearby lake. Straight ahead stood the walls of a great palace. The walls were tall and black and shiny like obsidian made from diamonds that had been forged together by dragon flame. Inlaid jewels of many colors decorated them as they sparkled in the sunlight.

David pointed to the palace. "That's the grand palace of Moria, home to the King, your father." The two landed inside the walls of the palace, near a group of maids and menservants. The men tended to Ballah as David dismounted and helped Sandy to the ground.

"These young ladies are your maidservants. They will tend to your needs and prepare you for dinner with your father."

As the maids took her in, Sandy glanced back at David, clearly uncomfortable.

"Relax, my lady. Everything will be fine."

Sandy nodded. "I'm holding you to that, David."

Sandy followed the women to a grand entrance near the courtyard and went into the palace. The palace was the most luxurious and beautiful place Sandy had ever seen. Precious stones and costly curtains decked the hallways. Everything sparkled, from the high ceilings and archways to the marble floors. Even the paintings and sculptures sparkled! As they turned a bend at the end of a ballroom and entered a grand hall, Sandy stopped suddenly as, right before her in gilded frames, were paintings of herself as a baby and pictures of her mother. Sandy's hand went to her mouth instantly as she stifled a sob. Next to them was a portrait of her mother posing with a rather handsome man. Tears welled up in her eyes as she stared at the picture. "Who is that man in the picture with my mother?" she asked the maids.

"That is your father, my lady. He is King Black."

Sandy stared at the portrait, a smile creeping up on her face. *They seemed so happy together; what happened?*

One of the maids broke the silence, "We really must prepare you for dinner my lady – you must not be late!" The maids ushered Sandy into a great room with a vaulted ceiling and Persian rugs. The bed was wide, with sheets of the finest silk. "This is your room, my lady. My name is Lilly, and I am the head of your maids. If you have any questions, please, ask me."

"Hello Lilly, it's a pleasure to meet you. I'm Sandy." Sandy extended her hand to Lilly for a handshake. Lilly in turn gave a deep curtsey.

"The pleasure is all mine, my lady. It is my honor to serve you."

Sandy furrowed her brow. *"This is going to take some getting used to..."*

"Lilly, when will I see my father?"

"As soon as we get you bathed and dressed, we will take you to see him. The King wants you to be as comfortable as possible."

Sandy clapped excitedly. "Well, let's get on with it."

Sandy was pampered with sweet-smelling oils then submerged in the refreshing waters of Moria's underground pools. Her hair was combed and pressed by the best stylist in all of

Moria. And after the oiling, polishing, and combing, she was given the most exquisite gown she had ever laid eyes on. The dress was a silver, sleek, and form-fitting mermaid dress with a halter-neck, and shoulder sleeves with jeweled cuffs. After her maids helped her into the gown, Sandy could not help but spin around in glee when she caught the image of herself in a floor to ceiling mirror near the boudoir.

Sandy looked at herself in the mirror in utter amazement. *"Holy..."*

Her hair was perfectly curled and cascaded over her shoulders. Gemstones were deftly woven throughout her hair with braids and silver thread in the most elaborate hairstyle she had ever seen. All at once this became real to Sandy. She was about to meet her father for the very first time, and he really was a King!

Lilly led Sandy to a long corridor that led to enormous, wooden, arched double doors and said, "my lady, the dining room is just ahead where the King is waiting for you. I am not permitted to follow, as only kitchen staff are allowed beyond this point. I must take my leave."

As Lilly bowed and prepared to withdraw, in a moment of panic Sandy gripped both of her hands tightly and asked, "Do you think he'll like me; my father?"

Lilly paused and spoke, "My lady, he has already loved you from the day you were born until now. Take heart; all will be well."

Lilly gave a brief half smile and exited the hallway, leaving Sandy alone. Taking a deep breath, she thought, *"It's now or never, girl!"* After taking a moment, Sandy steadied herself and made her way towards the doors.

"Hello, young princess," a voice called. Sandy spun around in the direction of the voice. "It is so nice to see you in person, the pride of my King. He speaks of you and your beauty every day. You look so much like your mother."

"Who are you?" Sandy asked as she moved towards the obscured corridor to see who was speaking.

"I am Queen Mika, the fairest in all the land. I wanted to meet my King's only child."

Emerging from the darkened hall, the beautiful queen stood tall and radiant. Her golden gown, crown and jewels sparkled as she came into the light.

"You are my father's wife!" Sandy paused for a beat, "How do you know my mother?"

"Can't you remember when last you were here? Your mother ran away and took you with her. You must have been too young to remember how she broke your father's heart."

Sandy stood, speechless.

The queen continued as she sauntered toward a nearby mirror, primping. "Yes, your mother was picked mistakenly as the most beautiful in the land to wed your father, the King. And then, one day," she turned to face Sandy with a haughty look in her eyes, "she decided he wasn't good enough for her, and left him."

Sandy snapped defiantly, "What do you mean mistakenly? My mother is — I mean she was — beautiful." Sadness crept into Sandy's eyes at her mother's memory.

"My Ladies," David said, appearing in the doorway. "His Majesty is ready for you."

Sandy scowled at the queen as they followed David down the great hall to the dining room. The queen smiled back, undisturbed. Sandy decided she didn't like her, not one bit!

Sandy followed David and the queen into a grand room with golden ceilings and extravagant chandeliers. At the heart of the room was a brilliantly decorated table with golden candelabras and centerpieces of black roses. The silverware was all made of gold and there were more glasses at each place setting than Sandy thought necessary. *"They don't do anything here halfway, do they? Sandy thought.*

By far what excited Sandy the most was the food. The table was filled with a plethora of delicious cuisine. Platters filled with fruit, meats, and pastries of all kinds made the room smell heavenly! As the aroma of the feast wafted through the air, her stomach growled, making her acutely aware that she hadn't eaten all day. She would remedy that shortly.

The table was huge and could easily fit fifty people. Sandy watched as the queen took her seat at the far end of the table while David led Sandy to a seat next to a much larger, ornate chair at the other end. This must be the King's chair; her father's! Sandy's pulse quickened in anticipation. She was to sit next to her father – she was going to meet him for the first time, any minute now!

Sandy's eyes widened as she stared at the smorgasbord before her. "David, do you guys always eat like this?"

"My lady, this is a special feast in your honor."

Sandy smiled shyly, humbled at the realization. Sandy wondered briefly why the queen was seated so far away from her father, but the thought was interrupted by a blast of trumpet fanfare. Following the blast, drums rolled rhythmically. "All rise," the trumpeter shouted. "His Majesty, the King of all Moria."

The doors swung open and in walked the man from the painting. Sandy's world stopped turning, her breath trapped in her lungs as she waited. He was a tall and rather imposing man, with dark skin and intense dark eyes. A full head of dark curls and a full beard framed his face. Sandy couldn't help but think that he looked ruggedly handsome. He walked gracefully but strongly as he made his way toward the table. He wore a regal blue robe and a golden crown that glistened in the light of the candles. It was almost like a dream. Sandy couldn't have envisioned a more perfect-looking father.

"My daughter," King Black said, his eyes filled with emotion. "Turn around so I can have a good look at you.

The King towered over Sandy. As she was 5'7" he had to be above 6'3" tall. Sandy, suddenly catching her breath, beamed at her father and spun around in her beautiful dress.

Taking her hands in his, the King said, "My, how you have grown. So beautiful, so much like your mother."

Sandy bowed before the King. Raising his hand to her face, he gestured for her to rise. Sandy leaned into his touch as she fought back tears that threatened to fall.

"You will most definitely be the most beautiful in all of Moria! Don't you think, My Queen?" King Black turned to the queen, who had made her way to this side of the room.

"Oh, yes. Maybe after she has grown some more. She has potential."

"Well, I think she is far more beautiful than anyone I've ever seen," King Black said, and Sandy blushed.

The queen rolled her eyes, jealous of all the attention Sandy was getting. "My King, perhaps I should allow you and your daughter to spend some time alone."

"Oh, that won't be necessary," King Black replied. "She needs to get to know you as well if this is to be her new home."

The queen gasped. "Are you sure this would be best for her? Don't you think this might be too much of a change?" The queen turned and faced Sandy. "Sandy, you really should return home and give it some thought."

The King's lighthearted tone suddenly became serious..

"Nonsense! I don't want to hear you speak of this again. My daughter is home!" the King bellowed. He turned to Sandy. "Sandy, you are my only child and I treasure you most in my life. You will stay here so that I can be the father I always wanted you to have."

At King Black's decision, Sandy swore she saw the queen stymie a sneer but in a split second it was gone, Queen Mika returning to her calm, smug demeanor. King Black turned to Sandy and smiled with open arms. Overwhelmed with emotion, Sandy threw herself into her father's arms and the two embraced as father and daughter for the first time. Tears flowed down Sandy's face as she sobbed in her father's arms. The King soothed his daughter and kissed the crown of her head. "So long have I waited for this moment, Sandy. You are safe and you are home. I'm never letting you go again."

Queen Mika excused herself from the table. "As I said before, the two of you need some time to catch up. Goodnight Sandy; My King."

The queen bowed and made her way out of the room.

After the feast, the room was filled with the sound of father and daughter's chatter.

"It has been too long, my daughter. I wasn't sure I would get to hold you in my arms again."

Sandy looked at her father, confused. "I don't understand. I thought for so long that it was you who had left us. Why have I never seen you again, till now?"

The King stood from his chair and knelt in front of Sandy.

"My darling daughter, losing your mother and you was the hardest time in my life. I didn't know how I would go on. Your mother was the love of my life, and I would have given up my place as King for her and you. Your mother didn't want that. She thought my place was here and that yours was in your world. I couldn't convince her otherwise."

Sandy thought of her mother's fierce, headstrong nature and smiled. That sounded like her. "You and Mom were from two completely different worlds… how did you meet?"

The King returned to his chair and gave a slight smile as he recalled the memory. "Lena and I met one night in the forest just outside this palace. I had been hunting in the forest near the doorway to your world. It had always been of interest to me. We can see your world, but your world can't notice us. Most don't believe we exist. This is why the doorway only opens at night when children sleep and dream."

The King shifted in his seat, his eyes sparkling. "On this night, your mother was sitting alone in a park. I was captivated by her beauty. I had never seen her equal. My father had told me stories of how I would find the most beautiful woman in all of Moria and that she would be my wife. I knew from the instant I saw her she was the one. I crossed through the doorway and introduced myself. She was startled, but never afraid. She always had a fearlessness about her. We talked for what seemed like hours as she tried to understand where I had come from and why I was dressed the way I was."

Sandy smiled, remembering her reaction towards David. The King continued, "From that point on, we met in that same spot at the same park every night."

Sandy's eyes brightened. "Yes, yes! There was a park Mommy would take me to when I was little. We would go at the same time every night, even if we had gone earlier in the day. She would tell me stories of a faraway land, and all of people she knew there."

Sandy smiled, "And of you."

Tears filled King Black's eyes. The two glanced at one another as they remembered the woman that meant so much to both of them. Sandy ran and clung to her father as they burst into tears mourning their loss.

King Black continue, "Your mother left, doing what she thought was right. I will explain everything to you." King Black looked Sandy in the eyes as he cradled her face in his hands, wiping away her tears. "Just know your mother did nothing wrong. She has raised you to be more than I could have dreamed you would become. I know this all seems so different but we will be together for this new journey, my daughter." King Black said the words again just to hear them fall from his lips while he gazed into the eyes of his treasure. Sandy and her father were together once again.

Now back in her chambers, the queen paced nervously before an ornate golden mirror. But this was no ordinary mirror. One of seven mirrors forged of dark magic long ago, this mirror was passed down through the ages and guarded in secret by those who would wield its power. Finally, indignant, she stood before the ancient, enchanted mirror and said,

"Mirror, mirror on the wall,

Who is the fairest of them all? In this land, or that land, or in between,

I know I'm the finest because I'm the queen."

She smiled as the mirror shook, its glass surface rippling like water.

"Lovely lady and queen of mine,

I tell you the truth because I cannot lie.

The fairest and finest of them all, from this land and that land that makes up them all,

is Sandy Black, the princess thought lost.

She is the fairest and finest, without second thought."

The Queen screamed in dismay.

"How can this be? She is a child and I, I am the queen! Mirror oh mirror, you must be wrong, tell me once more and make it me!"

The mirror smoked and shook.

"Oh dearest, my queen, whom I hold above all others,

I have searched wide to find the true answer.

The truth of the matter is the same as the last –

I tell you the truth, your beauty is surpassed.

Sandy Black, the princess, is the fairest of all."

The queen stomped her feet, enraged. "I can make her go away," she muttered, a wicked smile creeping up on her face. "I'll do to her the same as I did to her mother."

Chapter 3

The Next Morning

The next morning, Sandy woke up to the sound of birds chirping on her windowsill. Waking up in the biggest bed she had ever seen with the softest blankets and pillows, it was so comfortable she didn't want to move. Enjoying the luxury, she wished her mum was here to share the experience. Suddenly there was a knock at her door.

"Young princess, are you awake?" David enquired through the door.

"Yes, I am."

The double doors swung open as Lilly and David stood at the entrance with a staff of servants. Sandy's jaw dropped at the number of maids – there were about twenty!

Lilly and the maids entered the room to get Sandy ready for breakfast.

"Young princess, are you ready for your day?" David asked. "It's all planned out for you since your father wants you to see the kingdom."

"Oh, my goodness. How fun!" Sandy said.

All at once one of the maids brushed her teeth while others combed her hair, cleaned her nails, and sorted her clothes.

"You will be having breakfast with the King first. He has rescheduled his normal activities for you today. After breakfast, you will go horseback riding to see the rest of the kingdom. When you return, the maids will prepare you for the ball."

Sandy's eyes lit up.

"A ball; you mean like dancing, gowns and stuff?"

"Precisely, young princess."

"Wow, I never got to go to a dance at school. I was always with my mom, making sure she was taken care of. I've always dreamed of going to one though."

David smiled. "Well, today you will experience the grandest ball in all of Moria. The remnants from the eleven other kingdoms that survived the great war will be present. The King of the Isles of Far-Off will come too. Some say the next King will come from there. And who knows; maybe you will be the fairest in the land and the one chosen to be his queen."

Sandy was too excited about the schedule of events that she hadn't heard what David said towards the end. David, noticing her excitement, excused himself.

"My lady, I shall go to attend to some things I must do. I will be back to escort you to your father when you're ready."

"Thank you, David!"

David made his way to the queen's chambers. When he approached, he could have sworn he heard voices behind her door.

He knocked at the door. "My Queen."

Silence. He knocked again.

"My Queen, are you there? I have come as you have requested."

"Ahh, David, my husband's number one manservant. Come in."

David walked into the queen's lavish chambers. She walked

up to him, dressed in a figure-hugging black dress. Her silhouette was what stood out as all the curtains were drawn and only a small amount of light was in the room.

"I have called you here to speak with you about the ball tonight."

"The ball, my lady – what about it?"

"You know the King has invited many guests from the 11 past kingdoms, and the prince who might very well be the next King. I do not think it a wise idea to have this girl at this event."

"My lady?"

"David, I'm not done talking."

The queen circled David and traced his body with her finger.

"I know that you have always wanted to have your own land and family. I even know who you have eyes for. We both know the King is overwhelmed with emotions at the moment because of this girl. All I am asking is that maybe you suggest to him that it's not the right time to expose this child to the rest of our friends. I mean, how would it make him look? A child from another woman long before me, the queen."

"My lady, I'm sure he knows what he is doing and that he understands the impact this could have on all our guests. I do believe he was ruling the kingdom before he made you his queen. I don't think it wise to second guess-him."

The queen was clearly disappointed in the response David gave her.

"Well, I thought more of you than this, David. Your King is going to make a mistake and turn us into a laughing stock amongst the other nobles of the land. She shouldn't be here, and you know it."

"Well, if that's how you feel, My Queen, maybe you should be having this conversation with the one who has the power to fix it for you. Is there anything else?”

The queen gave David a deceitful and glaring smile—one that he knew meant there would be more headaches to come from her.

“No, you may leave. I’m so glad I now know that you really don’t care about the King or me. I will recommend you to be replaced.”

“Thank you, Your Majesty.” David left, shutting the door behind him.

Sandy was prepared for her day. First thing on the agenda was breakfast. As she sat next to her father in the dining hall, servants came in with large trays of food. They were served large eggs, cheeses, meats, and exotic fruits and vegetables. The eggs were so large that two would satisfy everyone at the table. Sandy had never seen many of the native fruits and vegetables before. She reached out for a large green melon-like fruit and turned to her father.

“What is this called and is it good?”

King Black chuckled in delight at his daughter’s inquisitive nature. He cherished every moment of her child-like innocence, moments that he had longed for, for so many years.

“My darling, that is a juju berry. They grow throughout the forests here. They are known for their healing properties. We make most of our wine from them. It’s the reason so many here in Moria live so long.”

Sandy smiled and turned around. As she looked around, she noticed the queen wasn’t at breakfast.

“Daddy, where is the queen?”

King Black smiled when he heard her call him “daddy”. How he had missed this!

"My love, she figured we should have our alone time to become better acquainted. It's just a day for you and I. The queen also values her alone time in her private gardens. She visits every fortnight to pay homage to the fallen people of her kingdom."

"I'm ok with that. One, I wanted all of you to myself anyway. Two, I don't really think she likes me, and I can't say I like her either."

The King laughed. "I do understand she is a bit stubborn and jealous, but I hope with time, the two of you will become friends. Though she is not your mother, she does have much knowledge to offer."

"I guess I can try, Daddy, but I'm not making any promises. She is just so stuck up."

The King laughed at his daughter's annoyance. "I know, darling.

"Shall we go for a ride to burn off some of this breakfast now?"

"A ride? Where are we riding to?"

"Come, my dear. It is a surprise."

They changed into riding clothes and strolled to the stables to saddle up their horses for the excursion the King had in store.

Chapter 4
THE TOUR

Just outside the palace walls, two white horses pulled a carriage into the forest. Inside the carriage sat the queen, who sat in silence as her coachmen spurred the animals along.

The queen was restless today, her dignified deportment crumbling by the second.

"I have to get rid of this little distraction," she thought to herself as the carriage meandered its way through the narrow pathway to her place of solitude, her private gardens. She needed answers on what she was to do, and she knew the only way to get them lay before her.

Racing down a hill into the forest, King Black and Sandy shrieked with delight. They both wore matching riding outfits—black leather jackets with the King's crest embroidered on the chest, flowing blue capes, black leather boots and hats. Both sat atop black stallions, looking like shadows as they galloped through the forest. Trees turned to watch and bow before the King as they galloped by. David and other dragon riders flew overhead, keeping an eye on their monarchs.

Slowing their horses, King Black and Sandy stopped in front of a Great Tree where a long bench stood. "Let us rest here for a while," King Black said.

King Black pulled out a satchel from his side, filled with food and other things meant for a picnic. He walked to a spot, spread a blanket and set out mouth-watering delicacies.

Sandy was so captivated by her surroundings that she paid attention to everything but her father.

"We will eat first and then we will go see a special place that no one knows about," King Black said.

"You mean a secret place that nobody knows but you, because you're the King?"

"Precisely." The King smiled and thought for a moment, "Well, I guess the food can wait. Let's go."

King Black looked up at the sky and signaled David to retreat. David nodded and whistled to his team. In no time, the dragon riders vanished from the air.

"Now my love," King Black said, "I am about to take you to a place that is very special to both of us."

"What do you mean 'both of us'?"

The King took Sandy by the hand and led her into a dark part of the forest. It was cool but pitch black. Sandy walked cautiously.

"Come," King Black said. "It's OK, my love. You're safe."

Sandy followed her father until they arrived at an opening with two great trees. In between them were two vines and bushes. The King walked to the flora and pushed them to the side, uncovering a pathway.

"I have been coming here for years. And because of my coming here, I have the most precious possession in my kingdom with me now."

Sandy frowned. "I don't understand."

"Sandy, this is the doorway to your world."

Sandy stared at the pathway. To her, it was like every other path she had seen. Nothing spectacular. "What do you mean 'this is the doorway'?"

"This was where your mother and I first met. She was on the other side, sitting on a bench." And almost like a movie screen, the image of Sandy's mother sitting on the bench appeared clouded in mist.

"Mommy? Is that really her?"

"Yes, Sandy. It's your mother. Well, a memory of her. This forest has a way of bringing memories to life. When an emotion is strong enough, they can be seen; almost experienced again."

While Sandy looked at the memory of her mother, the vision changed. She saw her parents playing and chasing each other around a picnic area in the same location. She saw them hugging and kissing. Next, they were riding horses through the forest, laughing. After that, they were in each other's arms and the King pulled out a ring, got on one knee and proposed. Then she saw a small yet beautiful wedding beside a pool, with David at her father's side.

But just as suddenly as the vision had started, it got dark. Sandy saw her mother carrying a baby and walking through the woods to this very same doorway at night. Being very careful not to be seen, she passed through the doorway and disappeared while, not far away behind a tree, the King looked on.

"You were there? Why didn't you go after her?"

King Black wiped a tear. "Sandy, that was the day my heart broke. That was the day your mother took you away and went back to your world." Her father's voice broke under the weight of his words. "Forgive me; it is still hard for me to talk about it. I never thought I would see you again. For now, just know your mother saved me by leaving. And when I have the words to explain it to you totally, I will. I would not still be King if it weren't for her."

Crash! Sandy looked up. "What was that?"

King Black surveyed the area—crash!

"Giants," King Black said. "Let's go!"

They hurried back to the bench and mounted their horses.

"What do you mean giants? You mean like fee-fi-fo-fum giants?!"

"I will explain later. They may be hunting or moving their territory. We need to get out of their way. The giants and I have an understanding – I don't bother them, and they don't bother my kingdom. Let us depart from here at once before they find us."

They rode back quickly to the palace. As they did, boulders crashed into trees, and they heard the giants' deep voices fading into the distance as they raced home.

Now safe in the palace, the King and his daughter dismounted. Sandy was still a bit shaken by the experience.

"Trouble yourself over this matter no more, my dear. The great forest of Moria has many inhabitants that we share our land with. The giants are but one of many potentially dangerous entities in our borders, but worry not. Though their ways are strange to us and they do have a temper from time to time, we have been peaceful with their kind for centuries. You have no reason to fear, my love. You are safe with your father."

Sandy sighs in relief. David dashed into the palace. "Your Majesty, is everything alright? My men and I noticed a pack of giants headed in your direction. When we dropped to get a better view, they threw boulders and trees at us. Some of my men were injured. We had to return to the palace to assess damage done, regroup, and come after you."

"David, I am not in the least worried that you would leave

me with no aide. We are fine. How are your men and the drag-ons?"

"Those that were injured were sent to the doctor and the dragons are being cared for now. Nothing major. They are just a bit angry."

Just then a burst of flame and a roar shot out from the dragon stables.

"Looks like you were very right," King Black said, shaking his head. "Ballah doesn't like being picked on. There is nothing more to worry about from the giants. They are a group that shouldn't be bothered."

The group laughed. Everyone was safe and accounted for.

***

Meanwhile, the queen arrived at the gates of her private garden. Stepping out of her coach she unlocked the gates, closing them behind her. No-one but the queen was allowed into her sanctuary on order of the King, so her coachmen stood guard.

The gardens were particularly nice at this time of year, with blooms of every color and fruit trees of all kinds. The queen paid no attention to any of it, however. She proceeded to the eastern corner of the gardens and made a sharp descent down steps carved from solid stone that wound deep into the woods.

After walking for some time, she came upon a wooden struc-ture covered in old vines. The building looked dilapidated and it didn't appear that anyone lived there, but looks can be deceiving. Smoke wafted from a small stone chimney as the queen ap-proached and knocked on the door thrice. The door opened in-ward, and the queen stepped into the darkened room. Inside were two elderly women seated around a fire. Now these were no ordi-nary women, for they were the queen's mother and grandmother;

the sole remaining Nefarains.

These three women were three generations of an old order of witches thought to be extinct. Their singular goal was to take over the land of Moria. This quest had been passed down from generation to generation before the last great battle appeared to have wiped them out completely, leaving only two women who were thought to have perished with time. What was unknown at that time was that the younger of the two witches was with child. This child was Queen Mika.

The women were hideous, as was typical of their race. Over the millennia, the dark magic that corrupted their souls had consumed their physical appearance. Nefarians had unnaturally contorted bodies with skin covered in festering lesions. They emitted a noxious odor that smelled of bile and rotten flesh, and when they spoke, foul secretions flowed from their orifices.

Raised by her mother and grandmother in solitude, Queen Mika was raised in the old ways of her people and had inherited their mission and their hated of Morians. Their numbers decimated, they had to resort to using subtle tactics of infiltration and manipulation. They used their collective powers to cast a powerful spell that would alter Mika's appearance from unsightly witch to become the fairest in the land. She then used her charm to ascend the ranks at court, obtain the King's favor and become queen. Through their influence they would destroy the kingdom from the inside.

All had gone well for the treacherous threesome until King Black—then the prince— had found Sandy's mother. Sandy's mother was a threat because Mika had planned to infiltrate the castle and win the prince's affection, so that one day she would seize power from them and return the control of Moria back to darkness.

The queen recounted the recent developments to her mother and grandmother and awaited their advice.

"What do you mean distraction?" Myala, her mother, asked regarding Sandy. "She doesn't know anything about Moria. She has no understanding of our ways. Why do you let such a little thing trouble you so?"

The queen stared back at the older witch. "Because the kingdom is mine. The King is ready to give her everything to make up for lost time. He would even make her queen!"

"Not to worry. There is nothing your mother and grandmother can't help you deal with," her mother said. The two were silent for a time and appeared to be in a trance, then abruptly returned with fire in their eyes.

"Trouble you have; I have seen it," her grandmother, Obeia, told them.

"Yes, Grandmother," the queen said.

"I have heard the mirror's words as well," the queen's mother said.

"Yes. Yes, my dear," her grandmother said. "Now what to do about this issue, we three generations must think."

***

After lunch, King Black and Sandy toured the palace. In the huge royal kitchen, she met all the kitchen staff. The head chef, a rather robust and cheery man, bowed before Sandy.

"My princess, if I may be so bold to introduce myself to you. I am Chef Tasty, the head chef. I want to welcome you home with a special meal this evening. Might I ask what you would like?"

Surprised by his name, Sandy stifled a giggle. Looking at his pot belly and thin mustache, she couldn't help but smile. "Well, I have been missing my momma's cornbread stuffing."

Chef Tasty smiled.

"Oh," Sandy said, "with macaroni and cheese. Maybe some potato salad, some greens, bread pudding, fried chicken, ox tails and gravy. Candied yams and some peach cobbler, with some ice cream on the side and some sweet tea."

"Is that all, young princess?"

"Maybe some red beans and rice too." Sandy paused. "Oh my goodness! Chef Tasty, I'm so sorry. You probably don't know these foods. What was I thinking?"

Smiling, Chef Tasty's cheeks turned red and the edges of his mustache curled. King Black laughed.

"My princess," Chef Tasty said, "this would be true for any normal chef but not for Chef Tasty. Food is a language we all understand. It is a medium we all must work with. You, my princess, will have your meal this evening."

Amazed at his response, Sandy smiled. "Thank you, Chef Tasty. I look forward to eating what you'll prepare for me. If you need any help, I am available."

Chef Tasty raised his finger to his lips. "Shush! I will not think of it, my princess. You have come from far away and have not experienced the taste that is Tasty."

King Black stepped forward to save Chef Tasty. "My love, we have much more to see and after that menu I'm sure Chef Tasty will have his hands full all afternoon, finishing dinner for three thousand guests."

Sandy's eyes widened. "Three thousand guests? Do you have a stadium in here or something?"

The King laughed. "You will soon see, my dear. Shall we?"

Sandy nodded and turned to Chef Tasty. "Thank you so much, Chef Tasty. Again, I look forward to your meal tonight."

"You are very welcome, my princess. I hope to help you feel

at home."

King Black and Sandy continued their tour. They passed the dining room where they'd first met the night before. Sandy admired the long table, big chairs, high ceilings and large, beautiful chandeliers. Gold drapes were pulled back to reveal giant glass windows through which the sun shone. The sunlight bounced off the gold and silver tableware on the table. Birds sat on the exterior windowsills, singing songs like children.

Passing the dining room, the two stopped in front of a great hallway. "I couldn't wait to show you this," King Black said.

Sandy stepped forward, peering down the hall. On either side of its walls were murals and photos of her family. Seeing a picture of her as a baby in her father's arms made her teary. The hall had nothing else – just the murals and photos. Sandy was speechless.

"I had this hall dedicated to the memory of my family—to you and your mother," King Black said. "So that on days when I was lost or not sure of what to do, I could come here and spend time with those I love and missed so much."

Sandy saw a picture of her mother when she was very young. Sandy gasped.

"Yes, I know," King Black said. "You look just like her. So beautiful. I wanted to let you see for yourself that you belong."

Sandy broke down in tears. "I miss her so much. I wish she was here."

"My love, it is OK to miss her. I have missed you both too. I want you to know that when your mother died, she did not go away to exist no more. She is now in the presence of God. So, we must live and be happy for her."

Sandy hugged him and he kissed her forehead.

"It will be fine, my love," he said. "This is your home now.

Let us see some more."

They walked arm in arm down the hall, cracking jokes and laughing. Turning right, they entered the largest room Sandy had ever seen.

"You asked about a stadium earlier, right? This is the ballroom where later our guests will be."

Sandy clapped in excitement. "This is amazing! You know, they say back home, 'everything is bigger in Texas'. Everything is way bigger here."

King Black smiled as Sandy looked round the huge room. Maids and menservants were busy cleaning, decorating, and arranging the room.

"So many decorations and hold on, where do we sit?"

"Well, the tables are not in yet, and that space in the middle of the room is the dancefloor."

"Wow; this is a dream."

"No, my dear. This is your home."

Outside the palace, the queen's carriage arrived. Lilly waited at the entrance to greet her.

"I trust you had a good outing, my queen."

"Yes I did, young Lilly. Where might my husband be?"

"He is with the princess. The last time I saw them, they were in the ballroom."

The queen smiled. "Thank you, Lilly. Is my bath ready? I need to clean the filth of the day from me."

"Oh yes, my queen."

"Good, good. You know, Lilly, you might become my number one servant if you keep this up."

Lilly bowed before the queen as she walked off to her chambers.

Chapter 5

NIGHT OF THE BALL

The palace bustled with activity as servants prepared the palace for the ball. King Black and Sandy walked arm in arm towards her room. As Sandy opened her door, she gasped. Elegantly hung on a mannequin was the most magnificent dress she had ever laid eyes on! It was a glorious white tulle dress with a sweetheart neckline and straps off the shoulder. At the bust, straps and hem of the dress, diamonds were intricately sewn with flowers – white lilies and black roses, to be precise. A pair of jeweled shoes with wooden soles lay beside her bed.

Sandy's mouth still agape, King Black explained, "These shoes are made from the wood of a walking willow. Shoes made with this wood are said to make one's feet as light as air."

"Please, turn around, my dear."

Sandy turned around and gasped when she saw a gold crown in his hand. "A crown…, for me?"

"Yes, my princess. This is a symbol of royalty. It signifies who you are in the kingdom of Moria. With this crown of royal heritage, I pray the grace of God will forever be upon you."

Sandy blushed as her father placed the crown atop her head and stood back to admire her. "I see it fits well."

Sandy laughed. "Thank you, Daddy. I'm speechless!

"I understand, my love. Remember – there will be times when you will have to make decisions that will impact many people. Not all will be fun or glamorous, but I am confident that you can do it. You will meet many of the remnants of the eleven kingdoms that survived the great war tonight. The King of the Isles of Far Off will also be present. Just be yourself, and most of all have fun."

"Sure, Dad. Hey, when will the party begin?"

King Black laughed. "As soon as you get dressed, my dear. I will take my leave now so you can get ready."

He kissed her on her forehead and stepped out of the room. As he left, maids rushed in to prepare Sandy for the ball.

"We are here to get you dressed for the ball, Princess," they all said in excited voices. Sandy smiled.

"You're all so sweet. Well, let's get started."

After her maids left, Sandy, ready for the ball, admired herself in front of a large mirror in her room.

"My, you are beautiful. You could be the next Queen of Moria one day." Startled, Sandy turned around and saw the queen standing at the door. She stared at the queen's outfit, a form-fitting red sequined gown with a plunging neckline that clung tightly to her curves and revealed much more than it ought to.

"Thank you."

The queen looked Sandy up and down. "It's my fault that we haven't gotten along so far. I apologize for being rude, Sandy."

"Oh really?"

"I'm really sorry, and do hope you'll give me another chance. It's just that I do have a bit of a jealous streak sometimes. You were new, and taking time I spend with my King."

"Yes, I guess that could have been a little difficult. I'm not here to change your relationship with my father. I mean, I don't even know you. I didn't come here by choice. It was the only option I had left after my mom died."

The queen, noticing Sandy's grief, stepped closer. "My dear, you don't have to recount the past. I know it must be hard after all you have been through. I too have lost family and know the sting of loneliness. I can never replace your mother and would never try. But what I can try to do is be a true friend whenever you need one. It is hard for us, as you will soon find out, to have friends, being royalty and all. I would like us to be like sisters."

The queen stepped away from Sandy and pressed her hands together. As she opened them, a diamond necklace appeared. "Please accept this as a token of friendship."

"This has got to be a dream! Since I got here, everything has been so perfect. Now the one person I didn't think I would like now seems cool, and with her own little magic act offers me a gift like none I have ever seen before.

"Is that a real diamond? I've never seen one that big before!"

"It is one of the benefits of being queen; or in your case, princess. All the best jewels that are mined come to the palace for us to select. We can have them made into whatever we desire."

Sandy's eyes lit up. "You mean I can go to some room in the palace where I can basically make my own jewelry?"

The queen nodded. Sandy jumped in excitement. "Yes! Where is it and when can we start?"

The queen smiled a megawatt smile. "If you are ready, we can go there now. I thought it might interest you, so I had some good pieces pulled out. Plus, you're going to want to accessorize before the ball."

The queen led her out of her room and towards the room of jewels.

***

Throughout the palace, the last-minute preparations were being made for the night's event. Chef Tasty gave instructions to his cooks as they chopped, sliced, whisked grated, and cooked. Maids and menservants pressed and folded linen and readied seating arrangements. David was busy supervising all operations from atop an indoor balcony that had the view of the entire palace. King Black stepped out onto the balcony from behind him. "Is everything going on fine, David?"

David turned to answer the King. "All is well, my King. Actually, everything is moving ahead of schedule."

"Good, good. Have you seen Sandy come out of her room yet?"

"Yes, my King, and might I say that the seamstress did a magnificent job on her gown. She was in the company of the queen. They were on their way to the jewel room."

"She is with the queen? Hmm, that's good. Maybe if they spend a little time to get to know each other, it will help ease the tension between the two of them. I knew the queen wasn't going to be happy with so much attention diverted to Sandy. I'm glad she is being an adult and trying to work things out. Sandy needs a female friend anyway, and the queen would make a perfect confidant."

"I do hope you're right, my lord. The two seemed to be laughing together as they walked."

"Excellent, I will now ready myself for the evening's events where I shall introduce the world to my princess."

***

Inside the jewel room, Sandy and the queen played in giant piles of gold and silver, sliding down hills of precious stones that covered huge wooden boxes.

"I've never ever dreamed of a place like this. There is more gold and silver and just everything than I've even seen on TV."

The queen stood up after sliding down a small hill of gold dust.

"What is this TV you speak of?"

Sandy stood next to the queen after sliding over the same hill.

"Oh, I almost forgot y'all don't have TV here. It's like a box that has a window in it, but you can see programs… or I should say, moving pictures in it."

The queen was very interested in what Sandy was saying.

"You mean, it's like a mirror that you watch pictures of moving people on?"

"I guess you could say it that way. We have TV shows, movies, cartoons and all kinds of things we can watch on it."

"Would you like to see a secret of mine?" the queen whispered.

"What kind of secret?"

"The most wonderful kind! But you mustn't tell anyone! Come with me to my chambers. Hurry."

They took off to the queen's chambers. The queen, closing the door behind them, led Sandy to the far side of her room and pulled back her drapes, revealing a large golden mirror.

"This was a gift given to me by my mother, who received it from her mother," the queen said, pointing at the mirror, "and so on for as far back as my family has kept record. This mirror on my wall is very special. It can answer questions and show you things."

Sandy was interested but she was kind of skeptical. "So, what you're telling me is you have a magic genie that lives in your mirror, and you can ask it to grant you wishes?"

"No, my dear." The queen smiled.

"Let me show you what I mean. Mirror, mirror on the wall

What fun should we look forward to at the ball?"

After the queen addressed the mirror, it looked to Sandy almost like a TV had been turned on. It hummed and turned into different colors—red, green and blue—and then a shadowy face appeared in it.

"Dearest Queen of all the land,

the ball shall yield a loving hand.

One of a lad not yet in his prime,

a prince indeed the lass will find.

He shall court through song and dance.

A time tonight like no others in past."

Sandy turned to the queen, confused. "What exactly did it just say?"

The queen smiled in excitement. "My dear, did you hear what the mirror said?"

"Yeah, I heard it, but could you please explain what it meant?"

"The mirror said you will meet a prince tonight who will sweep you off your feet and you will have more fun than you have ever had."

"Wow, you mean he said all of that?" Sandy laughed out loud. "I don't know if I can take the word of a psychedelic talking mirror."

The queen stiffened, eyes wide, offended by Sandy's reaction to her prophesies. Clenching her jaw and gritting her teeth, she composed herself. Sandy, noticing her words offended the queen, apologized. "Oh, I'm sorry. I know this is important to you and very much real. I do apologize. I guess I've just never believed in stuff like this."

"What do you mean?"

"I didn't mean to say it like that. I just don't believe I'm going to meet some prince tonight and have a great time. I mean, I just got here, nobody knows who I am and plus, I'm kinda shy most of the time."

"Young princess, you have much to learn about this place. As I said, this mirror has been in my family for generations. I trust what he tells me with my life. You shall see tonight. But for now, it is time we got ready to welcome our guests. There are a lot of people you must meet."

The queen led Sandy from her room, locking the door behind her with a key. They walked side by side towards the ballroom.

***

The guests had started arriving. They were escorted from their carriages and beast-drawn wagons to their tables inside the ballroom. Large black carpets with blue and gold borders paved the way to the ballroom. David stood at the top of the palace steps, greeting all who had arrived as they passed by with their escorts. Every small and large township, nation and village was represented with their own distinct style and fashion to show off at the night's gala. A drum cadence is played that is distinct to each group of guest, as they enter.. A light music played as all came together in the ballroom. Dancers danced and aerial performers performed using silks and hoops above the crowd. Sandy, King Black and the queen all waited patiently behind a curtain on their balcony. As each guest walked into the room, they were announced before they were seated. King Black took Sandy's hand in his and prepped her for her royal entrance.

"Sandy, after all the people are introduced, I and the queen will be announced and go out. I want you to stay here so that I can announce you myself. All you have to do is walk out to me."

Sandy was nervous but excited. "OK, Daddy. I'll do it; just remember, I've never done anything like this before."

"Don't worry my dear, I will be with you every step of the way."

Just as everyone was seated and enjoying the music and food, a trumpet and drums sounded. "All, please rise for the royal family of Moria."

The entire room stood to its feet, all noise and movement stopping.

"Ladies and gentlemen, the King and Queen of Moria."

The guests erupted in applause as the King and queen walked out hand in hand, the queen brandishing a dazzling smile. After a minute, King Black raised his hands to the people and silenced the room.

"People of Moria, and kingdoms of old from the surrounding lands. I have bid you to come not only for a celebration of our world's peace – but for a celebration of the homecoming of a vital piece of my life. Now my only child has returned to me. Unfortunately for us both, her mother has passed on to a better place."

The queen smirked.

"You see, my child's mother was from earth. The land that has left us behind in dreams and fairytales."

The crowd murmured to themselves. "I am aware that this may come as a shock to you. This is why, on this night, I am revealing all of myself to you. I would like you to meet the Princess of Moria who has come home for good. My daughter, my love. Princess Sandy Black." Trumpets erupted and music played as Sandy walked to her father from behind the curtain. The crowd exclaimed in admiration of her beauty and applauded the new addition to the King's family. Sandy blushed as she walked into her father's arms. King Black raised Sandy's hand into the air and twirled her around. "Isn't she beautiful?"

The crowd, still mesmerized by her beauty, whistled and clapped.

"Let us eat!" King Black said.

After this statement, David clapped his hands and about thirty waiters moved in unison delivering covered trays to each one of the tables. Sandy was now seated next to her father at the head table. "This is amazing, Daddy!"

The King smiled. "You are my greatest treasure and tonight is so that all of the world can see you shine."

Just then, Chef Tasty served Sandy her dinner.

"Madam, may I present to you the dinner you have requested for this event. Might I say that I have done some of my finest work, if I do say so myself; I do hope you agree?"

Sandy's plate was covered with collard greens, candied yams, fried chicken, stuffing and rice, cornbread, and ham. Other side dishes she'd requested were within an arm's reach. The aroma reached Sandy and she was immediately brought to tears. Chef Tasty's smile turned to concern.

"Is something wrong, my lady? You haven't even tasted it yet."

Sandy shook her head. "No, no Chef Tasty. It is nothing you did wrong; it is all so right. So perfect. The aroma reminds me of Momma and thanksgiving at home. I can remember it all like it was just yesterday. Nothing is wrong, Chef."

Sandy stood and gave the chef a giant hug.

"Thank you very much. Now I really do feel at home."

The chef, surprised by the response from Sandy, looked at the King for approval. King Black smiles and gave Chef Tasty a nod of approval.

"My lady, please, I am glad you are happy but I would feel much better if you would taste it too."

Sandy smiled after wiping tears away from her face. She took a bite of each thing on her plate.

"My goodness Chef Tasty, I didn't know you could do it, but you did. This is the best food I have ever eaten in my life. You might have made this better than my mother used to."

Chef Tasty smiled and then bowed. "I am glad to be of service to you, my lady." "The secret is love."

"That's the same thing my momma used to say when she cooked."

"There is no element that is more universal than love, my lady. I will now excuse myself so that you may enjoy the rest of your meal."

The King nodded and Chef Tasty walked away. It wasn't just Sandy that relished her meal. All the guests went "ooh" and "aah" as they ate the different meals they were served. From appetizers to dessert, it was a wonderful experience. The peach cobbler, ice cream, and banana pudding served to the guests was exactly what Sandy had imagined.

After the sumptuous meal, the band struck up a beautiful song and guests began to socialize amongst themselves. Sandy, deep in conversation with her father, barely noticed when a young man approached their table. "My King," he said. King Black stopped him before he could finish his introduction.

"I know you, Prince Shamma! Your father and I have fought many battles together. My, how you have grown into a handsome young man! Why, you were only a child last I saw you."

The prince smiled proudly. Wondering who her father was

talking to, Sandy looked up and locked eyes with the prince and it was as if time slowed to a halt. She couldn't breathe. It was like she'd had the wind knocked out of her. The young man before her had the most marvelous green eyes that sparkled like emeralds beneath long eyelashes. Pink full lips parted in a half smile as he took Sandy in. He had skin the color of caramel, and long dread-locks he kept in a mohawk secured at the nape of his neck. He had to be about 6'2", in his early 20s with broad shoulders and an athletic build. Sandy noticed he wore a white gold-trimmed suit with a mandarin collar that framed his angular jaw. He really was a thing of beauty. There they stood, gawking at each other until the King cleared his throat, bringing them both back to reality.

The young prince smiled brightly and bowed before the King and his family, and spoke with what Sandy thought was a slight Irish accent.

"Great King, on behalf of the people of the Isles of Far Off I would like to congratulate you on the reunion with your daughter. And if I may be so bold, I would like to welcome her in a custom-ary fashion in my land – with a song."

Sandy was so floored by what she was hearing she just sat there staring at her father like a deer in headlights. The prince struggled to keep his focus away from her to address the King. The King replied, "Well, you are right – that is one of the old cus-toms of the land and I have heard that you have quite the gift. Be it so, young prince."

The prince smiled and extended his hand to Sandy.

"My lady, it would be my honor and great privilege to wel-come you to your new home with a song. If you will," Prince Shamma offered his hand, "it is only right that you stand with me."

Sandy blushed and heat rose behind her ears. She was sure

that if she were lighter of skin her face would be beet red about now. "Well, I don't know, umm..."

"Sandy, it is only polite that you make yourself seen in order to be welcomed," said King Black.

Sandy hesitantly stood and took the prince's hand. The two walked out to the terrace in front of the King's table.

"OK, what do I have to do?" Sandy whispered to the prince.

"Nothing; just be yourself," Prince Shamma replied.

The prince helped her down the steps to the terrace below their table. Though she was still nervous about being under a microscope, she was so captivated by the handsome prince that she barely noticed everyone else. The crowd watched in anticipation as the prince cued the musicians. The band started to play music and the prince addressed the crowd.

"I would like to welcome the Princess of Moria to our lands in the customary way. With a song."

The prince stepped away from Sandy for a moment, looked into her eyes and his velvet voice rang through the room. He sang of new beginnings and times gone by. Sandy froze like a statue.

The guests were captivated by the story of the song. The song reminded Sandy of all she had gone through as the song spoke of things in the past and the new beginnings ahead. Memories of her childhood flooded her mind of her mother and the fun they had; then the time her mother went to the doctor and found out about her illness. As she flowed with the song, it seemed the crowd was on the journey with her. Sandy thought of her trip to Moria and all the events to that very moment. Finally, the prince ended the song with a bow. The crowd erupted into cheers. Sandy did not realize that tears had welled up in her eyes, but this time tears of happiness.

Prince Shamma turned back to Sandy. "Welcome, Princess

of Moria." Sandy beamed back at the prince as he raised her hand and pressed his lips to it before leading her back to her seat. The King stood to address the guests.

"That was a beautiful welcome, Prince Shamma. Your gift is welcome here anytime. For now, let us dance."

The King clapped and music played. All the guests rose and moved to the dance floor. The prince turned to Sandy.

"May I have this dance?"

Sandy blushed. She'd been doing a lot of that today.

"Well, I don't know, because if you dance as good as you sing, I won't be able to keep up! Plus, I just ate."

The prince laughed. "Trust me, singing is by far my most developed talent. We will take our time. Shall we?"

Sandy took the prince's hand as he led her to the dance floor. The queen and King were already in the middle of the floor, dancing amongst the guests.

Prince Shamma placed his hand on Sandy's lower back and raised her arm in preparation to dance. Sandy noticed a heat beneath his touch that ran throughout her entire body. Her breathing became shallow and her stomach fluttered. *OMG! This guy is giving me butterflies!*

"Ready Princess?" Shamma offered her a cheeky grin.

Is he flirting with me? Sandy countered, "As ready as I'll ever be!" And off they went twirling on the dance floor. David, looking on from the King's table, smiled in contentment. Just then, Lilly the head maid grabbed him by hand. "You're not getting away from me this time," she said as she pulled him out to the dance floor in a rush. They all had fun dancing and laughing.

The dancing stopped as the evening pressed on and the crowd and the royal family mingled. King Black left the queen to where Sandy was still in the company of Prince Shamma. The two appeared to be totally enthralled with one another, him rarely leaving her side.

"Prince Shamma, may I steal my daughter away for a moment? I have some friends to introduce her to."

Prince Shamma bowed. "By all means, please. The princess has many she must meet."

The prince kissed Sandy's hand. "And a pleasure it has been, my lady."

Sandy curtsied and thanked the prince for such a beautiful song.

"I do have to say, Prince Shamma, you have a beautiful voice. Nobody has ever done anything like that for me. I think I'm still in shock. I hope that we might see each other again so that you can tell me stories of your homeland."

Prince Shamma nodded. "It would be my honor, Princess Sandy."

Noticing the attraction between them, the King led Sandy away and smiled. "My queen, if only I had the prince with me in Moria's last war, he might have sung a song to make everyone so happy and in love we might not have had to fight at all."

King Black and the queen laughed but Sandy didn't get the joke. She stood there with a quizzical look on her face. "Will someone tell me what is going on?

"Maybe someone needs to look at herself in the mirror again," the queen said.

At the queen's words, Sandy suddenly remembered what the mirror had said concerning her, the party, and finding her true love.

Sandy blushed. "Ermm, I'm fine. It's just that the song was so nice and all. Prince Shamma is nice but he's really not my type. I like guys who are uglier than him... and shorter, you know."

The queen and King glanced at each other and smiled. The group walked over to King Ananias, King of the Isles of Far Off. King Ananias, his queen, Prince Shamma and King Black's family were the only royals at the ball. In fact, their families were the only monarchs who had survived the war that occurred 300 years ago.

"So, this is the young princess that the King of Moria has called us all here to see," King Ananias said. "I knew it wasn't going to be foreign policy he was so excited about."

King Black smiled. King Ananias laughed as his slight Irish-accented voice filled the air.

"And yes, a beautiful young princess you are. Shamma did tell me you are even more beautiful up close. He is very right."

Sandy blushed at the thought of Prince Shamma thinking her to be beautiful.

"Don't you think she will make a lovely queen one day, my love?" King Ananias asked his queen. The Queen of the Isles of Far off had a quiet strength about her and a regal demeanor. Her tawny brown skin contrasted with the same captivating emerald green eyes as her son. She was stunning.

"Yes, my King. She is very pretty but true beauty springs from the heart, and as far as I can tell, young princess, you shall be the most beautiful in all of the land in not much time. I can see it in your spirit."

All smiled as the flattery continued. All except the queen, who became more rigid and began looking around the room to avoid the conversation. It was evident that she was jealous of all the attention Sandy was getting.

"Well, enough of the compliments," King Black said. "I think your son has that covered for this evening."

The two smiled.

"I wanted you to meet my daughter. I wanted her to know you as well."

King Black turned to Sandy. "You see, my dear, King Ananias is my most trusted ally."

Sandy wondered how big the land really was. "Ally? It seems as if everyone here is a friend and getting along. Is there more out there?"

Sandy looked out of one of the windows into the dark night, wondering how much more there was for her to learn and understand in that world.

"Yes, my dear. There was a time when our two kingdoms were just two of the 13 kingdoms of man. That's not including the beasts and monsters that plotted against all of the kingdoms long ago. But the great war happened 300 years ago when my father, your grandfather, was King. Only two of the 13 kingdoms still stand to this day. The battles we have fought in my rule have been with some of the dark foes that come from the deepest parts of the forest.

Sandy, interested in more history of the two kings, listened on as her father spoke.

"There was a time when the entire world was covered in darkness. An evil brood of people lived among us and they had only one purpose and goal—total control over all. They were witches whose magical powers seduced nation after nation."

Sandy interrupted her father.

"How come they didn't take over control of this world if they were so powerful?"

"This was many centuries ago, my love, before the rule of the fairest. You see, witches are a foul and grotesque group of women and men. So, our original thirteen tribes that made up the great kingdom made a rule. This rule of the fairest was put in place to make sure one of them wouldn't get too close to power.

"Well, why didn't they use their magic to make themselves beautiful to hide among the people of Moria?

"Nefaria, their progenitor, forbade them from using that type of magic, seeing it as weakness," King Ananias interjected. "She was a powerful witch who wanted complete domination. Prideful as she was, she believed that representing herself in any other way than what she truly was, was beneath her."

"Their clan was isolated away from all others and it is believed that all of the witch's order are extinct. We haven't heard from them in a very long time."

Sandy looked at her father, intrigued by his story. When she was about to ask more questions, the queen gave a small yawn and excused herself from the group.

"My King, I am a bit tired. I shall retire early tonight as tomorrow I have much to do."

The King looked back at his queen. "My dear, I was hoping you would stay a bit longer to meet some more of our friends with Sandy."

The queen smiled. "Oh, that doesn't seem necessary. You have all that under control, my love. The young princess has already met the most important guest here. And it seems as though Morians have accepted her with open arms. She will be fine without me; we had some girl time earlier."

Looking at Sandy, she continued, "Maybe tomorrow, Sandy and I can have lunch and share some girl talk?"

Sandy smiled. "That would be nice."

"Then it is settled. I shall retire for this eventful evening and will see you all in the morning."

The queen smiled at Sandy as she passed, and kissed the

King on the cheek before curtsying to King Ananias and his wife. All said goodnight to the queen as she exited the ballroom. The King and Queen of the Isles of Far Off looked at each other as if to say, "What was that?" The night continued as King Black and Sandy greeted the guests. After most of the guests had gone, Prince Shamma and Sandy stood together.

"It has truly been a pleasure to have met you, Princess Black. I do hope that it would not be too forward of me to ask if I might be able to come and see you again."

Sandy smiled. "That would be nice, Prince Shamma. This has been the most exciting day of my life. Again, your song was beautiful."

The prince took Sandy's hand.

"I did what I could to make it represent the lady for whom it was sung."

At this Sandy was speechless and she felt another unfamiliar flutter in her stomach. *Those darn butterflies again!*

"I shall send you something tomorrow; a gift. Take it as a welcome home present."

Sandy raised her eyebrows and willed words to come out of her mouth, but she was yet again speechless. She had to stop doing that.

"I will not take no for an answer, Sandy. I will deliver it myself before noon tomorrow. Then shall I see you again. Goodnight."

Shamma kissed her hand, gave her a dashing grin then turned and mounted his golden dragon in one fell swoop and took off into the sky. Sandy waved as Shamma grew smaller and smaller as he flew into the silhouette of the moon. Her father watched from a distance and smiled.

"Prince Shamma is a handsome young man."

Sandy turned to see her father walking down the palace steps to escort her to her chambers. Sandy sighed, starry-eyed. "I don't think there are any guys like him in LA."

King Black laughed.

"My dear, I do think you have had enough for today. Let's get you to your bed, shall we?"

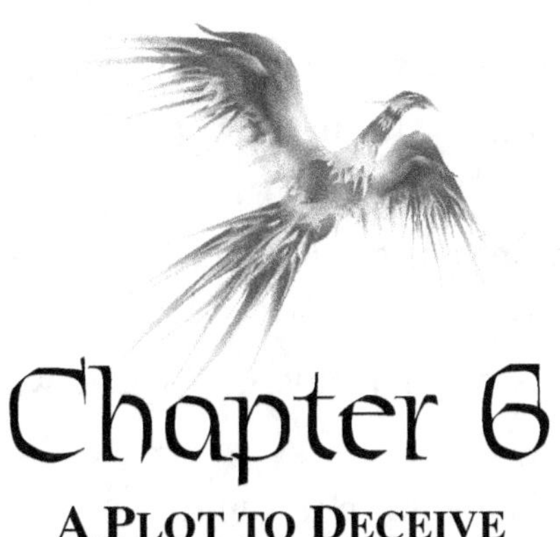

Chapter 6
A PLOT TO DECEIVE

While most were asleep, the queen stood in front of the mirror.

"Mirror, mirror on the wall,

whom I stand before and call,

I ask of you this very night,

of what to do to make things right,

to change the course of present time,

to make this Kingdom forever mine."

The mirror was still for a moment before speaking to the queen.

"The plan at hand you have will be,

the plan indeed to give to thee.

What it is you seek to find,

the kingdom you wish as yours for all time,

you have but make these to come true,

the death of one; no, the death of two.

Once you make it so then right,

the kingdom's yours once you dim the light."

The queen danced and sang like one intoxicated. "It shall be mine, all mine. The power that has evaded us for so long will finally be mine to wield. I shall crush this land and all its people. I will enslave the world with my power. All that come against me shall meet the edge of the sword."

The shadows in the room came to life and danced with her around the room. As

the mirror glowed and pulsed, "Speak with them this very night,

prepare the trip and keep in sight,

the goal of three whose seed your right,

to carry out this crude birthright."

The queen stopped dancing. "I will make haste to my mother now."

She flew out the door, hopped in her carriage and zoomed off into the wilderness. Atop the palace walls, David stood watching the departing carriage.

The palace was a hive of activity the next morning as the maids and menservants cleaned up after the last night's festivities.

The King greeted some of the workers as he strolled down the halls to Sandy's chambers.

"Good morning, Lucas,"

"Good morning, my King," Lucas replied with a bow.

"Good morning, Artimus and Hilda."

"Good morning, Sire," Artimus and Hilda replied simultaneously.

King Black was close to Sandy's room when David intercepted him.

"My King, may I speak with you for a moment?"

King Black observed David's face and knew it was a serious matter. "Yes of course, David. What troubles you?"

As they spoke, Sandy opened her door. King Black and

David stopped talking immediately when they saw her. Noticing their silence, Sandy glanced at both and grew worried. "Is there something wrong?"

King Black walked up to her and kissed her forehead.

"No, my princess. Hope you slept well?" Before Sandy could reply, a trumpet and drumbeat sounded that announced the arrival of Prince Shamma. David rushed off to the entrance to welcome the prince but Sandy stood, bewildered.

"Who could that be, Dad?" Sandy asked. King Black smiled, "You have company, my dear. What an impression you must have made."

"What are you talking about, Dad?"

King Black held her hand. "Let's go see your visitor."

King Black and Sandy met David rushing towards them in the hallway. Right behind him was Prince Shamma. Sandy blushed when she locked eyes with the prince.

David announced the prince's presence.

"My King, and my lady," David said as he bowed then turned in reference to the prince. "Prince Shamma."

"Good morning, King Black. I hope I haven't interrupted any of your plans today. But I was hoping to go horseback riding with your daughter, and maybe help her learn more about Moria."

King Black crossed his arms and frowned, a skeptical look on his face.

"Does your father know that you are here?"

"Yes, my lord. He does."

Prince Shamma cleared his throat and wiped the sweat from his brow while David stifled a smile.

"I informed him I was going to come to see if there might be any help I could render to you this day, my King."

"Hmm... help, you say? Didn't you say you wanted to help

my daughter learn more of Moria? A task that I am sure the King of Moria, her father would be better suited for, but what you really meant is that you wanted to go horseback riding with Sandy?" Prince Shamma blushed and nodded in agreement.

"David," said King Black, "what's the report like from the forest? Are the giants nearby today?"

"My lord," David said with a bow, "no giants have been sighted so it should be safe to ride today."

"Well then. Shamma, you may have lunch with the princess but be back before the fire flies dance. Do you understand me?"

Prince Shamma nodded. "Yes, King Black."

"Oh, and Shamma, I must warn you. She is a princess and is to be treated as such."

Prince Shamma bowed. "Of course, my King. You have my word as Prince of the Isles of Far Off."

"All right, children, have fun. David, we should be going."

While King Black and David continued their discussion in a private room, Prince Shamma and Sandy descended to the stables, mounted two horses and galloped off into the forest.

Deep in the forest beyond the queen's garden and nestled amongst a canopy of trees that blotted out the sun stood a cottage. The trees surrounding the cottage were covered in strange symbols written in red.

The queen, and the other witches dressed in hooded robes, held hands and chanted simultaneously in a dark room in the cottage.

"Oh, great spirit that is most powerful and wise, we ask of you this day for our rightful place. Bring about the rise of an oppressor from the east to smite the land with a curse. Bring about our rule once again that we may hold all power once more. May all of the kings of this world and the most powerful among them,

King Black, be consumed by this oppressor and its might. That we three, the Order of Shadows, might reign supreme once more and forever. You have promised us this in your ancient words, oh spirit of all power. We ask this of you on this day. Hear our voices oh great spirit."

As they chanted a great, shadowy figure loomed over them in the room. A loud, blood-curdling scream resounded throughout the forest. And then, silence filled the air. The three witches burst into laughter. "It is finished," said the eldest witch. "The great spirit has heard us, and chaos will reign down on this land."

The older witches look at the queen and said, "Daughter and fairest of the land, you will soon have the throne. Do not forget our plan and remember, our power is greater united."

The queen smiled. "I will do all that is required of me. I will send for you soon to be with me so that we might rule what is rightfully ours."

The three cackled with insidious laughter while embracing in the darkness.

***

"So, Princess, have you learned much about the forest and the creatures that live in it?" Prince Shamma asked Sandy.

"I've only heard about the giants and their attitude."

"Yes, they are a bit moody. But they are not the worst you can come across when in the forest. You see, my lady, everything in Moria is alive."

Sandy, a bit confused by the prince's statement, asked, "Alive? What do you mean?"

The prince stopped his horse, jumped down and stretched his hands towards Sandy. "Come with me. I will show you."

Prince Shamma pointed at a grove of giant oak trees.

"You see those trees, Princess? They talk."

Sandy giggled. "Trees that talk! What's next? Birds that really sing?"

Suddenly, giggles filled the air.

Sandy turned around. "What was that?"

The prince laughed. "It's the trees, Princess. They are laughing at you."

Sandy surveyed the trees and saw small faces on all of them. "Are you laughing at me?"

Sandy approached them to get a better look. The trees shushed each other and one of them, a large tree, spoke. "We are sorry, Princess, but it was quite funny that you didn't realize we were here."

Sandy fumed, a little upset that she was kept in the dark for so long.

"That's just rude. I could have done something embarrassing. You know it's not polite to spy on people."

The trees bowed in fear. "We are sorry, Your Highness," said the large tree. We will not do it again. Please do not hold this against us."

Suddenly aware that her words may have been a bit harsh, Sandy smiled at the large tree. "Oh, please don't be afraid. I'm just being fussy. You know who I am already. What's your name?"

"You're right, my princess. How rude of me. We are the builders of the forest as you would understand. We are called the Wajenzi. Without us there can be no forest. I have no name in the language that you know. There is no direct translation for our language, so it is very difficult for mankind to understand."

Sandy paused for a moment. Then she smiled. "Hmmm, I will call you Eve, because you are my first new friend from a new world."

Eve shook her branches in excitement.

"I am honored to have you call me your friend, Your Highness."

"My pleasure!" Sandy exclaimed.

"As my friend I must warn you, Princess, that there are others who are not as we are. They are evil; near to them do not stay! They are bound by the magic of the old order which was long and forgotten in Moria but which still exists to this day. We are friends of the King, but they are sworn enemies because of the oath they have sworn to darkness. You will know them by their red markings. Magical spells are placed on those who inhabit enchanted areas of the forest."

The prince stepped in front of Sandy.

"That's enough now. The princess doesn't need these rumors of times past and of evil not seen in a millennium."

Eve turned to the prince.

"Young prince, you would be wise to listen and know what it is I speak of. Even to this very day, darkness does not sleep. Especially with your arrival, my lady."

Sandy's eyes widened at Eve's last statement. The prince cleared his throat. "Alright, alright, I understand as there is good in the world there will always be bad, but let's not assume that because there is bad that it is going to somehow notice or pursue Princess Sandy. We have spent enough time here, my lady. We should be on our way. Thank you for your time, Eve."

Sandy still looked at Eve intently.

"Thank you, Eve," Sandy said.

"The pleasure is all mine, my lady. I do apologize if I have said too much, and maybe the prince is right. All of this could just be a rumor in the forest. I bid you farewell."

As the prince and Sandy mounted their horses, Eve shook her leaves.

"Princess, I hope I am wrong but if I am not, mind the skies. For they shall be as night even in the day, and the light of man shall not shine through when that hour arrives."

Sandy nodded and continued away with Prince Shamma. Soon, they stopped at a spot with odd-looking plants. The plants had big purple bulbs with long stems. Prince Shamma jumped down and helped Sandy down. "This is very special," Prince Shamma said, pointing at the plants. "It is very strange for this to be in season right now."

Sandy clueless, walked towards the plants and peered at them. "What are you talking about?" Prince Shamma knelt to one of the plants and pulled it off the ground. He tore the bulb in half and the smell of fresh-baked bread filled the air. "This is a manna plant."

Sandy looked at the prince like he had lost his mind.

"A what?"

"A manna plant."

"You mean like manna from heaven? Like what God fed his people in the desert with?"

The prince stood, amazed. "Yes, you know the story? Our history from the Isles of Far Off tells of this great gift God gave our forefathers. This plant was created from one of those loaves being planted into the ground as a reminder for us. In its season, this plant produces a bread that is life-sustaining. People say one giant loaf can fill your needs for a year. Hunters and people who get lost in the forest, as well as the poor, seek out this plant. I'm surprised to find it at this time because this is not its season. Normally, you don't even notice this plant until it's ready to be picked."

Prince Shamma gave Sandy half of the manna. "Try it!"

Sandy shut her eyes for a moment, put the bulb to her mouth and tasted it. When she opened them, they were bright with excitement.

"This is amazing! It's like having a full meal all in one bite. It doesn't taste like bread at all. It's more like eating six or seven different courses at once. Kinda tastes like Mexican food!"

The prince chuckled, flashing her a dazzling white smile.

"It is said that the manna plant will take on the flavor of whatever your heart is seeking as far as food goes. I guess for you, it is this Mexican food."

Sandy smiled as they mounted their horses. She rubbed her tummy. "This is amazing. I feel full."

Prince Shamma nodded. "Yes; it's a miracle, isn't it?

***

While they continued back into the gates of the palace, King Black and David were still deep in discussion.

The queen was announced as she entered the King's private room. David bowed before the queen, and the maids left the room. The queen gave a nod to David and walked up to the King with a huge smile on her face. The King spoke, "Where have you been??"

"Your Highness?" the Queen asked, pretending not to have heard the question.

"You forgot that I have instructed you not to leave the palace grounds without letting me know first?"

The queen embraced the King.

"Oh, my King, I do apologize. I had received word that my mother was ill, and I needed to go tend to her."

"If this is true, why didn't you inform me so that I could send the best physicians with you?"

"Great King Black. I wanted to confirm that the report was true before I asked for your assistance." The King, unconvinced, pulled away from the queen.

"I will not tolerate disregard for my word from you. There are far too many matters I have to deal with, and I won't have you adding to them."

The queen bowed.

"I am sorry I have offended you, my King. What must I do to regain your trust? May we spend some time together tonight? I could spend some time with Sandy this evening so as to give you time before dinner to address your matters. Then later we can spend a romantic evening together by the lake. How does that sound to you?"

"I don't think you fully understand what it is I need from you, but I do need some time to handle some pressing matters. And I do think you need to spend time with Sandy, but don't think you can pacify me with your charm. I will see you later tonight. Till then, have a good time with my daughter."

King Black kissed the queen on the forehead and walked out of the room. Close to the dragon stables, Sandy and Prince Shamma said their goodbyes.

"I wish I could spend more time with you, Princess, but I have some matters to deal with at home."

"I do understand, Prince Shamma. You've got responsibilities. Handle your business."

Shamma wasn't sure what 'handle your business' meant but he liked the sound of it.

"I will handle my business. And once I am finished, I will come to see you again; that is, if that is alright with you?"

Sandy smoothed her hair. "I think we can do that. I had a great time with you today. I can only imagine what else I have to see and learn."

"Oh there is much for you to see and learn, my princess. It's impossible to see it all in one day. I look forward to many fun days with you in the future."

"I can't wait."

They gazed into each other's eyes. "It hurts to leave you, Princess."

"Please, call me Sandy."

Prince Shamma pulled Sandy close to him and kissed her on the cheek.

Just then they heard a loud CRACK and they jumped away from one another, startled by the sound. David rushed to the scene while one of the stable-hands came out with his hair singed and clothes tattered.

David looked him over. "What happened in there?"

"I'm all right," he said. "I was giving the dragons their shots and Ithros wasn't very happy about the needle."

Thankful it wasn't King Black that had showed up, Sandy and Prince Shamma breathed a heavy sigh of relief. David smiled at both of them.

"Prince Shamma, I believe it's time for you to go home. Princess, I believe you need to meet with the queen now."

"Yes, Sir," Prince Shamma said as he mounted his dragon. "I'll be on my way now."

He looked down at Sandy and their eyes locked together.

"I will be waiting for our next adventure," Sandy said as she played with her hair.

"That shall be sooner than you think, Sandy," the prince said with a bow. He mounted his dragon and took off into the sky.

David glanced at Sandy as she stared at the sky. "A new friend I should say, Princess."

Sandy walked towards the door and paused. "You could say that, David, but don't tell my father please. I don't know what you saw..."

"Don't worry, Princess. I saw nothing. There's no need to alert the army when there is no war brewing."

Sandy glanced nervously at David. "Thank you, David."

David ushered her into the palace.

"The queen awaits you in the garden."

"Oh, ok, another girls' bonding moment. Cool, I'm on my way."

Sandy hugged David and scurried into the palace.

Chapter 7

THE STORM

Sandy walked over to the palace garden. On her way, she met Chef Tasty who had his hands full with a basket of various vegetables.

"Hello Princess. How are you?"

Sandy smiled. "Oh, hi Chef Tasty!"

She looked at the basket in his hands. "My goodness you've got a lot of plans this evening, I see."

"Of course, Princess. Tonight, I will prepare the most delicious vegetable soup you have ever tasted, with an assortment of cheeses and fruit. And that's just the first course. Hmmm mmmm! I'm getting hungry just thinking about it!"

Sandy laughed. "That's wonderful. I can almost taste and smell it now."

"You know, Princess, the secret to this wonderful garden is in the dragons."

"What do you mean by that?"

More than happy to tell her the story since it had to do with food, Chef Tasty's eyes lit up. "Well Princess, this very garden was the first garden our people created. The reason they chose this location was because this was a dragon dung heap."

Sandy frowned. "You mean this was a litter box for dragons?"

"Sandy darling, you must understand the beasts." Sandy turned around and saw the queen suddenly behind her, smiling.

"They are very protective and clean with their homes," the queen continued. "So, they used this place long ago as a public restroom."

Chef Tasty nodded. "Yes, yes, and you see their dung fertilizes the ground better than anything and it produces fruits and vegetables of the greatest quality." Chef Tasty held up a giant carrot. Sandy reached for it, "May I?" "Of course, Princess. But be careful, it has some weight to it."

Sandy took the carrot, carefully supporting its weight and marveled at how large it was. It must have weighed over 20 lbs. The queen looked at the orange root with disgust, lifted it slowly out of her hands, and dumped it back in the chef's basket. "Chef, I believe you have a lot of work to do."

Chef Tasty nodded, knowing full well the queen wanted him to leave.

"Yes, yes, I do. Princess, it was nice chatting with you. I will reserve some of this soup for you."

"Thank you so much, Chef Tasty," Sandy replied. Chef Tasty bowed before the queen and skipped to the kitchen, singing to the vegetables as if they were babies.

"Wonderful, wonderful food,

wonderful, wonderful food,

I love to make, to eat, to bake!

Wonderful, wonderful food."

Sandy and the Queen looked at each other in amusement.

"Princess, I'm very happy we could get some more time together. I am eager to know more about you."

"Same here," Sandy said.

The queen led Sandy to a small bench near some of the largest sunflowers Sandy had ever seen. As they sat, the sunflowers started talking.

"Hello, hello, how are you? How are you?"

Sandy turned and saw two sunflowers smiling at her. *First it was the talking trees, and now talking flowers! This place is sur-real!*

The two sunflowers continued,

"Hey, hey Queeny. Isn't it sunny out here today?"

The queen hissed, unamused.

The sunflowers smiled the more. "Isn't it sun-flowery to you? Ooh and the princess, ooh she is beautiful. Yeah, the birds said you look like an angel, and sleep like a baby."

Sandy giggled. The queen fumed. "SILENCE!"

Immediately, the two sunflowers stopped talking.

"What's wrong with you?" Sandy asked, annoyed. "Why did you do that? They didn't do anything wrong. I didn't like you when I met you, but lately you have been trying to be nice to me so I've been giving you a pass. But I can tell you are faking it, just like that smile you gave me a few minutes ago. What is your problem?"

Reining in her anger, the queen feigned regret and put on her most pitiful expression. "I apologize, Sandy, for my behavior. I have been irritable lately. You see, my mother is sick and I'm not sure how much longer she has left."

"Well, you can't go around being mad at folk. It's not any-one's fault your mother is sick. It's just how things are some-times. I know because my mom was sick for a while before she passed on. It was hard to watch her get worse as time went by, but I had to be strong for her. I didn't want her to worry about what was going to happen to me since she had enough on her plate. But I guess that's kinda how I ended up here. She already had a plan."

Sandy surveyed the beautiful garden surrounding her and sighed. "I know God has a plan for everyone and everything comes or goes in its season. Things are happening really fast."

The queen, seeing Sandy's vulnerability, seized the moment. "Sandy, have you ever thought of going back home for a while? I know things happened so fast. You should go back and visit your mother's gravesite. Wouldn't that be nice? I mean you did leave everything so quickly."

"My mother is dead. The Good Book says to be absent from the body is to be present with God, the Father. And in Moria, I've been given something I didn't have back in Los Angeles. A fresh start and a father. I'm alone back there; here I have my dad and he truly is better than any dream I could have ever come up with. I can't go back now; there is too much for me here. Too much to learn and understand. Like how did you end up with my father anyway? I know he loved my mother. So why did he choose you?"

The queen faked a smile, "I am the fairest in all of Moria. The most beautiful woman in all the land. It is the law of the land that the most beautiful woman marries the King."

"Well, if you're so fine, how come you're so ugly on the inside? You've got a bad attitude and you are never really happy."

The queen shrugged. "Princess, I am the most powerful woman in all of the land. I can do as I want. What woman doesn't want to be feared by all?"

Sandy rolled her eyes. "Sounds like you're a gold digger to me. Hasn't anyone ever told you beauty is only skin-deep? You're only going to be fine for so long. Then your butt will droop and your skin will wrinkle. What are you going to do then? It's not what's on the outside but what's on the inside that makes you beautiful."

The queen laughed.

"Ooh, Sandy You are so naive. No one can see what's on the inside of you. So, in Moria, beauty is everything for a woman."

"Well, it doesn't seem like my father thinks you're all that. You have no kids."

The queen laughed again. "You're very confident, like your father. I can see now that we may never get along. You are very bright and beautiful, but your naivety will cost you here. I will give you some advice, young princess. Go back to your home and remember not what you have seen here. This is all a dream to you. It can become a nightmare if you stay past your time."

Sandy fisted her hands.

"Stop threatening me, you old ugly witch."

The queen, thinking her true identity had been exposed, covered her face and backed away from Sandy. Sandy stood and faced the queen, her hands still fisted. "This is my home and if you think I'm going to go back so you can find some way to try and mess with my father, you're tripping!"

Sandy took off her earrings and slippers.

"I'm from LA, baby, and we don't take crap. I think I need to teach you a lesson."

The two sunflowers woke up. "You go girl. That's right, she is a witch, get her! Make her shut up!"

The queen dashed off to her chambers. "You and I will have our time, Sandy. Very soon! Hahahahahahaha!"

"I'm going to go tell my daddy!" Sandy screamed.

"Yeah, go tell your daddy, girl," the sunflowers said. "That will teach her. Why you running? Huh? Huh, Queeny?!"

Sandy smiled at the sunflowers. "Thanks you two. I'll come back and talk to you later. Right now, I have to go tell my father what just happened."

Sandy ran off to find the King.

As night fell over Moria, a dragon rider approached the palace gates. David and some of his men waited to welcome the rider when he landed. As the rider and the dragon approached, David noticed an arrow lodged in the dragon's side and blood flowing from the rider's head.

When they landed, David commanded his men to administer first aid immediately. One of the men attending to the rider ran to David. "Sir!" he said, "there is a message for the King!"

David ran over, his heart beating hard. As he got closer, he noticed that the rider was from the Isles of Far Off. David's heart sank at the thought of the news to come. The rider sat up. "Tell your King, the Isles of Far Off is under attack from a dark army. They are attacking from all sides. I barely made it out."

David, concerned about the King asked, "Is your King safe?"

"Yes; for now. We have moved him and the rest of the royal family to the refuge. We will need all your army to overcome this enemy. They are too much for us."

David turned to his men.

"Take this man and his dragon to their respective infirmaries and treat them as the King's family."

"Yes, Sir."

David rushed to the King's chambers. Sandy, still unfamiliar with the palace, got lost while searching for the King's chambers. Fortunately she met Lilly, the head maid, on the way. "Excuse me."

Lilly bowed. "Yes, Princess?"

"I need to get to my father's room but I can't find it.".

"Oh, you go back down the far corridor, turn left at the statue of your mother, climb the staircase and turn right. You will see the doors."

"Thank you so much, Lilly."

"You are welcome, Princess." As Sandy searched for her father's room, David was there already. He met the King on his knees, praying. "My King, we have a problem."

King Black rose to his feet.

"What is the problem?"

"The Isles of Far Off are under attack."

King Black was shocked. "What of King Anannias?"

"My King your friend, as I am told, is safe for now. His family are also safe. I am told they might not be able to resist for long and that your entire army is needed."

"Who dared attack one of my allies? Was it the empire of Gog, or Magog?"

"My King, I am told this is like no enemy we have known. An army of shadows. Much like that which your father dealt with many centuries ago with the Nefarians."

"Assemble the army. We must leave immediately."

David rushed out of the King's chambers to carry out the King's order. The King hurried to the armory to get prepared for battle.

Sandy found herself on an upstairs open patio. Frustrated, she turned around and walked down a hallway. The blast of a trumpet, the beating of drums, and stamping of feet almost made Sandy jump out of her skin. Down the hallway, she overheard some of the maids talking.

"Did you hear that the King is leaving with the entire army to help King Ananias?"

Sandy panicked. *I need to see Dad as soon as possible!*

Outside, the dragons were armored and set for their riders.

The army filled the courtyard awaiting the King. Clad in black armor that looked like black rose pedals with thorny points throughout, King Black strode to the balcony to address the soldiers. He turned to David who was by his side.

"Where is Sandy? I must speak to her before I leave."

"The last time I saw her was when she went to spend time with the queen." As if on cue, Sandy ran towards King Black. "Dad!" she screamed. What's going on?"

King Black turned and hugged Sandy. "Sandy, I must leave at once. A terrible enemy has attacked King Ananias." Sandy's face fell. "You mean Prince Shamma's father?"

"Yes, darling. I must go now before it is too late to help."

"I want to go with you. I can't stay here with the queen. She doesn't like me; we just had a fight. She is no good, Dad. Something isn't right about that woman. She threatened me." "Sandy, are you sure all this happened or is it that you just don't like her?"

"Dad, I'm sure."

King Black looked into her eyes and remembered when Sandy's mother had the same serious expression.

"I don't know what's going on but I believe you. I cannot bring you with me, Sandy. It is too dangerous." The King turned to David.

"David, find out what's going on between the queen and Sandy. Protect the princess too!"

David bowed. "Yes, my King. I will protect her with my life."

King Black nodded. "I know you will."

King Black turned back to Sandy.

"Sandy, David is your personal bodyguard. If something goes wrong while I am gone, trust him to keep you safe. I will write to you every day. As long as you reply, I will know you are safe."

"Dad, I'm scared."

King Black smiled.

"All will be fine, Sandy. You will see."

The King hugged and kissed her forehead and took her hand in his. He then walked with her to the balcony overlooking the great courtyard to address his army. The soldiers all wore shiny armor and carried shields and swords. The armor and shields had the royal symbol of the flower — a black rose with a dragon encircled around it. The soldiers echoed a loud war cry when they saw King Black. King Black lifted his hands and there was silence. Sandy looked around and saw servants watching through the windows and standing in the doorway.

"Our friend and ally, King Ananias of the Isles of Far Off, was attacked by an unknown enemy. We must assist our ally and vanquish this threat. I know we have the greatest army in all of the lands in Moria and beyond. We will prove it today as we crush this enemy. Let us pray." Everyone bowed their heads.

"Heavenly Father, I stand before you now as King of your people, before your army. Father, as we go to battle, we ask that you watch over us and protect us as you have always done. And that for those you will take home, that you bless their family with peace. Lord, we pray this before you this day. Amen."

"Amen," everyone chorused.

"Now, if God is for us, who can be against us!" King Black raised his sword. "Onward, we fly into battle."

The entire army echoed a war cry, raising their shields and swords in salute. The dragons spat fire high into the sky.

King Black pulled David to his side. "If things get bad over here, take Sandy back to the portal and send her to her world as she will be safer there until I get home. Do you understand?"

David nodded. "Yes, my King."

"Keep your eyes open and keep me informed of anything unusual."

"Yes, my lord."

"And keep my daughter safe."

"I will, my lord."

The King walked over to Sandy.

"Remember, David will be your protector. If anything seems strange, just call on him and let him know."

"Yes, Dad," Sandy said with uncertainty.

"I love you; remember that."

"I love you too, Dad."

Sandy hugged King Black fiercely and put on a brave face for her father. He kissed her forehead and turned and jumped over the side of the balcony, landing on his dragon who whisked him off into the sky. David and Sandy watched as the soldiers joined King Black in the air. Sandy held David's arm as tears rolled down her cheeks.

David turned to Sandy. "All will be well, Princess. Come; it's time for dinner. I heard Chef Tasty is making a wonderful meal for you tonight."

Sandy wiped her tears. "You are right. I need to relax. Everything will be ok," she said as she walked towards the dining room. Somehow Sandy didn't believe that at all.

David, knowing he had to keep an eye on the queen, stopped.

"Sandy, go ahead. I need to inform the queen about dinner."

Sandy rolled her eyes.

"Does she have to eat with us?"

"Yes, she does. I need to keep a close eye on her."

Sandy sighed. "OK, but I'll knock her out if she starts tripping. I just want you to know." David laughed as Sandy strolled to the dining room. As David approached the queen's chambers, he heard the queen talking. Curious to see who she was conversing with, he opened the door carefully. The room was as black as night. Suddenly there came a blinding light from the mirror across the room and he squinted as his eyes adjusted to the scene before him. The queen stood in front of the mirror, breathing heavily in a deep drawl.

"Mirror, mirror on the wall,
My spell has been cast and soon a war,
Shall engulf this land and make them pay,
For memories past and misplaced days.
The reign of the spirits shall be once more,
The King slain attempting to help before,
I take back what is mine and that's all I see,
All will bow and fall before me."
The mirror shook and smoked.
"Oh ruthless queen who stands before me.
All shall be yours; everything you see.
But first you must make an end to the King,
and after that Sandy Black must not be.
Since she is still more fair than thee."

The queen cackled. "My plans won't change. I will kill the princess and erase her name."

She laughed and danced like a drunk and as she did, loud thunder shook the palace. A sudden downpour took over. David slipped out of the room and rushed to the dining room.

How come this evil has been happening under our noses and we didn't know? We didn't know the queen is a witch!

Reeling from his discovery, he tried as much as he could not to attract attention to himself as he made his way down the hall. He didn't know how many servants were on the queen's side. David had never taken a liking to the queen but it was not until Sandy showed up that her actions had become out of the norm.

They had all been caught off guard. How had she not been found out? Why was she so beautiful? Why was she waiting so long to launch an attack? What was she waiting for? All of these questions swirled around David's head as he thought of the best plan to address the circumstances. First and foremost he must get Sandy some place safe, but not move too quickly as to draw too much attention to them.

David crashed into the dining room, causing Sandy to jump to her feet. "David?"

David shushed her and whispered in her ear. "Princess; to-night…"

The door opened and a trumpet blasted as the queen sashayed into the room wearing a long flowing black gown, headdress, and dark makeup. She took her seat at the end of the dining table and smiled at Sandy and David. "David, how come I wasn't informed about dinner?" David faked a smile.

"I apologize, my queen. There was a lot going on with the King's departure and I had a lot to explain to the princess as to what to expect."

The queen cackled. "I'm sure Sandy understands things well. She is a smart and strong girl."

Sandy hissed and David's heart raced in his chest for fear of the queen's reaction. He heaved a sigh of relief when he saw the queen admiring her long, jet-black nails.

Not too far away, Chef Tasty's melodic voice rang loud and clear.

"Veggie tables, veggie tables,

How I love your smell.

Cooked down in this broth of mine.

Where you cook and swell.

As if on cue, the kitchen staff brought in steaming portions of food and served their patrons. David left his food untouched. His eyes were locked on the queen, who was humming to herself. Steadily, Sandy glared at the queen. Nudging David, she whispered in his ears.

"I'm trying to be nice, but she is driving me nuts with her humming. Could you please tell her to stop or I'll throw a dinner roll at her!"

David turned to Sandy, "Finish up quickly. I need to tell you something."

One look at David's face sent a chill down Sandy's spine. His face was ashen and beads of sweat clung to his forehead. Scared, Sandy rushed her dinner like a child threatened by her iron-fisted parent. Chef Tasty bounced in, grinning from ear to ear. He bowed before the queen, then turned to Sandy. "Princess, I hope you are enjoying your meal?"

Chef Tasty, this is the best soup I've ever had. In fact," Sandy yawned, "it was so good it made me sleepy." She rose to her feet and hugged Chef Tasty.

Chef Tasty looked at Sandy with a puzzled frown. "I never get sleepy when I eat something good. It just makes me want to eat more of it. I'll take that as a compliment. I guess where you are from, good food has that effect on you." He smiled, "Have a good night's rest. You will love breakfast."

Sandy nodded, stealing a glance at David who was wiping his brow. "I'm sure I will. Mr. Tasty, you're the best chef ever."

Chef Tasty, now on cloud nine after that statement, giggled

and skipped to the kitchen. David stood. "Princess, I will escort you to your chambers now. You had questions for me earlier, right?"

Sandy played along.

"Oh yes; thanks for reminding me, David, I just have a few questions."

They walked out together when the queen called after them, "David?"

David froze. He turned back slowly and met the queen's steady gaze. "Yes, my queen?"

"Can I see you later in the evening?"

"My queen, I have so much to do this evening. Could we meet later in the morning?"

The queen turned back to her dinner.

"That will be fine, David." She dipped her spoon in her soup bowl.

David bowed. "Thank you, my queen."

Lightning flashed and thunder clapped as Sandy and David hurried down the hallway. David pulled Sandy into the palace library and locked the door. Squatting close to a shelf, he brought out a dusty book with an inscription on it that read, *"The First Book Of Man,"* and dumped it on the table. Sandy coughed as a dust cloud filled the air.

"Sandy, I don't expect you to understand all of this, but I have to get you back to your world."

"What? Why?" Sandy replied.

"This book contains the beginning of recorded history of the rule of man in this land. Before this history the first men in Moria came from your realm, escaping persecution or disaster. Some formed tribes to protect themselves from the darkness that controlled this world full of monsters and beasts. Mankind fought amongst themselves for ages over resources, gaining nothing and losing much. Until the representative of the almighty above, the Great Tree of the forest sent a light to guide the heads of each tribe to a sacred place for a meeting that would change the course of history. Peace was ushered in the place of this meeting and flowers bloomed of many different colors. Each leader chose a different color which then represented the beginning of a new house or kingdom. Hence your father, King Black - house of the black rose. King Ananias White of the Isles of Far Off, house of the white rose, and so on and so forth. Thirteen kingdoms were formed that day. Yet there was one leader, Nefaria, who rebelled against the idea of peace. Nefaria vowed to gain her own power for her people and then subjugate all 13 kingdoms. The newly formed kingdoms were given territories throughout Moria by the Great Tree. Each kingdom was to flourish in its lands, not to impede upon the others. Refusing to be a part, Nefaria took her people and went to the darkest parts of the forest. There, she and her people were corrupted by the dark power they found. It changed them; made them grotesque and evil. Between the 13 a pact was made to protect the realm from an endless war for power. This pact brought about the Tournament of Roses, a month-long contest of skill, wit, and power held at the site of the pact's creation that determined the ruler of all of Moria for a season. After many millennia of peace, the great war happened. Nefaria's people caused a great tragedy that created the great war and in it the loss of 11 of the 13 kingdoms and their royal lines. All would have been lost had not your grandfather not been able to rally those who survived to this palace for a last stand. After defeating Nefaria's people, all that remained was a woman and her daughter. Your grandfather, seeing no threat from them, banished them to the forest to live out their days and die."

Sandy was still confused. "You're right, that is a lot to digest, but you said these evil people are ugly, right, so it should be easy to identify them?"

David responded. "You are right, Sandy. But this time I have seen one who is different. I don't know how she has changed her appearance, but she has."

"So how do you know she is one of these evil order women?"

"I've seen her use a device rumored to be used by Nefaria herself. A mirror you can speak to, and it will tell you of things in the future."

Sandy's face turned white as she remembered her visit to the queen's chambers.

"David, the queen has a mirror like that."

David looked back at Sandy. "I know. This is why I must get you back to your home world so she can't harm you."

"I knew she wasn't right. I knew it! The sunflowers in the garden called her a witch and that's exactly what she is."

David calmed Sandy down.

"Shush! We have to behave as though we are unaware. I don't know who may be working for her and how powerful she might be. You need to go to your chambers and don't let anyone else in. I'll come for you. Take only things that you need. We will leave tonight under the cover of darkness, get you back to the portal and you will be safe until your father gets back; then I will come for you again."

Sandy agreed to the plan. She went to her room while David walked up to the King's chambers to make some final preparations.

As all was quiet and still in the palace and, as the maids and menservants closed doors and drapes for the night, David made his way towards Sandy's chambers. Vigilant, he listened to every noise and watched every shadow. Who knew who could be working for the queen? The sound of howling wind and rain beating the rooftops and walls made it harder for David to be sure no-one was following him. Thunder crashed and lightning flashed outside the windows.

"These are the perfect conditions for this situation," David said to himself. Finally, he reached Sandy's door. As he was about to open it, Lilly showed up.

"My lord, is there something you need me to get from the princess for you?" Lilly asked.

"No, Lilly. The King asked me before he departed to check on the princess at night, just to make sure she is comfortable."

"Well, if you would, my lord, I can go and check on the young damsel. I wouldn't want her to be indecent upon your entering her bed chambers. After all, she is a young lady."

"No, Lilly. Things will be fine – you may leave now."

Lilly bowed her head. "As you wish, my lord. I shall go see to the queen now."

David raised his eyebrows as he knew it won't be long before the queen got wind of him in Sandy's bedchamber. He must move quickly. Lilly walked off towards the queen's chambers. David opened the door, after looking for any other distractions or witnesses. Sandy inside was dressed and ready to go.

"David, when are we going and to where?"

David shut the door.

"Listen to me, Sandy, this could get dangerous. You need to stay as close to me as possible. Don't make any extra noise and don't talk. We are going through a secret passageway, and then out to the forest. If anything happens to separate us along the way, you run back to the spot your father took you for lunch near the portal to your world. Do you understand me? You go there and as soon as you see the portal open, you go through. You will be safe in your world." Sandy was a bit uneasy.

"I don't have a good feeling about this, David. I'm scared. What if we get separated and I get lost? What if the portal doesn't open? What if we get caught?"

David walked over to Sandy and grabbed her by the shoulders.

"You will be fine. We will make it to the portal. And you will be safe. You must believe this. You are a member of the Black family. You are stronger than you know."

"OK, we are going to make it. I'm ready." Sandy hoped her steady affirmation would overcome the fear that rocked her to the core.

David pulled out his sword and opened the door carefully. He grabbed Sandy by the hand. Sandy's eyes grew wide when she saw David's sword. The full weight of the situation was starting to sink in. Slowly, down the hall they went. Lightning flashed and thunder rumbled. Sandy was afraid, but determined not to show it. Closer and closer, the two got to the King's chambers when suddenly, they heard footsteps coming from the floor below. The queen's voice ran through the hall. "Find them and bring her to me!"

Quickly, David pulled Sandy as they ran to the King's chambers. They passed by a flight of stairs and saw a group of soldiers who were loyal to the queen, who gave chase. Finally, they got to the door of the King's chambers. David opened the door and pushed Sandy inside, shutting the door behind.

"Quick, Sandy! Find something we can place behind the door."

On the wall next to a bookshelf were two lances. Sandy

grabbed them off the wall and handed them to David.

"Here, will these work?"

David jammed them across the door to stop their pursuers from getting in. As soon as the doors seemed secured, the servants behind hit the door with a huge object. Wham!

David yelled at Sandy. "Sandy - on the far wall is a black stone. Lean against it and touch it with your birthmark."

Sandy rushed across the room to the far wall, trying to find the black stone in the wall. David leaned against the door, attempting to prevent the doors from opening.

"David, I can't see it!"

"It's just past the center line of the wall."

Sandy looked harder.

"I see it. OK, so I'm just supposed to lean against it with my birthmark, right."

David, struggling with the door, yelled. "Yesss!"

Sandy pulled her hair to the side and leaned back against the black stone. A blue glow emanated from the stone and a passageway opened in the wall.

"I've opened it."

David set himself to move from the door. "OK. Go on. I'll be right behind you. Go now go, go."

Sandy turned and ran into the dark passageway. David pushed the door with his feet and dashed towards the doorway. The two of them ran into the dark corridor. Their pursuers tore down the door with axes, making their way into the corridor as well.

Deep in the corridor, Sandy saw an exit up ahead when lightning flashed.

"There is the exit. We are almost there, David."

David looked back to see if anyone had got through to follow them. He saw a group of men in pursuit with swords and axes.

"Sandy, remember what I told you. Get to the portal. I must stop here."

Sandy slowed down.

"No, we are almost out. Come on, don't leave me! We can make it remember; you told me we can make it!"

David stopped just as they are at the end of the corridor. His eyes were already used to the darkness. He knew he had to stop and fight to save Sandy. Sandy was already outside in the rain at the edge of the forest outside of the palace walls, with the wind whipping through her hair and lightening flashing above. She saw David standing at the mouth of the corridor.

"David!" Sandy yelled. "David come on; we are here! We are out now, let's go."

David motioned Sandy to keep going. The soldiers were close already. The first to attack met the edge of David's sword. He dodged his falling body and prepared for the next attack. Sandy screamed as she saw the men attack David. She wanted to help but she knew David was trying to protect her and there was nothing she could do. David jumped over a thrown spear and for-ward-rolled over an axe on the ground from the next attacker. Throwing it at the remaining attackers, he created enough time to look back at Sandy to tell her to run.

"Run, Sandy Black. Get to the portal; don't worry about me!"

Sandy, still scared, stood watching. David noticed a beam that was holding up the roof to the corridor.

"For Moria!" he yelled, and cut the beam. The roof collapsed on him and the pursuers. Sandy screamed

"David! No!"

Alone, cold and afraid, Sandy turned around and ran.

Chapter 8

ALONE

Sandy ran as fast as she could through the stormy night into the forest. Not paying attention to where she was running, she slipped in the mud and slid off the trail and down a small hill. She brushed past some bushes and splashed into a stream. Sitting in the cold stream, alone and scared, she cried. "David, you said you wouldn't leave me. Mommy, what am I supposed to do now, huh? What now?" Sandy glanced around, not knowing where she was in the dark forest. "Daddy is gone, I'm alone, and this crazy woman is trying to kill me."

She staggered to her feet and moved to a place under a tree. Curling up and rocking herself to keep warm, Sandy cried out to her mother. "Mommy, I'm scared. I need you. Please, Mommy. I don't know what to do." As Sandy cried, she heard a familiar voice in the rain. "Sandy girl, calm down."

Sandy looked around, trying to locate the speaker. She rose to her feet. Not far away, a glowing figure moved towards her. "Sandy, you know crying ain't fixing nothing."

Sandy now knew this voice.

"Mommy! Mommy it's you! But how?"

"Sandy, don't worry about that. This place is special. Just like you. And sometimes when your heart really needs something, the forest will provide it for you.”

“I understand. Mommy I miss you so much!” The tears began to stream uncontrollably down Sandy's face.

“Baby girl, it's not safe for you here. You have to move. That woman is evil, and you must hide.”

Sandy was feeling overwhelmed with the situation. “Mommy, I don’t know where to go. I don’t know where to hide.”

“Sandy, find Eve. Follow the fireflies; they will light your path.” Out of her hand flew a swarm of fireflies.

“Remember, baby, I’m always with you. You have to keep your head and think, or she will find you. I love you Sandy, my sweet girl. Now get moving!” She vanished.

“Mommy, Mommy. Don’t leave.”

In the distance, dogs barked. Sandy quickly collected herself and heard a small group of voices. “Princess, follow us,” the fireflies said, their voices sounding like children. As she ran, she looked back and saw lights flashing. Torches! She turned back and ran after the fireflies like her life depended on it. They made their way through twists and turns and around rocks and up hills.

“How much further?” she yelled. “I think they are gaining on us.”

“Not much further, Princess,” the fireflies replied in unison. “Don’t you worry.”

As they got to a grove of trees, the dogs’ barks sounded very close. The fireflies spiraled up and flashed their lights in bright blue, red and yellow. Sandy stood watching as a tree limb swooped her up into its canopy. Almost immediately, the group that was chasing her arrived. The fireflies burst into hundreds of colors and then their lights extinguished with a flash! Then, darkness. The dogs barked and the men flashed torches around, searching the forest. High up in the tree, Eve whispered to Sandy, "Shush! They will pass soon. Just be still."

Sandy nodded. The group below searched for hours. Then they gave up and moved on. As the sound of the dogs slowly faded away, the rain stopped. Sandy sighed in relief, laid back on the branch she was on, and from exhaustion fell fast asleep.

A few hours later, very early in the morning, A voice woke Sandy up.

"Princess, Princess, wake up, please."

Sandy found herself high above the ground on a moving tree. Sandy, not sure of what was going on, thought the events of the last night had been a bad dream.

"Where, what's going on?" Sandy looked around and could see from atop Eve a group of trees moving through the forest.

"Good morning, Princess," Eve said. "You are awake."

"I guess last night wasn't a dream after all." Sandy remembered David. "Oh, my goodness. Eve, we have to go back to help David!"

"Princess, I'm sure he is fine. He can take care of himself. What is important now is that we hide you as best we can until your father gets back. The queen will most certainly send out another group to find you soon. We are too close to the palace, so now we move deeper into the forest."

Sandy held on to Eve as the convoy of Wajenzi moved deeper into the forest. Stepping over large hills and streams, the group moved while animals and beasts scurried out of their way at their swift movement.

Curious, Sandy asked, "Is this what you were talking about when we first met? Is this what you were telling me to watch out for when it got dark?"

Eve, paying more attention to the movement of the group

than Sandy's question, suddenly halted the group. Eve whispered to Sandy, "Something is up ahead, and if it's what I think it is, we are not safe here."

Sandy heard the cry of what sounded like a large child. Recognizing the sound, she wasn't scared anymore, but the trees were still on alert. She jumped down from Eve's branch. "Princess, stay put! You don't know what that might be."

Sandy rolled her eyes. "Eve, I'm not going to sit up here and be scared forever. Plus, it sounds like somebody could use some help."

"Princess, it would be unwise to go forward now. Please let me look ahead."

Sandy reluctantly allowed Eve to investigate the strange sound. Sitting atop one of Eve's branches, Sandy waited for the outcome.

Eve sent two of the other tree folks ahead to check the source of the sound. The crying and sniffing got louder as the group passed through bushes. Suddenly, a twig snapped on the ground and the crying and sniffing stopped. The trees stood still, waiting to see what would happen next. Without warning a giant, taller than the trees in their group, roared from beneath the trees surrounding them. The giant rose to his feet and towered over most of the trees in the group. He was 30ft tall, and clad in orange-colored clothing that looked similar to overhauls. He threw up his hands in a display of anger towards the Wajenzi. Scared at first, Sandy remembered her first encounter with the giants. She thought of what her father told her. "Eve, if we leave him alone, he won't bother us."

Eve and the rest of the trees backed off as the giant growled and yelled at them. He knocked over boulders and tree stumps to show his power. As the giant started moving towards them, Sandy noticed him limp. She looked closely and noticed a splinter underneath one of his toenails. *That must be what he was crying about. It looks like it's too far in for him to be able to dig it out.*

Sandy jumped down from the branch she was sitting on and walked towards the giant. Eve tried to grab her but Sandy rolled out of her reach.

"Princess, what are you doing? He is dangerous."

Sandy looked back at Eve as she walked towards the giant. "He is hurt. If I can fix it, maybe we won't have to be afraid of him."

Eve couldn't go after Sandy because she was afraid the giant would think she was launching an attack. She slowly followed Sandy at a distance, close enough to react to help Sandy if need be. As Sandy walked up to the giant he growled and displayed his teeth, trying to scare her off. As he did this, he protected his toe from touching anything. Sandy again looked at his toe and then looked up at him. "Hey, stop all that fussing. I know your toe hurts. I'm trying to help you."

The giant rushed at Sandy to scare her off and in doing so, he bumped his toe and stumbled to the ground. The giant cried out as he fell. Eve and the rest of her group moved up to secure Sandy. Sandy moved towards the giant. Crying, the giant held his toe and sobbed.

"Now I told you I was trying to help you. We can do this the easy way or the hard way. Let me see it."

Knowing he needed help as soon as possible, the giant let go of his toe and showed it to Sandy.

"Princess, be careful!" Eve yelled.

Ignoring Eve, Sandy checked the toe. A sharp piece of wood had jammed under his toenail, and he couldn't reach it. Sandy grabbed it and the giant screamed. As she tightened her grip, she called out to Eve for help. "Eve, grab onto me. He's going to pull away."

Just as Eve grabbed Sandy, the giant pulled his foot away because the pain was too much. Out came the splinter and the large creature sighed in relief

"Ahh, thank you."

"I couldn't get that out for a long time. I was getting so frustrated; all I could do was cry."

Sandy walked over to the giant.

"Maybe if you weren't so scary when you first meet people, you could just ask folk for help next time."

The giant looked at Sandy and focused on her for a moment. "You are the new princess, aren't you? King Black's daughter, yep yep it has to be you! You talk just like him. Follow me."

He motioned for them to follow. Sandy looked back at Eve. Eve was very hesitant, as the giants weren't known for hospitality.

Sandy tries to reason with Eve. "Come on, let's go. You said we had to move and get me some place safe, right? Well, who's going to guess I'm kicking it with giants?"

Eve reluctantly motioned the rest of her group to follow the giant.

As the giant walked up ahead, the journey seemed as though it would go on forever. Sandy, who was riding on the branches of Eve, noticed a difference in the forest.

"Eve, why is it so gloomy? I thought it was just from the rain, but it's a feeling. You can see the forest isn't as alive as it seemed when I first got to Moria."

Eve listened to Sandy and responded. "Yes, Princess, you are right. I fear something very terrible may be coming. The queen has already shown herself to be of the long-forgotten evil clan of Nefaria. The sisterhood of the dark place will soon re-unite. Some of us can remember the carnage and destruction that came with that age. It was terrifying. Their power turned brother against brother, wiping out entire villages.

"Deep into the forest we go, and where we will stop, no one will know."

Sandy nodded. The group kept trekking through the thick forest as colorful birds flew away and the stillness of the forest grew eerie. The giant stopped in front of a tree surrounded by giant flowers. The tree folk stopped as well, wondering why he'd stopped.

Sandy jumped down from Eve to investigate. "What's the deal? Why are we stopping? Are we here finally?"

The giant inspected the flowers. He pulled one off its stem and drank the water that had filled it from the night's rain. He turned to Sandy and offered her a drink.

"Are you thirsty, Princess?"

Sandy nodded. He handed it to her and she drank. "Thank you."

The giant turned to Eve and offered the drink. "We are all right, giant. We drank our fill overnight."

The giant nodded. A distance away, Sandy noticed something familiar. She took a few steps towards a small group of trees trying to figure out why. Unsure of what Sandy was looking for, Eve drew close.

"Princess, what is it?"

Sandy paid no attention to Eve. The giant sniffed the air, looked around, and told Eve to relax. "There is no one here but us," said the giant. Sandy knelt before a small plant. She pulled it up and found three large bulbs of manna.

"Ahh, Princess, someone has shown you the elusive manna

plant. That should satisfy your hunger."

Sandy smiled as she remembered the wonderful experience she'd had the last time she had tasted the manna. The giant's eyes widened, and he was very excited at the sight of the manna.

"Princess, Princess, you have found the manna. My brothers and I love this; it is one of the only things that makes us feel full. And it reminds us of our mother's cooking. Ahh, so tasty – if you will share some with my brothers, I'm sure it will make your introduction smooth."

"Sure, I'll share, especially if it will help us be friends with your brothers."

The giant turned to start walking again.

"Good, cause they usually just throw people they don't like into the ocean."

Sandy confused by the giant's statement.

"The ocean? I haven't seen one of those since I've been here. Where is it?"

The giant kept walking, not having heard Sandy's question. Eve took the moment to explain the giant's worry.

"Princess, the ocean he speaks of is over five hundred miles away. This is why I told you we are cautious of the giants."

Sandy was concerned, but soon cheered up. "Well, at least I found some of this bread," she laughed.

The group continued onward. As they moved closer to the giant's camp, the giant talked to himself.

"Oh boy, I hope they are in a good mood. I know we don't usually like visitors, but this is the princess, and King Black is our friend."

Sandy and Eve heard the giant's conversation with himself. Eve spoke up first. "Giant, are you sure your brothers will welcome our visit?"

The giant stopped for a moment, scratched his head and smiled. "Sure, sure. Everything will be OK. Your friends will be OK."

Sandy, bothered by how long it took for him to respond, spoke hesitantly. "Uhmm, it took you a little time to answer that question, almost like you were unsure if, when we meet your brothers, they are going to throw us into the ocean."

The giant looked at Sandy with concern.

"No, no. I would never let that happen. They might be hungry though, so they would try to eat you first."

Sandy looked back at Eve wide-eyed as they wondered if this was worth the danger.

"But you have the manna, Princess. Everything will be fine. Trust me."

The journey had taken them all day but because the giant's steps were so long and Eve could keep pace, they finally arrived at the giant's camp. There was a large lake with a rolling waterfall and tall trees that masked the huge house where it sat at the base of a mountain. Eve looked around cautiously; Sandy looked around in amazement. The giant motioned for them to sit near a very large campfire. Sandy jumped down from Eve to make herself comfortable as the giant went inside the house. Eve had the other tree folk with her on alert for any threat. Sandy, trusting her new friend, tried to make herself comfortable. From inside the house, deep voices could be heard arguing. There was a rustle in the trees to the right, then to the left. From outside looking into one of the windows, Sandy saw a large eye look out and then pull a curtain. She jumped at the size of what she had seen. The arguing from inside continued. Just as things seemed to calm from the left side, Sandy, Eve and the tree folk were charged by another giant holding a flickering fiery sword. He growled and moved, twirling his sword in the air. Suddenly, from the right side from out of nowhere, the three other treefolk that had been there to help protect Sandy were grabbed all together by one massive hand. The largest giant—Sandy couldn't even imagine his size—stood from the forest floor. Eve moved to cover the princess, and as the sword-wielding giant drew closer, a commanding voice from inside bellowed out.

"Hold!"

The angry sword-wielding giant stopped, but looked back at the house and responded in a deep and raspy voice. "Why should I stop for the likes of men and these twigs? This small one should be but food to us."

Then again, from inside the commanding voice rang out.

"Hold!"

The other massive giant with his grip around the three tree-folk spoke as well.

"Uriel, listen to your brother. Let us first find out why they have been brought to us." Immediately, the giant with the sword jumped over near the waterfall. Steam rose off his blade as the water touched it. The door to the house opened and the giant Sandy had helped came out first. Eve, covering Sandy, looked at the giant and said, "This does not look like a warm welcome for us. Tell your brother to unhand my kin and we shall be on our way."

As Eve spoke, four more giants came out of the house. The last spoke with the voice heard earlier. "You now know our home. It would not be wise for us to allow you to leave until we understand what you want."

Sandy stood from underneath Eve's protection. "I am Princess Sandy Black. Eve is my friend, trying to help me. On our way through the forest, we came across your brother here."

Sandy pointed at their escort. "He hurt himself and I helped him. So, he said he would bring us to meet his brothers and here we are."

The giant that had led them there turned to his brothers. "I told you. She is King Black's daughter."

The massive giant with the grip on the treefolk slowly released his grip.

"If this be true, you are welcome here."

The giant who had spoken from inside the house responded to his brother's gesture.

"We should still find out more, Gabriel, before we let our guard down."

The giant in the steamy waterfall replied, "If they are lying, they are dying."

Eve looked over at the aggressive one. "Maybe we should all sit near your campfire here, so we can see all of you and you can see and ask all of us what questions you may have."

Another giant standing in front of the house agreed with Eve.

"This sounds like the best solution to our issues now. Brothers, please let us learn more before a decision is made."

The giants nodded and took their places near the fire. As they sat, the giant Sandy had helped earlier leaned over to tell her something.

"It would be a good time to show them the manna now."

Sandy nodded and uncovered the manna from the large leaves. "First, my friends. I bring a gift."

The giants' eyes all got big in delight at the sight of the manna. The young one spoke. "She knows of the manna plant and has found this on our way here. She is willing to share." Sandy handed one of the big bulbs to him. He took a small bite and passed it to his next brother until all had bitten into it. This pacified the group as they were content, with their bellies full.

The brother who had spoken from inside the house sat with a great spear in his hand. He said, "Since you have brought this very special gift and shared with us, we shall share with you. King Black is our friend and since you are his daughter, we shall treat you as our friend."

The daylight, what little there was through the clouds, had gone away, and all that was left was the flickering of the campfire that illuminated the area around them.

"It is late. You and your friends may lodge here for the night. In the morning, we shall ask our questions."

Sandy looked at Eve, knowing they had no other choice. Sandy thanked them for their hospitality.

"We thank you for your kind gesture. We will lodge here with you tonight."

The giants rose to their feet and made their way into the enormous house. The young giant looked very pleased that Sandy had been accepted, and took Sandy and Eve to where they must sleep.

"Come Princess, come this way - I will show you to where you may sleep tonight. Didn't I tell you to trust me?"

Sandy looked at the excited giant. Eve looked at Sandy to give her instruction.

"Princess, it would be better if for tonight you sleep here with me. They have extended their trust to us, but I must be totally sure of their intentions."

Sandy understood Eve's hesitations and request. "Yes Ma'am."

She looked at her new giant friend. "I will sleep here for the night. We should talk more in the morning."

The giant was disappointed but happy she was still there. "OK, Princess. Much will happen tomorrow. Goodnight."

All said goodnight and the night set in on them.

Chapter 9
TREACHERY

Darkness had fallen over the palace. Torches burned like giant candles around the perimeter of the palace walls. The citizens surrounding the palace were rounded up and trapped.

While all the commotion went on at the surface, deep below the palace David hung by both of his arms in chains in the dungeon. As he hung motionless, a voice from the other side of the cell called him. "Mr. David, can you hear me?" David couldn't reply in his state. Again, the voice called to him. "Mr. David, can you hear me?"

No response still. Chef Tasty emerged from the darkness of the dimly lit room. He walked up to David with a cup filled with a sweet-smelling liquid. He winced when he saw the state David was in. "Goodness; you look like some half-cooked meatloaf. Let's get this in you."

The chef emptied the contents into David's mouth. "That's it, Mr. David. Drink it up. It's going to make you feel so much better."

As the fluid entered David's body, his wounds started healing. His injuries disappeared and his eyes opened. David tilted his head back from the cup and looked up.

"Chef Tasty. How are you? What's happening up there?

"Shhh. You need to let what I just gave you work. Soon it

will be as if nothing ever happened to you. Don't you worry about what's going on for now. You're going to need your strength. That wild woman up there is tripping, and she's coming down to stir you up to try and find Sandy soon. You have to find a way to get out of here and warn the King. I'll do what I can to help."

David nodded, his strength returning to him as they spoke. He looked up at his hands and arms in amazement. "What is in that stuff?"

"It's nothing but some juices and berries." David looked at the chef in disbelief.

"Juices and berries?"

Down the hall, they heard the queen's footsteps. "I must go now; pretend to be in bad shape. I'll come check on you later. Don't worry, I've got things under control."

Chef Tasty sneaked out of the cell and down another staircase just before the queen arrived. David dropped down into his previous-looking state.

The queen, wearing her seductive dress, strolled into the dingy cell. "Stand up, David, head manservant to King Black. Stand before your queen, and soon the one true ruler of all the land. I know that you have strength now. I am unsure as to how, but your wounds are healed and you have the look of a very fit man. Rise so I may speak with you."

David opened his eyes, standing before the queen in tattered clothes. "I stand before you, witch! What is it you would have of me?"

The queen smiled, circling him and running her fingers over his shoulders. "I have but one question for you. But first I make you an offer."

David glared at the queen as he tried to figure out his next move. "Join me, David. Join the darkness that is night. Join me and all of your desires can and will be. I have seen your diligence with your master and admire your loyalty. I would just require one thing from you. Tell me, where have you hidden Sandy Black? Tell me of her location and no harm shall come to you. You will be given the nicest clothes and the best food. I can give you pleasures your heart has no knowledge of yet."

"It is not by your power that men are given position to rule and reign. It is not of your will that the world was made. And it is none of your business where Sandy Black is."

The queen whispered into David's ear. "Your last chance is now to choose me. You will tell me where the child is! There will be no more opportunity to escape my wrath."

David looked the queen in the eye. "If you plan on torturing me to get me to talk I would advise you to pack a lunch, because we are going to be here for a while."

The queen smiled, stepping back from David. "You have made your choice. Don't beg me to kill you while I have my fun."

David laughed. "Hahahahaha. You think your threats mean anything to me? The pain you cause me cannot be compared to the agony you will receive once the King knows what you are doing. You and whatever is left of your people and those who follow you will be deleted from history by his wrath. Oh, and should anything happen to his daughter, your suffering shall never end. No, I do not worry about what you will do to my body. I lay in wait for the end of you."

The queen glared at David. She clawed at his face with her sharp nails, drawing blood and leaving large wounds. She licked the blood on her fingers. "I shall shed more of this before your time is over."

The queen and David stared into each other's eyes for a moment, then the queen turned and exited the cell as she motioned to Lilly who had been standing afar the entire time. As Lilly turned to follow the queen, she stole a glance at David. Their eyes met. Lilly could see disappointment in his eyes. Lilly sighed, ashamed. As the queen and Lilly exited, the queen gestured for a small man who was half-clothed with bluish skin to deal with David. "Doctor, he is all yours."

The small man's eyes glowed yellow as he smiled and nodded. "Yes, yes, my queen. Much fun I will have with him. Much fun!"

"Now remember, Doctor, he must stay awake for everything. He must not die."

The bluish man smiled, salivating.

"Yes, yes. Much fun, my queen."

The queen then turned and exited the corridor. The bluish man placed his leather bag on a table near David's cell. He talked to himself as he opened the leather bag and started pulling out surgical tools and devices from it.

"Yes, we are going to have a lot of fun with this one. Many things we will see, much we will learn. Yes, yes, fun, fun, fun!"

David recognized the slender built small bluish man. "You are Doctor Cain. The King locked you away forever to live in darkness and alone so that you wouldn't try anymore of your experiments on anyone again. You killed your brother because of jealousy, and then when judgment was passed to you, you decided to try and bring him back from the dead through your own practices and experiments. Trying to right the wrong you had done."

The doctor stopped talking to himself as he looked up at David.

"You are right, Sir, in your understanding of who I am. I was locked away in darkness with no hope of bringing my brother back, having to live with the curse of never dying. But now that the queen has shown me grace, I can continue my work and hope to make right what I did wrong."

David cringed a bit at the sight and smell of the doctor, as well as the thought of what he might do to him. "You think I look distasteful, right? These last hundred years in that cell alone and in the dark makes you change mentally and physically. Oh, don't worry, David, high servant of the King. I will take good care of you. I must not kill you because my queen desires you alive, but I will find other ways to get out of you what I need to rebuild my brother."

As he finished his statement, he picked up a saw and a small knife from the table and walked towards David. "Now, you hold still. I want to get this right the first time."

David's eyes widened as Doctor Cain moved closer with his tools of pain in hand. The door to the prison cells shuts and a loud scream of pain rang through the halls. The queen smiled with delight as she heard the scream.

The next morning, the queen stood on the same balcony the King addressed his army from before leaving for battle. A crowd had gathered below the balcony, whispering among themselves. In place of the normal guards were the queen's servants and those who had decided to be loyal to her. As she emerged from behind the curtain, a large Minotaur helped her onto the balcony. Her beautiful flowing red dress and head covering were made just for this occasion. She raised her hands as she addressed the masses. "People of Moria, I know that you are confused as to why I have summoned you here. I would like to thank you for all that you have done in the past to make Moria the wonderful place that it is. And thank you for allowing me to share this land with you."

The entire crowd stood still, confused. A loud shout from the crowd, "Do you have any word from King Black?"

The queen smiled.

"I know, I know. You want to hear of news about your King? I am here today to give that news to you."

The queen glanced around. "Your King, unfortunately, shall never return. I will be taking control over all of Moria and all those who oppose me shall die."

A panic and an uproar broke out amongst the crowd. The Minotaur came out next to the queen and raised his hand, signaling to the guards. The gates around the courtyard were closed and all were locked into one confined area. The queen smiled and raised her hands and began to laugh. As she did, lightning flashed and thunder crashes rumbled in the skies. As the masses panicked and tried to scatter, a troop of the queen's soldiers rushed into the crowd, beating and moving the people into cells. "If you do not resist and choose to serve me, then your families, your homes and all that you know will last and not be destroyed. But if you fight against me and do not serve me, I will destroy you and all you know. Your families will be broken apart, your homes destroyed. Everything that has ever been a part of your life will not remain. For I am due praise and worship, and none should oppose me."

At this, one third of the crowd made up their minds to follow the queen. The guards ushered those who choose to serve the queen to one side where they were given a mark, branded upon their hand. Those who resisted the queen were set aside for slaughter with the queen overseeing the carnage. Lilly, standing in the background, had no sign of outward sadness, but her eyes showed a pain that couldn't be explained in words. The queen turned to Lilly.

"Soon, all of this land will tremble at my presence and worship me. Now go and tell that chef we are to have a feast tonight."

Lilly bowed before the queen and left. The queen walked back onto the balcony to watch the destruction as if it were some type of wonderful play.

In the kitchen Chef Tasty worked feverishly, hiding food and giving his staff orders.

"Move all of those breads and put them in the pantry. Take these and lock them in the secret cabinet. Don't let anyone see you."

As the chef's staff hurried to their destinations with trays of food in their hands, Lilly came through the door. The chef saw her and acknowledged her presence.

"Hello, high servant Lilly. What can I do for you?"

Thinking she had noticed what he was hiding, Chef Tasty was a bit nervous. Lilly glanced round the kitchen with a sad but confident look in her eyes. "The queen would like you to prepare a banquet for her."

Lilly walked around the kitchen, looking through the bowls of fruits and vegetables. Chef Tasty walked over and stops her. "Is there anything else that the queen wants, Lilly?"

Lilly stopped, and thought for a moment. "I would say make her something very special for the occasion." Afterwards Lilly turned to make her way back to tend to the queen.

Chef Tasty nodded. "Lilly, are you sure you're doing the right thing?"

Lilly, with her back to the chef, stopped as a tear fell from her eye. "Chef Tasty, I'm doing what I have to do and you should as well. I will inform the queen that the banquet shall be served at dinner's usual time."

Lilly walked out of the kitchen with Chef Tasty still staring at her departing figure and sad at her response.

King Ananias, Prince Shamma and the rest of the royal family, along with their personal guards, were locked away in a fortified room with one entrance. They had been in there since the battle began to spiral out of control. The King's guard stood at the bolted door. They had been tormented by the sounds of death from outside that door for almost two days now. Caught off guard, their army never had time to defend the land. The enemies stormed in late at night with no warning. Their masses covered the kingdom like a swarm of bees, where they stung the Kingdom of the White Rose almost to extinction.

White Trolls, from the subterranean world of Moria stood 10-feet tall with bodies covered in white hair. They were extremely strong with long arms and legs. Their exceptionally long noses looked like the beak of a bird. They had red eyes that they were mostly blind in. Extremely agile, fast, and strong, Trolls were ruthless hunters that hunted in packs relying upon their senses and basic weaponry to attack and destroy their prey. They cover themselves in tribal war paint and light armor made of bone. Those in charge wore teeth and claws from kills around their necks.

Prince Shamma was awake at the time of the attack and was able to get his family to the fortified room. The guards watching the perimeter were overwhelmed as suddenly as the attack started. The fortified room was the only safe place in the kingdom. The enemy noticed them inside and made efforts to break down the heavy door; they clawed and banged as they tried to gain entrance. The room rattled as the enemy hit and smashed the door continuously. Prince Shamma, his father, and King Ananias stood beside their guards as they gripped their swords. The Queen stands behind them.

"Hold men, hold," King Ananias said. "Remember, whatever

comes through that door will be shown no mercy."

He sighed, "I don't know if He will, men, but our Father in heaven can deliver us from anything. We must trust Him. As we know, a call for help was sent. We must hold firm, for the future of our people depends on this day."

The King's words give the scared and tired men strength. As they lined up in front of the door, weapons drawn and shields ready for war, they banged their shields on the ground in anticipation of what may come. The shields being banged equaled the sound of the door being rammed. A small crack appeared in the door, and the light of torches from the other side could be seen. One of the guards inside the room peeped through the crack and an arrow flew through the cavity and struck him in the eye. He screamed and fell to the floor, dead. Cracks showed up more and more on the door, and the guards scrambled to cover them with their shields. The door began to crumble as the enemy smashed it with a huge metal object. King Ananias, afraid of what might happen, glanced at his son and all the guards. He whispered a prayer under his breath.

A loud trumpet blasted, announcing the presence of King Black. The dragon army of the King of Moria arrived! Dragons spewed fire over all the hordes of enemies. The fire blasted close to the door of the room, and screams from the enemy's soldiers were heard as they all melted away. The men inside jumped back from the excess heat. Cheers erupted inside the room as King Ananias shouted for all to praise.

"All hail King Black and his army. Hail! Hail!" all of the men echoed out, raising their weapons high.

King Black's armies had taken control of the palace. Loud whooshing sounds from the dragons' wings sent the enemies scampering into the surrounding forest. King Black's dragon,

Ithros, landed in front of the room. The King dismounted as Ithros spoke in his ruff voice, "They are all inside. I can hear their hearts beating."

King Black rushed to the door and pulled it open forcefully. The door crashed onto the floor and the dim light of the day filled the room as King Ananias, Prince Shamma and the rest of their men hailed King Black.

"Your men were holding this door up. I'm glad we could get here when we did. It's a good thing trolls are stupid; they kept pushing in rather than pulling out."

King Black laughed as King Ananias and the prince approached him. The two kings hugged.

"Oh, I knew you could deliver us," King Ananias said. "I never gave up hope that our rider had gotten word to you."

King Black responded, "I am sorry we didn't get here faster, my friend."

King Ananias put his hands on King Black's shoulders. "Don't think of things we have no control over, my friend, at least you made it when you did. Because if not, I don't know if we'd still be alive."

Prince Shamma bowed before King Black. "I thank you, King Black."

All who were in the room bowed before King Black. One of King Black's soldiers came to the entrance to the room.

"My lord, the enemy has been pushed back into the forest. We will refortify the palace before nightfall."

"Thank you," King Black said. He turned to King Ananias. "Shall we go see what we have to work with?"

The two kings and Prince Shamma strolled around the palace, assessing the damages done. A large part of the palace was burnt, and dead bodies littered the floors. Smoke and rotting flesh filled the air. Looking over the kingdom, some buildings were still burning. "Trolls! This land hasn't seen their kind in ages," King Black said.

"What manner of evil has awoken this foe?" King Ananias asked.

"The kind of evil that has knowledge of things past. I am unsure of what else this evil has in store for us, but I will say that there will be much more pain and heartache ahead."

"My lord, was it only in our land that this enemy came?" Prince Shamma asked.

King Black smiled, understanding what the young prince was concerned about. "So far, young prince, yes. All is safe in Moria." The prince sighed in relief.

King Black looked up at the sky as the rest of the army landed with their dragons. "Well, let us build back what we can, and fortify your defenses before night. Those beasts most certainly will return."

"But this time we will be ready for them," King Ananias said.

The crippled city and palace sat on a peninsula that connected to Moria with an assortment of island cities surrounding it, and once again life strived to hang on. The army kept busy working through the day to restore some of the protection the kingdom once had, but all found comfort in knowing they were now safe. And King Black was happy knowing that Sandy was far away from this danger.

Chapter 10

HOME

Sandy woke up and saw the youngest giant standing and staring at her like a new toy. He grinned from ear to ear as she stretched and sat on a branch.

"He has been standing there for about an hour," Eve said. "We should leave soon, Princess."

Sandy smiled at the giant. "We should find out more about them before we leave. You never know what they can help us with."

"Ok, Princess," Eve said. "As long as you are safe, I'm OK with it."

Sandy climbed down the tree and walked over to the giant.

"What is your name? Where I'm from, it's rude when you meet someone and don't introduce yourself."

The giant stood at attention. "I apologize, my princess. I am Remiel, the youngest of my brothers."

Sandy walked around Remiel with her hands behind her back. She stopped right in front of him and stretched out her hand. "It is a pleasure to meet you, Remiel. I am Sandy."

She grabbed his huge pinky finger when he stretched out his hand. "Now that wasn't so hard, was it?"

Remiel laughed. "Come; I'll introduce you to the rest of my

brothers, Sandy."

They walked towards the giant house, which was built on the side of a mountain. Along the way, they met one of Remiel's brothers picking leaves and sorting through herbs. Remiel tapped his shoulder. "Raphael, Raphael."

When he didn't respond, Remiel turned to Sandy and shrugged.

"He is into forest plants and fixes you if you're sick or hurt."

Raphael turned to face them. He wore glasses made from windows with frames from large iron bars. He noticed Sandy had a few cuts and bruises on her face, arms and legs.

"Yes, yes. I can fix this. Come, come. I will make you better."

Remiel nodded to Sandy as a sign that she was safe. Raphael motioned for Sandy to follow him as he walked over to a large chair and sat. "I, Raphael. You, little princess?"

Sandy looked up at the giant. "Yes, I am a princess. Sandy is my name."

Rocking back and forth in his chair, Raphael clapped in excitement. "Ooooh, I have always wanted to meet a princess. Come, come. I make you better."

He grabbed a large leaf, mixed herbs together in it and rolled it up. "Princess Sandy, hold out your hands like this."

He cupped his hands and Sandy did the same. Raphael squeezed the rolled leaf between his fingers and sweet-smelling oil trickled into Sandy's palms. Remiel smiled as he watched his brother with gusto.

"Now, Princess Sandy," Raphael said, "rub the oil on your body."

Sandy shrugged. "Oh well. I guess I'll get moisturized." She rubbed the oil into her skin—her arms, face and legs. Her body tingled and like magic, the scratches and bruises healed and faded away. Sandy watched in amazement as a small scratch on her arm vanished before her eyes. "Oh my God. That was cool." Sandy smiled at Raphael. "Thank you, Raphael. Thank you so much."

Raphael's eyes glittered behind with excitement. "You are welcome, Princess Sandy."

A flight of swallows flew across the sky and Raphael observed them with undivided attention.

"Let's go on, Sandy," Remiel said. "I have more brothers for you to meet. Raphael is in his own world right now."

Sandy laughed. "Ok."

As they passed a campfire in front of the house, two of Remiel's brothers stepped out. One of them roared like a lion as he stretched and yawned.

Sandy walked with Remiel over to the campfire. Remiel clapped. "Brothers, let us not be rude. She's our guest. Come, let's have lunch."

Raphael took his eyes from the birds when he heard it was time to eat. "Hmmmmm food. I love food." He dashed over to the campfire, holding his glasses in place.

The giants sat with Sandy in a circle, ready for breakfast. Sandy eyed the huge pots of food in front of them. Eve stood neatly, on alert. Remiel leaned over to whisper into Sandy's ear. "That's our eldest brother Michael," he said, nodding towards one of his brothers.

Michael, the first, had a long grey beard and a large afro. His clothing was red in color. Sandy noticed the giants were color coded. With a large spear in his hand, Michael had the look of a man that had seen many battles.

Michael stood up. "Princess, my brothers and I are pleased to have you as our guest. I am Michael, the eldest of the seven."

He walked round the circle, introducing his brothers. Sandy noticed later on that they were seated according to their age.

"The largest of us all and second eldest," Michael continued, "is my brother Gabriel."

Gabriel stood, clad in a large blue robe. "Pleased to meet you, young princess."

With his long braided hair and goatee, Gabriel looked a bit menacing. Michael introduced the next brother. "And third amongst us is Uriel. I believe you have met already."

Uriel bowed. "I am Uriel and as long as you are friend, my sword will protect you."

Sandy remembered seeing Uriel standing in the nearby waterfall with the steam rising from his flaming sword. Uriel sat, twirling his sword. His bald head shone in the sunlight. His yellow vest had pictures of battles and strange writings Sandy couldn't make out.

Michael pointed at Raphael. "This is the fourth brother in order of birth – Raphael – I believe you have recently benefitted from his knowledge of healing."

Raphael stared intensely at the food pots. "Raphael is very special, a genius in the understanding of medicines, poisons and plant life. He is a genius, but he lacks social skills. He gets distracted easily as you can see."

Raphael, still staring at the food, licked his lips. His green sweater blended with the leaves in the forest. Raphael looked away from the pots of food and turned to Sandy. "Hello, Princess. We are going to eat soon," he said, rejoicing like a child over a favorite dish.

Sandy smiled at him. "Thank you again for that oil you had me put on. I'm completely fine now."

Raphael nodded, licked his lips again and then focused on

the pots of food again.

Michael moved on to the next brother. "This is our brother Raguel, the fifth in order of birth."

Raguel was a brawny giant with inviting eyes. His white armor sparkled in the sun. "Hello, Princess. It's wonderful to meet you. I'm thankful I have someone else to talk to other than my boring brothers." Raguel looked around and noticed Eve. He whispered to Sandy. "My brothers would tell you I'm a little off, but don't look now - but I see tree people." Sandy looked back at Eve, who didn't hear what was said and laughed. Raguel laughed too.

"You're funny, Raguel," Sandy said. "I can see we will get along for sure."

Raguel bowed as he laughed and sat back in his place.

Michael moved to the next brother. "This is the sixth among us. Zerachiel." Zerachiel was a thin and dark giant with eyes like night and jet-black hair. He bowed and smiled at Sandy. Sandy nodded and admired his long purple cape.

Michael moved on to the last of the seven. "And him who you have met already. Remiel, the youngest of us all." Remiel stood, smiling at Sandy. His baggy orange overalls flapped in the winds. He was pleased that she'd met his family.

Michael rubbed his hand. "Now that we all have been introduced, let us eat before Raphael goes crazy again."

"LETS EAT!" the giants all said in one voice.

The pots were opened and breakfast was served. Remiel grabbed a large leaf and dished a brownish, mud-looking substance from the pot on it. He handed it over to Sandy. Sandy held her breath as the odor hit her nose. The brothers devoured the brownish mess like it was the greatest food ever. Dodging the drops of food falling from the mouths and hands of the giants,

Sandy was at loss for what to do. When she saw Raphael reach out in need of more food, she threw her dish into his hand. He gobbled it right up and smiled, satisfied. Sandy heaved a sigh of relief and pulled out a small piece of manna she had left. She ate the manna and felt satisfied within a few minutes.

Wiping his mouth, Remiel looked down at Sandy. "Sandy, can I get you some more?"

Sandy shook her head. "Oh no, no. That won't be necessary, Remiel. Thank you."

Remiel clapped excitedly. "It's good having you as a guest. You don't eat much; you don't take up any space. That's nice."

Sandy smiled. "Eat up. Make sure you all eat it all up."

The brothers were too busy throwing food into their mouths to hear or respond to Sandy. She looked back at Eve, wrinkling her nose. "I can't wait for this meal to be over."

Eve laughed. "You wanted to stay, young princess."

Loud belches erupted, signifying the end of breakfast. The giants sat, their faces smeared with the brownish meal. They looked like they had just finished competing in an eating contest.

Remiel wiped his face and smiled at Sandy. "In a minute, I'm going to show you where we all sleep."

As if a spell was cast, they all fell asleep. The ground shook as the giants snored.

As they napped, Sandy got up and looked around. "I can take this time to explore the surroundings."

"Princess," Eve said, "I know you're entertained by your new friends, but I believe it's best we move on now. We don't want to be here when the giants have a mood swing. Regardless of what they've showed us today, their kind was a warring tribe at one time, an instinct that is passed down in their genes."

Sandy rolled her eyes. "Eve, you're so worried about who

folk used to be, or what they used to do. Do you know I grew up in the hood?"

Sandy frowned when she saw Eve's blank expression. "Maybe you don't. We don't have too many trees in the hood outside of the one I had in my front yard. But all I'm trying to say is that people where I'm from used to get in trouble. They would join gangs and do bad things. Most times, they did it to belong, or have a family. They weren't really bad people; they just lived in a bad place. You've got to know an animal is in its most aggressive state when it's cornered. These guys here are a family. It doesn't seem like anyone has taken the time out to talk to them and see if they needed anything, or get to know them. Trust me, they're not bad. I've seen bad. These guys are some giant teddy bears. We will be fine."

Eve shook her leaves. "Ok, Princess. You are very much like your father. You seem to be able to find the good in things. Go on, Princess. Look around."

"Thank you, Eve, for understanding me and trusting my judgment."

Eve bowed. "I am here to help, Princess."

Sandy rubbed her hands. "Hmm. Let's play a little CSI. Let's see if these guys live as bad as they cook."

Sandy walked to the giant house and stared at the huge door. She noticed a slight opening she could fit through. She looked back at Eve before going in. "Let me know when they wake up."

Eve gave her a twig up. Upon entering the dark, smelly house, Sandy saw the largest sizes of dusty furniture she had ever seen. Standing close to them made her feel like an ant. She saw a huge piano, a huge chandelier, huge sofas and tables. Moving farther, she walked down the hallway to their rooms. She sneezed as the buildup of dust and dirt increased. The windows were thick with grime and fish bones, and bits of food littered the dirty floor. Huge overflowing trash cans stood at the door of each room, making it difficult to get in. Sandy covered her nose because the odor was overpowering.

How can they live like this? she wondered She heard the sound of tree limbs breaking. *That must be Eve. They must be waking up.* She dashed back to the living room, sneaked out of the opening in the door and stood in front of Eve.

"Did you find anything interesting?" Eve asked.

Sandy looked up at Eve. "It's horrible in there. I don't know how they live in that. Eve, was it you that made the sound earlier like snapping branches?"

"Oh yes, Princess. I make that sound when I snap my twigs together. Hey, I'm a tree."

Sandy laughed. The giants all roared at the same time as they woke up. Remiel got up and rushed to Sandy. "Sorry if we startled you. it's just a defense mechanism. You see, if an intruder was around and we roared like that we'd scare them away."

"It's OK, Remiel. I understand. it's like a wake-up alarm. So, what do you guys do the rest of the day?"

"Well, we have our normal chores to do today."

"Do you guys go hunting or have a smokehouse?"

"Yes, we have a smokehouse. It's at the back. Come, I'll show you."

"Ok. Remiel, can you help me with a surprise?"

Remiel rubbed his hands in excitement. "Sure, sure I can."

Sandy motioned for him to come. When he did, she whispered in his ear. His brothers got up and got busy. Michael and Uriel went hunting, Gabriel stood guard by the trees, Raphael went back to make medicines, Raguel told himself jokes near the lake and laughed, and Zerachiel was nowhere to be found.

<u>Remiel</u> and Sandy walk to the smokehouse. "Remiel, we are going to need some help from Raphael since he knows about the plants and herbs in the forest."

Remiel smiled. "Oh, don't worry about that. He will do anything for food."

"Good."

They walked inside the smokehouse and Sandy looked around for cooking tools. Remiel dashed out to talk with Raphael.

A few hours before nightfall, the other giants returned home. The smoky smell of barbequed meat filled the air of the camp. Raphael couldn't stop drooling as he and Remiel assisted Sandy in the smoke house. The aroma reached the nose of Gabriel, making it difficult for him to keep watch. Michael and Uriel, afraid an enemy had set the house on fire, ran towards the camp. Uriel pulled out his flaming sword and Michael gripped his spear tight. On getting close, they paused as the smell of the cooking meat hit them. Zerachiel jumped from the top of a mountain.

"What is that wonderful aroma?" Zerachiel asked.

"If I aint told ya once I've told you a thousand times—" Raguel stopped in the middle of another one of his conversations with himself to follow the smell. "Ha, ha, now that smells like some good food." He traced the aroma with hungry intentions.

As Michael and Uriel got to the camp, Michael looked out for Gabriel. He wasn't in his normal position. They looked around for the rest of their brothers at their normal spots. None of them were there. Scanning the camp, they found everyone seated around the fire with Sandy.

"Princess, what is going on?" Michael asked. "Why are my brothers all seated so?"

"Yeah," Uriel chipped in. "What kind of magic are you using to control them?"

Sandy smiled as she opened the lid of a pit Remiel had built. "I hope this isn't a big deal. I wanted to do something special for you guys since you let us stay here last night. Besides, breakfast wasn't exactly five-star."

As she lifted the giant lid, the grilled meat aroma filled the air. The giants' mouths watered and they couldn't remember when they'd last had something like that. Uriel's flaming sword died down as he grabbed a seat. Michael stared at him in shock. Uriel looked back at his brother. "What? Do you smell that? I'm ready to eat, I don't know what you're doing."

Michael grabs a seat too. Gabriel patted Michael's shoulder. "Michael, the princess is trying to be nice. Besides we haven't smelled anything this nice in ages and—"

"I know, Gabriel. I know, we will eat."

The brothers all sit in anticipation of the savory meat.

With Remiel's help, Sandy made plates from large green leaves from a tree nearby to serve the food on.

Raphael drooled in anticipation. "That smells sooo yummy."

"Thanks to Raphael and Remiel I was able to get the help I needed to make all of this, so thank them."

The giants' eyes widened as the food was distributed. Remiel stopped his brothers from attacking the grill as they had done in the morning. Uriel reached out to grab a piece of meat off the grill and Sandy slapped his hand. His sword lit up.

"You're going to have some manners if you want to eat," Sandy said. "I didn't spend all day cooking all of this so you could be some kind of animal when you eat."

Uriel bowed his head, feeling sorry. "Sorry, Princess. It just smells so—"

Sandy handed his plate to him. Grabbing it, he took a deep breath and inhaled the savory meal.

Sandy handed plates of food to all the giants as she explained what she had made. "I didn't have all of the ingredients I usually use, but I did what I could with what you guys have. That's barbequed roast along with some potato salad, and some greens I happened to find with the help of Raphael. I even made dessert."

"Well, I don't even care what the rest of you think," Raguel said. "The girl can cook. We need to keep this little princess around just so she can cook."

Raguel pointed at his plate. "This food right here, I'm in love with it."

Zerachiel, the thin, dark giant, stood. "Princess, if I may, I must salute you for your contribution to our family. This is an exquisite meal. I don't talk much, but I must say you have brought me back to a time before we were out here."

Gabriel looked over at Michael, who was enjoying his meal like his brothers. "Princess, maybe Raguel is right. Maybe you should stay with us, at least until we can get you back to your father."

Sandy was dishing more food for Raphael, who then looked at Gabriel. "That sounds good to me."

Eve shook her leaves. "Princess, we must not stay here and disrupt the giants' way of life. By now, the queen must have taken full control of the palace and will still be looking for you. We can't afford to stay in one spot for too long."

Sandy looked back at Eve. "Eve, think about it. The crazy old queen is looking for me, but would anyone expect me to be here with the giants? Everything in this forest seems to be afraid of them. I wouldn't be surprised if the queen was too. If you ask me, there is no safer place than for me to be here with them."

Uriel burps. "There is no safer place in all of Moria than with us."

Eve nodded. "Princess, you are right. There is no safer place for you to be than here. The queen will not know you would be safe with them, plus her scouts would be too afraid to try and come near here."

Sandy smiled as she opened the dessert she'd made. "Who is up for juju berry cobbler?"

All of the brothers put out their leaf plates, and she piled the hot cobbler onto their plates with a giant spoon that might as well have been a shovel to Sandy. The instant Michael tasted the cobbler, his eyes begin to water. Gabriel looked up from his food and looked sadly at Michael. Michael peered back at Gabriel. A giant-sized tear dropped from Gabriel's eyes. Michael stared at his food, stood from his seat and excused himself. "I am sorry, Princess. Thank you for the dinner. It was delicious."

The stoic and composed Michael's eyes glistened with tears as he tried hard to keep his emotions under control. "I shall retire for the night. And since it hasn't been said, you are welcome to stay with us for as long as you need."

The great lumbering giant turned away right before a tear dropped from his eyes. The atmosphere turned gloomy. The other giants ate slower now, as if someone had died. Sandy walked over to Gabriel. "What's wrong? Was it something I did?"

Tears rolled down Gabriel's cheeks. "You must first understand our people's history in order to understand our pain now."

"Please tell me about it."

"Long ago before your father was even born, Moria was a land of hostility. There was much suffering when the old evil clan of Nefaria sought after dark power. They wanted to rule everything and were relentless in their quest to control Moria. In the beginning, the kingdoms of men didn't know what the other inhabitants of this world did. Nefaria and her tribe had grown so demented with power, they tortured and killed or controlled most of the beasts or monsters of the darkest parts of the forest. Your grandfather, the King at that time, as well as the rulers of all 13 kingdoms of men, formed an alliance with the tribes of giants. There were a great number of us in those times. Too many feared what Nefaria was doing in the dark. So man and giant made a vow to help one another to rid Moria of the evil order, and keep peace in the land. This wasn't long before the tournament they had at that time. The order heard of the new alliance and, fearing that they would be overpowered if we stood together, came at night with their troll armies and wiped out our villages. One by one, our villages fell that night. With no advanced warning; no sign of danger. That night, we were all just children. Michael and I were the eldest. Our village was attacked. Our father was the chief of our village, so it was his duty to lead in the fight against the dark army. Our mother, fearing for the lives of her children, gave Michael and I instructions to take our brothers and hide in the forest. We did as she said. We were so young. As we hid on that rainy night, cold and scared, we wondered what would happen next. We could see the flicker of fire in the night and hear the yells of war. Sometime later, when all was quiet and we could no longer here the clashing of blades or the footsteps of our soldiers, we wandered back to see our mother. When we arrived at what was once our village, there was nothing left. It had been burned to the ground and not a soul was found. We have no idea what they had done with those that had fallen in battle. So, since that night, we have been alone. Orphaned in the forest of Moria, wandering from place to place, trying to find home or any sign of our people. Michael keeps blaming himself for not fighting with our father, and eventually not restoring us to our people. Your food tonight has been the closest thing we have had to our mother's food since that night. And it has reminded us all of what we are continually searching for—home."

Sandy sighed, feeling sad. "When my mother passed away, for a moment I didn't know what I was going to do or how I was going to move on. Then my father, who I had never known, brought me to Moria. And now I've seen things I never thought possible. I sit in the company of giants who no longer exist in the land I come from. I await to hear news from a father that I have gained. But as it looks now I have lost. I am alone in this world, much the same as you. Chased away from my future and not sure what to do. All I can offer is hope and my friendship. I know things will get better."

Michael came back outside to the group. Uriel stood to his feet. "Princess, your road has been one of pain and loss. Much the same as ours. We don't have many we can trust, or any that we bring into our home. To you, I would like to extend my hand of friendship on behalf of my brothers."

Sandy smiled at Uriel. She put her hand on his finger and they shook. Michael coughed. "Brothers, I apologize for my weakness. Princess, I have heard your words and appreciate your knowledge and perspective. It would be an honor to have you stay with us until King Black can be contacted." He looked at Eve and crossed his right arm over his chest. "You have our word as the last sons of the giants of Moria; Princess Sandy Black will be safe with us."

Eve and the rest of the treefolk, who had been with her the entire time, bowed before the giants. "I thank you all for accepting the princess. I apologize for my people's ignorance about your actions." She turned to Sandy. "Princess, since you are in good hands, I will go on my way to meet the wisest of my people - the Great Tree of Moria. There I hope to find answers as to how to get you to your father, and what may be coming ahead."

Sandy ran over to Eve and hugged her.

"Thank you so much, Eve. I couldn't have gotten here by myself. Please be careful and do come back."

"I will, young Princess. You just stay with your new friends until I return."

Eve and her group turned around and made their way through the forest, heading for the Great Tree of Moria. Sandy stood with the seven giants behind her, watching Eve disappear into the forest.

Chapter 11

WAR FAR OFF

It was night in the Isles of Far Off Kingdom of the White Rose. Fiery arrows from King Black's army and the troll invaders decorated the dark sky. King Ananias's soldiers stood with King Black's troops, fighting off the trolls. A group of dragons circled about, spewing flames of fire around the palace walls and creating a perimeter of flame. King Black and King Ananias sat on the high balcony watching the battle.

"It looks as though your dragons could protect our gates until we totally rebuild if need be. The trolls can't pass through the wall of fire they have created."

King Black nodded towards his dragon. "Ithros! What is that approaching the east wall?"

King Black's dragon flew to inspect what the king had asked. When he returned, the news wasn't good. "My master, they have dispatched an army of stone Golems."

Both kings' eyes opened wide. "GOLEMS!"

"Yes, my master. They are an old adversary of my kind. Inanimate material built into a large figure. With a spell, this figure becomes alive and serves the purpose of its master. These stones are impervious to our flame. The only way to stop them is to take the ornament from their necks that hold the spell. Then they will return to that which they were made of.”

“I can help,” Shamma said to his father and King Black. He walked towards them. “I can fly a dragon better than anyone here. I can get those talismans.”

King Anannais looked sadly at his son. King Black waited for King Anannais’s decision. King Ananias was hesitant to give his son the go-ahead. He had lost so many in this battle, and more would be lost. He knew Shamma was telling the truth.

“You are a man now, son, and I have raised you to succeed me when I am gone.” He put his hands on his son’s shoulders. “This is your decision, son. If you believe you can help your people from this evil, then fly.”

Prince Shamma bowed to King Black and hugged his father. King Black walked up to King Ananias and patted his shoulder. “You have made the right decision, old friend. He is the best rider in both kingdoms, and a fierce warrior. He will make you proud this day.”

The prince took off his heavy armor and dumped it. He jumped on his dragon and flew away.

The Golems slowly approached the outer wall of the palace defenses. They passed through the first ring of fire the dragons created. The arrows stopped as both sides anticipated what the Golems will do next. Their large, rock-filled frames glowed white -hot after passing through the heat of the fire wall. But they kept advancing. High above the palace beyond the glow of the fire, a lone dragon and his rider approached the Golems. As stealthily as a shadow at night the prince and his dragon, cloaked in darkness, sped through the night sky. King Black ordered a unit of his soldiers to a point where the defense was weak. The Golems were almost there. It would be difficult stopping them if they breached the wall. Shamma rolled into a dive that only the most skilled riders would be able to pull off. As he dove down, the two rows of Golems marched side by side all the way up to one of the fire walls. The prince and his dragon passed right in between the Golems closest to the final wall. He snatched the talismans from their necks as they passed, thereby freezing the rock figures. His dragon arched his shoulders to protect him. He tucked down tight as the two Golems slammed into the ground. Their momentum helped them burrow a tunnel then they resurfaced between the next two Golems in line. Shamma snatched their talismans as well. He and his dragon continued in a weaving pattern up then back underground, stopping the Golems as he snatched their power source. King Ananias could see the result as his son moved at blinding speed, leaving in his wake the frozen figures of golems. King Black, sensing this was too easy, noticed the real plan of the trolls. "They knew we would figure this out." He turned to King Ananias. "Get the prince out of there!"

King Ananias was caught off guard, not sure of what King Black meant. "What! He is stopping them; why, what is wrong?"

King Black pointed to the formation that the inanimate golems had formed. "They are forming a tunnel through the fire with the golems."

As they looked back out at the fire ring, they saw the golems locking themselves together to form a safe place for the trolls to pass through.

"At this rate, if the prince continues freezing them, we will have helped them build a corridor that is fortified from our arrows all the way to the inner wall."

King Black whistled and almost instantly his dragon, Ithros, arrived with a large gust of wind from his powerful wings.

"We have to change tactics; the golems aren't attacking. They are building a corridor to the wall for the trolls. They must have known we would figure out the talismans would stop them." Ithros listened intently as the King spoke to him. "Can you contact his dragon to stop their attack of the golems?"

"Yes, my King," Ithros bowed. "I think I can." Ithros rumbled and soon enough, other dragons, who weren't spewing fire joined in. Like a wolf pack howling to make contact with another pack, the dragons' rumble reached the prince's dragon. Just as the prince burst out of the ground to take two more of the golems' talismans, his dragon bolted them straight up into the night sky.

King Black called out to the troops. "Knock down that section of wall! We need to get a better angle on their attack since these big piles of rock are in our archers' way now."

The army crushed the weak section of the wall, exposing them to the row of golems. Some still lumbered towards them.

King Black turned to King Ananias. "Can you ride? Thema was injured in the attack but I believe she can make it."

From behind them a dragon landed with a loud whoosh of air. It was King Ananias's dragon, Thema. "My King, I can fight."

King Ananias patted her neck and mounted her. He glanced at King Black. "What are you waiting for? Let's go have some fun like the good old times."

King Black jumped on Ithros and off they flew. They headed down towards the golems to try to repel or block off the corridor. The soldiers at the wall had formed a living wall to repel the enemy. The two kings flew in and their dragons picked up the inanimate rock golems. They shot into the air with the rocky masses in their claws, flew over the moving golems and dropped them. Some got crushed and some got stuck in place. The trolls, not concerned about being hit with arrows, flooded through the shielded area, charging at the soldiers who had been protecting the fallen wall. The kings flew back to their perch to direct the next phase of the attack. King Black jumped down just before Ithros landed. He yelled, "Archers on the ready! Archers on the ready! Once you smell the stench of their breath, you fire."

The squad close to the wall moved backwards to give the archers room. The archers shot at the charging mass of evil. The first wave of trolls went down. The archers reloaded their bows and fired again. The more they shot their arrows, the more the trolls came close. King Anannias watched as they inched closer and closer to their men. "They are going to breach the wall!"

The dragon flyers were unable to torch them because they were too close to their own men. Instead, they kept a perimeter around the palace to keep the hordes of trolls surrounding the palace at bay. Looking around, it seemed darkness was about to overcome. The evil creatures, waiting to devour the men, were held back only by a wall of fire.

The queen's plan was working to perfection. With the King gone, she had taken over the palace and all of Moria. They were all under her rule. So sure of her success, she ordered a redecoration of the entire palace. According to her, "everything must change."

Chef Tasty, staying below the radar, heard about the order. In an effort to help protect the King's most beloved assets, he hid as many of the pictures and paintings of the King, Sandy and her mother as he could find.

In the queen's chambers, Lilly received instructions concerning the queen's visitors. "Go and make sure everything is set for their arrival. They must be very comfortable."

Lilly bowed. "Yes, my queen." She dashed out of the room, shutting the door behind her.

"The little princess, that slippery rat," the queen spat, "I will soon find you. And when I do, you're dead. Your father will never know what happened, because as soon as he comes back—if he makes it back—I'll kill him with our power to show the people how strong I am. But you, little princess. Yes, you. I will not tolerate your existence any longer."

The queen gazed into the mirror and admired herself.

"Mirror, mirror on the wall.

I pray to thee as I have before.

I ask of you this very night,

To show me the life of Sandy Black."

The queen stepped back as the mirror shook and changed color. The mirror responded,

"A haze, a mist, enshrouds her path.

Sandy Black, the princess, has lost your grasp.

She is safe, well deep, into the forest,

More time will it take; for you to know where."

The queen screamed as she smashed a vase of flowers on the wall. "I must find this child before her father hears of what has happened, and they find each other."

The mirror then shook again.

"Oh Queen of mine, do not worry. For time is on your side.

Your strength will grow, when you three are one,

And much more, much more you shall know."

The queen smiled. "Yes, you are right. Once our powers are united, we shall know more and be more powerful than anything in all the lands. Hahahahahaaaa."

She stopped cackling when she remembered her prisoner. *I wonder if he has any information for me, after his playtime with Dr. Cain.* She gazed back into the mirror.

"Mirror mirror on the wall,

I ask you now of the battle and war,

That rages on between man and beast,

How long must I wait for the beasts to feast?"

An image of flames appeared in the mirror.

"The time of war is at hand,

The battle waged it shall be forged by flame.

King Black will hold strong, and his armies the same.

It is too early to tell as it is mid-fight.

Give him hope to remain as his inquiry is in flight."

A raven croaked as it flew by the queen's window. The queen hurried out of her chambers and followed the croaking raven. On getting to the top of the stairs, Lilly ran towards her from the bottom of the staircase with a letter in hand.

"My queen. It is a letter from the King to the princess."

The queen looked back at Lilly. "What does it say?"

Lilly scanned the letter. "It's asking how she is and wanting to know if David has everything under control."

The Queen cackled. "Reply to his message as if you were her."

Lilly gasped. "You want me to act like the princess, my queen?"

"Yes, Lilly. We must give the King what he is looking for. Comfort, until my power is complete and his daughter dead."

Lilly bowed. "Yes, my queen." Lilly walked to the library to write her reply. The queen strolled to the dungeon.

Inside the dungeon, Dr. Cain stood barefoot in his brown leather shorts with a contraption in his hands. His yellow eyes glowed through a dark set of welding goggles. He turned a knob on the contraption and lifted up two metal rods. An arc of electricity charged between the two rods. Hanging from his chains, David's eyes widened as the mad doctor approached him with the rods in hand.

"Unfortunately for you, this will hurt," Dr. Cain said with a smirk. "Actually, it will be extremely painful. Hahahahaha."

David clenched his teeth as Dr. Cain put the rods on him. "Aah!"

The door banged open and the queen strolled in. "Oh doctor, doctor. I didn't mean to interrupt you while you are working."

Dr. Cain turned around with the rods in his hands. David sighed in relief.

"My queen, it is fine you are here, yes. I was going to do some more tests." The queen smiled as she looked at the damage done to David's body. She walked past Dr. Cain to get a closer look at David. Dr. Cain stumbled as he made way for the queen. The queen walked around David, observing his battered and bruised body. She smiled when he glared at her. "Dr. Cain. You are truly an artist."

Dr. Cain grinned from ear to ear and hopped up and down. He loved the compliment.

"Dr.," the queen said, "the contraption you were about to use; may I?" The queen stretched her hands to Dr. Cain.

Dr. Cain's eyes light up, since he had never had any interested in his crafts or his work. "Why yes, Queen. I would be honored if you would use my tools."

He handed the electrified rods to the queen. She grabbed the rods and scowled at David.

"I don't want to play games with you anymore, David. I want to know where you sent the princess. I will find out, one way or the other. Why not spare yourself great suffering and just tell me. After all, what is she to you but a little girl?"

David, with his energy renewed, stood and looked the queen in the eye. "You have no power over me, witch."

The queen smiled as she placed the rods on David's head.

The palace rang with his piercing screams. The queen lifted the rods and he panted as fat drops of sweat and blood rolled down his face. She placed the rods on his face and watched with relish as his face contorted and veins stuck out. His body shook like a chicken as the charges flowed through him. The smell of blood and melting skin filled the room.

"Give me more power, Dr. Cain. I want to make a lasting impression on him."

"Yes, my queen."

David dropped on the floor, twisting and turning in pain. His body sizzled and emitted smoke like roast turkey on a grill. As Dr. Cain's finger touched the switch, a loud trumpet blasted. The queen's visitors had arrived. The queen placed the rods on the table.

"Thank you, Dr, Cain, for this enjoyment. I will have no more need for this slave. You may do with him whatever you like."

The doctor's eyes grew wide. "My queen, does he need to stay alive?"

The queen looked back at David's smoky body. "No."

Dr. Cain smiled wide, salivating and snorting as he hopped around.

"Yes, yes, yes. Thank you, my queen. Might you come by later, I should have a surprise for you; something very special."

"If I am not too busy I will come." The queen left the room as the Dr. Cain rubbed his hands in excitement.

Outside the palace, a wagon pulled by two beasts pulled up. The trumpets and drums thumped as Lilly rushed out to welcome the guests. She opened the door to the wagon and gasped. Two hideous women sat with bulging eyes, crooked teeth and mottled skin.

The two witches stepped out of the wagon and surveyed the environment. One of the hideous figures moved like an old woman while the other, who was much more fluid in her movement, turned to Lilly. "Where is the queen, child?"

Her deep black eyes made Lilly feel the witch could see her heart. She bowed and didn't look up. "I am Lilly."

The elder witch walked up to Lilly, grabbed her chin and looked her in the eye. Lilly froze. "I know who you are, child. You are Lilly, the servant that betrayed her master to serve another. We know you. No one can serve two masters; remember that."

Lilly's heart pounded so hard she feared it would explode. She breathed a sigh of relief when the witch released her chin. "Please," she said with a shaky voice, "come in."

The old witch waved her off. "Inform the queen of our arrival. We will wait for her to take us inside."

Lilly bowed and dashed into the palace. The queen walked out of the dungeon and up to the main floor of the palace. Lilly, with fear spreading over her like a blanket, bumped into the queen as she ran up the stairs.

The queen grabbed her and held her up. "Lilly, why are you out of control?" She peered into Lilly's eyes and saw horror in them. She sniffed Lilly's face and perceived the odor of death. "Mommy and Grandma are here!"

She let Lilly go. "Clean yourself up and get the chef to make us a grand meal - ensure that the meat is raw."

"Yes my, queen." Tears strolled down Lilly's face. "Right away. I am sorry for my actions. I will take care of everything." The queen dusted off her dress and strolled out of the palace. Lilly rushed to maid's quarters without looking back.

The two witches were still surveying the environment when

the queen ran out of the palace with her hands stretched out.

"Mommy, Grandma!" The queen hugged and kissed the witches. "I am so glad you are here. I have missed you. Come see what I have done with the palace."

The trio toured round the palace with the queen acting as the tour guide. Servants carried their luggage behind them, heading for the guest room as directed by the queen. As they dragged the heavy luggage, one of the servants dropped a box. Crashing onto the marble floor, the box burst open and potions, seashells, pebbles and amulets sprawled out.

The witches stopped and looked back. The eldest witch strolled over to the opened box. She looked at the servant and at the items on the floor. The servant, afraid of the witch, shivered like a leaf. Lilly stood at the top of the staircase, out of sight, and saw everything.

"It's not your fault, child," the eldest witch said as she caressed the servant's cheeks with her long fingernails. "You haven't been trained properly." She turned and smiled at the queen. In a split second, she dug her fingernails into the servant's throat and tore out a large chunk of flesh. The other servants gasped in shock. The servant held his throat, gasping for air. He fell to his knees as the old witch bit and chewed the flesh in her hands. "If you had been taught correctly you might not have had to die. But since you are careless and know not how to respect an elder's things, you will pay with your life." She drooled and bits of flesh fell from her mouth as she spoke. Finally, the wounded servant fell to the ground dead.

The younger witch stepped forward and addressed all the servants. "From now on, you will respect the things of the three that rule you. If any disrespect is shown to us or our belongings, you will pay with your life or one that you love." She smiled at the eldest witch. "Mother, I am hungry as well. Grab me a piece, will you?"

The eldest witch pulled another handful of flesh from the dead servant's throat and handed it over to her daughter. The queen looked on with a blank expression on her face.

In the queen's chambers, the eldest witch addressed the queen. "You have grown soft in your position. Let me remind you why we have placed you here." She stepped in front of the queen and slapped her hard across the face.

The younger witch—the queen's mother— stood over the queen. "We have placed you here so that we can rule this land once more."

The queen staggered to sit up and wiped blood from her mouth. The eldest witch continued the tirade. "We have not forged alliances with the evils of the ancient times to allow you to wallow in your beauty," the eldest witch yelled. "You are too soft with these worthless and weak people."

The younger witch stretched out to help the queen up. "Come, my daughter. Let us show you how to rule effectively."

The queen's mother helped her up as the eldest witch opened the doors. They strolled through the palace, observing the activities taking place. Lilly tiptoed behind them, her heart pounding mercilessly against her chest. The trio turned around and Lilly gasped in fear. She bowed before the queen, Myala, the mother, and Obeia, the grandmother. "My queen, I have sent the letter to the King."

The two witches squawked like crows. "What?"

"Why are you sending a letter to the King?" the younger witch asked. "I have directed her to, Mother," replied the queen.

After the queen was done explaining, the eldest witch smiled at Lilly. "Ahh, a good servant - you have proved to be obedient after all. So, you sent him a letter telling him what?"

Lilly stumbled over her words. "Uhh, I told the King that all is ah well and that David is taking care, I mean good care, of the palace."

"What about me?" the queen asked. "Did you include anything about me in the letter?"

"Oh yes, yes my queen," Lilly replied, nodding. "I said the two of you are getting along quite wonderfully." The three witches smiled. Lilly bowed. "My queen, I'll take my leave now to make the arrangements for dinner."

The eldest witch grabbed Lilly's hand and sniffed it. "Yes, I am a bit famished. I do hope it is a good meal."

Shaking, Lilly gulped and pulled her hand back. "Yes, it should be wonderful. Chef Tasty is the best chef in all of Moria. Let me check on him and ensure he's started preparing dinner."

The queen dismissed Lilly and walked alongside her mother and grandma outside the palace. Villagers gathered outside the palace. The younger witch turned to her daughter. "It is good to be with you again, daughter. Our powers will grow as long as we are all together. We have made you beautiful, to be in this position for this purpose. Now we will make you terrible, and ruler of the whole world."

As they walked by a bucket of fruits, the older witch grabbed some of the fruits. Still walking, she pulled a vial containing a purple liquid from her neck and poured it over the fruits. The fruit absorbed the liquid and the witch sniffed the fruit and smiled. They approached an outdoor makeshift prison with palace guards that refused to pay obeisance to the queen. The older witch pressed her head against the bars of the cell and waved the fruits. The prisoners smacked their lips and stretched out their hands with their eyes on the fruits. Smirking, she tossed in the fruits.

"You will like this, my sweets." The prisoners jostled for the fruits like monkeys. Within minutes of devouring the fruits the men choked, grabbing their throats.

Villagers converged on the scene, watching the men gasping for air.

The younger witch faced the villagers. "You will follow and submit to the queen who rules with the power of three. Or your fate will be much worse."

The villagers stared in horror as the prisoners began to swell like balloons. Their skin turned red as blood vessels in their bodies burst from all the pressure. Their eyes burst as they fell to the ground, five times larger than their original state. One of the chef's helpers hid behind a pillar, witnessing the whole event. Chef Tasty had sent her with a tray of delicacies for the soldiers but on seeing the witches, she hid behind the pillar. When the prisoners burst, she dashed to the kitchen to tell the chef what she'd seen.

Lilly banged the kitchen door behind her. Glad no one else was in the kitchen, she grabbed a stool, sat and cried her eyes out. Chef Tasty trudged into the kitchen with his arms full of food. Lilly wiped her eyes quickly with the back of her hand. Chef Tasty, pretending not to have seen her tears, placed the food on a table. Lilly ran to him and hugged him from behind. Tears rolled down her face. "Dad, it's horrible, just horrible. I can't do this anymore. They are killing the people of Moria. We have to stop them."

Chef Tasty turned around and hugged her. "Oh, my child. I knew something wasn't right about you. What happened to you?"

Lilly lifted her head from Chef Tasty's shoulders. "We have to stop them. They are evil. They killed a servant for dropping a bag and I just heard they killed a bunch of prisoners. The soldiers who refused to serve the queen, they died some horrible way. I'm so sorry for helping her get control of everything. I was afraid of her power. I have been upset with you after Mother died but nothing you did can compare to this; I am sorry."

Lilly grabbed Chef Tasty's hands. "She has that mirror and the things she has seen and shown me – it reminds me of what you told me about when you fought in the great war."

Chef Tasty opened a doorway in the kitchen and placed a finger on Lilly's lips. "Lilly, my daughter, I am just glad your safe. We will have time later to fix our problems but first, we must leave at once! The situation has gotten out of hand, much faster than I had originally calculated. First, David needs my attention." He grabbed Lilly and ushered her down a hidden path.

Chapter 12
THE FOREST

Early in the morning, Sandy was busy preparing a breakfast of giant-sized eggs along with slices of wild boar meat. Her humming filled the quiet house where all the giants slept. All but Zerachiel.

Like a shadow, he sneaked out of the house, jumped on a nearby tree and watched Sandy cook. Sandy stopped humming when she sensed someone was watching her. Scared, she turned around and saw Zerachiel on the tree. "Now that's not nice," she yelled. "Didn't your mom teach you it's not polite to sneak around unannounced? You scare folk like that and that ain't right."

Zerachiel bowed his head, sorry. "I apologize, young princess. I did not mean to scare you."

Sandy noticed his sad face and felt bad for yelling. "You are Zerachiel, right?"

He nodded.

"You're the quiet one. Why are you up so early?"

From his vantage point, Zerachiel glanced over the forest. "I love to be up as the sun rises, as the new day comes to be. I love the smell of the air; the dew that waters the plants and gives the bugs a pool to drink from. I love the shimmer of light that reflects off the surface of the river as each new day begins." He took a deep breath. "The smell at dawn is like no other time of day. It's peaceful. It's quiet, like me."

"Nice." Sandy smiled at his reasoning. "Well, I guess you have been here long enough to know I am making breakfast for everyone. I figured I can be of some use around here."

Zerachiel smiled. "I thank you, Princess, for taking this duty on yourself. None of us can cook like you."

Sandy smiled back. "Well, it's not hard to learn how to cook. You just have to be patient, that's all."

"Would you perhaps teach me this art of cooking?"

Sandy smiles and checks on her food. "It's a deal. You'll help me prepare lunch and dinner."

He leapt from the tree in excitement and stretched out his huge hand to her.

"Thank you, Princess. I hope I'll make a good student."

As Sandy and Zerachiel talked, the aroma of the food woke Remiel up. Like a kid anxious to see what gifts Santa brought on Christmas day, Remiel followed the smell to locate its source. After making his way to the front door of the house, he heard Sandy singing, "The Old Rugged Cross."

Remiel smiled as he swayed gently back and forth, listening to Sandy's angelic voice.

Unable to resist, Remiel slowly opened the front door. He saw Zerachiel standing near the fire pit as Sandy sang and cooked.

"That is beautiful, Sandy."

Sandy looked up and saw Remiel. Behind him, his other brothers huddled together, listening to her sing. Sandy smiled. "I'm glad you all are up. It's time for breakfast."

The giants rushed out of the house, aiming for the fire pit. Sandy stood in front of the brothers and waved a large wooden spoon with both hands. "We aren't going to do this like you're used to. We are going to have some manners and take our time today."

The brothers stood still, surprised.

"Now, you'll all go and wash your hands first," Sandy said, pointing at the nearby river.

Michael nodded and turned to his brothers. "It is only fair that we listen to the young princess. After all, she has prepared a fine meal for us. It won't hurt to follow her guidelines before consuming it."

The brothers muttered amongst themselves and then headed over to the river. Zerachiel stood near Sandy, wearing a large purple apron.

Raguel looked back as his other brothers and begrudgingly started moving towards the river. "Hey, why isn't he coming?" he asked sternly. "You think you're special, Whispers?"

Sandy frowned as she stepped in to defend Zerachiel.

"Hey, what's your problem? Mind your business, Mr. Raggedy. He has been helping me make breakfast, so he has already washed. Go on and stop bothering him."

Embarrassed, Raguel scratched the back of his head. He turned around and muttered as he walked. "She is a feisty one, isn't she?"

"Stop muttering!" Sandy hissed. She turned and tugged at Zerachiel's apron. Zerachiel looked down. "Why did he call you that?"

A look of surprise crossed Zerachiel's face. "What did he call me?"

"Why did he call you Whispers?"

"Ohh, that's what my brothers call me. They call me that because I'm so quiet."

"OK; maybe we will have to come up with another nickname for you."

"As you wish, Princess."

The brothers came back after washing their hands. Raphael was soaked, Raguel was laughing his head off, and Uriel was soaked and upset. Sandy, wondering what happened, walked up to them. Raguel rolled on the floor, laughing like a hyena. Michael stood off to the side, shaking his head. Sandy turned to Gabriel. "What happened?"

"Well Sandy," Gabriel said, "as we all took off to wash, Raphael figured it was a race. But he was losing as we were all in front of him. As we approached the water, I guess he figured he would make his last attempt to try and win."

Gabriel glanced at Raguel, who was clapping his thighs and laughing harder. "So he jumped over us and as he did, he knocked Uriel over and they both splashed into the river."

Sandy cracked a smile, trying hard not to laugh. The other giants burst into laughter. Uriel stamped his feet. "That's not even funny!" he growled.

Sandy nudged Zerachiel to hand Uriel the first plate. "Here, Uriel," Sandy said. "A little water won't hurt you. Have some breakfast."

Uriel's eyes widened as he stared at his plate of food. All the giants were served, but Sandy didn't let them eat yet. She looked around to make sure everyone had their portion. Raphael drooled, eager to consume his meal. The other giants all had their eyes on their breakfast. Sandy clapped. "Now, where I come from, we pray before we eat. Everyone, bow your heads so we can say grace."

The giants bowed their heads. "GRACE!" Raphael blurted out. He raised his plate close to his face, ready to gobble down his meal.

"Stop!" Uriel shouted. "Wait for Sandy to say what she has to say. You know better."

Raphael slumped his shoulders and put his head down. Sandy glanced around again to make sure every head was bowed. "All eyes closed. Dear heavenly Father, we come to you in the name of your son, Jesus. Lord, we thank you for this food we are about to eat. We ask that you keep it safe for our consumption. We thank you for our safety, and the company you have given us on this new day. We ask Father that you protect our friend, Eve, and those who travel with her."

Sandy sniffed as tears rolled down her face.

"Lord, we ask that you keep David safe if he is not already with you. Please keep all the good people of Moria safe from the evil queen. I ask, Lord, that you keep my father safe, and that we will be with each other soon. In Jesus' name we pray. Amen."

The giants teared up as they chorused 'amen'. Sandy's head remained bowed as she tried to hide her hurt and tears. Michael leaned over next to her and lifted her chin with a finger. He wiped her tears with another finger.

"Princess, God has heard your prayer. All will be fine." He smiled at her. "But it is important we finish this business."

Raising her head, Sandy sniffed. "What business?"

"We need to eat this food before it gets cold."

Sandy smiled. "Of course! Let's eat!"

The giants pounced on their plates and within minutes, breakfast was over.

One by one, they got up to carry out their routine tasks for the day. Sandy turned to Remiel. "Remiel, will you help me clean out the pans I used in making breakfast?"

Remiel, happy to help, clenched his fists in excitement. "Yes, Sandy. What do you need me to do?"

Sandy pointed at the dirty, gigantic pans made of wood. "Can you bring the pans over to the river for me?"

"No problem, Sandy. I can do that."

Remiel picked up all the pans at once and carried them over to the river. Sandy walked behind him, observing the other giants. Michael and Gabriel made plans for the day, Raphael was in his lab, making medicines, Uriel practiced his fighting techniques, Zerachiel was nowhere to be found, and Raguel was sitting on top of a large rock fixing nets and fishhooks. "Remiel, I want to check something."

Remiel turned around. "Can I come with you?"

"No, Remiel. I need you to finish cleaning the pans. I'll be right back to check them."

"Ok."

The front door was wide open when Sandy got to the house. She walked inside and glanced around. "This house is a mess! Clothes and dirt everywhere. It's a wonder how they find things in here."

Sandy sighed. "I need this sorted out quickly." She dashed out of the house to the river to inspect Remiel's cleaning. Sandy gaped as she watched him wash. He busied himself dunking the pans in the river over and over again, trying to get rid of food particles stuck in them. He frowned, frustrated. Sandy chuckled. "Remiel, that method isn't working. Haven't you noticed?"

With a defeated look on his face, Remiel sighed.

"Remiel," Sandy said, "you need soap. Do you have any soap?"

Remiel had a puzzled look on his face. Sandy thought for a

minute. "Come on, Remiel. Let the pans soak in the water. Let's go check Raphael. He might be able to help."

Remiel put the pans in the water and walked with Sandy to ask Raphael for some soap.

Sandy and Remiel strolled to the side of the house where Raphael's lab was. Hearing bubbling and sizzling sounds inside the lab, Sandy knocked on the door. Raphael didn't respond. Sandy knocked again. Remiel, who was standing behind her, tapped her shoulder. "Sandy, remember it's Raphael. He is always focused on whatever he is studying. Let him know it's you 'cause he likes you."

Sandy nodded, remembering how Raphael had helped her with the cuts and bruises. "Raphael, Raphael," Sandy called, "it's Sandy. I need your help."

"Princess, is that you?"

"Yes, Raphael. It's me. Do you have soap?"

Raphael opened the door, smiling down at Sandy. "Is it time for lunch now?" Sandy smiles and responded, "No not yet Raphael, but I need your help with something."

Walking into the lab, Sandy glanced at the shelves filled with bottles and containers of different shapes and sizes. They were all labeled and had either powder or liquids in them.

"Soap?"

"Yes, you know, something I can use to clean the dishes. It smells good and becomes foamy."

Sandy looked around the lab as Remiel encouraged his brother to think of something he could make. "Raphael," Remiel said, "you're the only one who can make something for us to clean the pans with."

Raphael, still focusing on the problem in deep thought, sat on his chair and scratched his head. He spun around in his chair and Sandy dodged him to avoid getting hit. Raphael reset his glasses and scanned a shelf with bottles and jars. He pulled out a jar with a blue, powder-like substance. He reached out of the window and grabbed a flower. Putting the powder and the flower into a cup, he crushed them with a pestle. He added water to the mixture and placed it over heat. Sandy and Remiel stood afar, patiently waiting for the mixture. The mixture bubbled and turned green. Soon, the lab was filled with a fruity smell. Raphael took the frothy mixture off the heat, poured it into a small glass container and swirled it around the glass. He sniffed the jar and smiled. "Try this, Princess. Yes, yes, that should do it."

He lowered the jar so Sandy could take a sniff. Sandy smiled. "I'm not even going to ask what you put in this. It smells good and I believe it will work."

Raphael handed the jar to Remiel and told him to use a little bit of the solution. "It's concentrated," he said. Remiel nodded, excited because Sandy was happy. "OK. Thanks, Raphael." Remiel, eager to test the soap, turned to Sandy. "Can you show me how to clean dishes now?"

Sandy hugged Raphael's leg. "Oh, thank you, Raphael. You are one in a million."

Raphael giggled. "Hmm, Princess. You make me feel special. I like you, Princess. I will always help you when you call."

Sandy rushed off with Remiel to the river to wash the pans. "I think if we move the pans over to the waterfall, we will be able to wash the pans properly."

"Whatever you say, Princess."

Remiel got into the water and Sandy stood on a nearby rock giving instructions. She had to shout because of the rushing waterfall. "OK, Remiel. Pour a little bit of the soap into the waterfall."

Remiel gave a thumbs-up and began pouring out the contents of the jar. As he poured, he stepped forward, trying to get a small amount closer to the falling water. He slipped on a slippery rock and a lot of the soap poured out into the water.

"Are you hurt?" Sandy asked.

"I'm not, but so much of the soap poured into the water!"

"I don't think it's that bad."

As Remiel regained his balance, the bubbles from the soap started forming. Under the force of the waterfall, the bubbles grew. Raguel, who was fixing his net atop some rocks near the waterfall, noticed the giant-sized bubbles. Shocked, the piece of straw he was chewing fell from his mouth. Sandy stood, mesmerized by the amount and size of the bubbles being formed.

Zerachiel appeared out of nowhere and stood next to his brother Uriel. He looked at the bubbles forming and looked down at Sandy.

"Princess," Zerachiel said, "was this what you planned?"

Sandy pulled her attention away from the soapy mountain to respond.

"No," Sandy said. "I've never seen so many bubbles!" She laughed.

"Oh my," Remiel said, feeling bad about the incident. "I'm sorry, Princess. I didn't mean to-"

Sandy cut him off mid-sentence.

"Oh Remiel," Sandy said. "It's not your fault. It will be fine. It's just bubbles."

Remiel breathed a sigh of relief. "Hey look. It's like snow. It's just not cold."

He grabbed giant-sized soap suds and blew them over to Sandy. The soapy cloud engulfed her and almost floated away. Zerachiel pulled her out from the cloud. He placed her on his shoulder. Remiel laughed on seeing a soapy moustache on Sandy's face. Sandy laughed too. Michael and Gabriel came over as they noticed the bubbles. Raguel jumped down from the rock near to the waterfall with the largest bubbles.

"Hey, Michael, Gabriel look! I'm melting, I'm melting, ahhh!" He got covered in bubbles till he couldn't be seen any longer. They all laughed.

Raphael, distracted by the laughter, ran out of his lab to see what was going on. His eyes widened when he saw the bubbles. On seeing Raphael, Raguel called out to him. Raguel was engulfed in soap suds. "Hey Raphael! Raphael!"

Confused, he adjusted his glasses. "It's a talking cloud."

He clapped his hands in excitement. "I have never ever seen a talking cloud. I always knew they could talk. I told you guys." He rushed over to the river to get a better look at the talking cloud. His brothers burst into laughter. Gabriel reached out and grabbed a handful of the suds. He clapped his hands, causing the bubbles to fly. Sandy watched and smiled as the white bubbles floated all over the trees and down to the ground around them. They all stood and watched as Gabriel did the same thing a few more times. When they realized the bubbles were all gone, they looked around and noticed that the bubbles had cleaned everything they had touched. Sandy looked at her clothes, and ran her hands through her hair, smiling and saying to herself, "Wow, I wish I would have had some stuff like that at home. I got cleaned with the bubbles!"

She looked at all the giants and noticed their clothes and armor had been cleaned as well. Everyone was happy except Uriel. He looked at his new shine and it upset him. "No!" he shouted, upset. "What is this? Do you know what it just washed off me?"

Confused, Sandy turned to Michael. "Michael, why is he

upset? He is clean. He should be happy."

Michael shrugged. "Princess, Uriel doesn't believe in washing off past battles."

Uriel, hearing Michael talking to Sandy, rushed over. "That's not it, totally." Uriel knelt before Sandy and looked at the sky. "Our great father used to tell us something when we were little. He would say, "If you stay ready, you don't have to get ready." Then he and his brothers howled like a pack of wolves.

Sandy gaped as they howled. "I'm sorry. Does it still bother you to talk about your father?"

Uriel looked down at Sandy with a puzzled look on his face. "Oh no. That's just how our father always said it. With the howl at the end."

Sandy nodded. Uriel looked up at the sky again. "So in tribute to my father, the great King of our people, I do not wash off the memories of wars past. Because for me, if I can always remember the last battle, I will stay ready for the next one."

Raguel walked near Sandy and whispered in her ear. "It's just a shame we haven't had a fight in years. So, he has been funky for no reason. Sometimes breakfast and dinner are battles for him."

Sandy covered her mouth to stop herself from laughing. Raguel laughed out. Enraged, Uriel stood up to face Raguel. "Well, I guess I was ready for this moment cause I'm about to show you how ready I am."

Sandy stepped between the two giants with her hands raised. "Raguel," Sandy said, "stop talking about your brother. He has been very loyal to the memory and philosophy your father gave you all." Sandy turned to Uriel.

"And Uriel, calm down. Where I come from, it is proper for a warrior to go into battle clean and with a shine to his armor. So when he wins his battle and hasn't covered himself in dirt or grime, he can show his enemy how easy it was to defeat him. And then talk about him in a shameful way." Uriel thought about the statement Sandy had made. "Besides, I think you look very handsome with your new clean armor."

Uriel looked over his shiny armor and blushed. "I guess what you say of the warriors from your homeland will work for me as well." He walked off admiring his new shine.

Michael approached Sandy. "Princess, I thank you for your wise heart. You give a refreshing viewpoint to my brothers even in times of frustration."

Sandy looked up at Michael. "You're welcome."

In the afternoon, Michael called out to his brothers. "It is time to go get supplies. Remiel, stay with the princess. Everyone else, let's go."

Sandy walked over to Remiel. "Where are they going?"

"We have to go out to restore supplies every few days. Raphael also needs to find new plants for his study."

"How long does it usually take?"

"Don't worry, Princess. I won't let anything happen to you."

Sandy, comforted by his words, smiled. "Well, I guess since they are going to be gone, I can show you how to make dinner for them."

Remiel's eyes lit up. "That would be wonderful, Sandy. I hope to do better with cooking than I did with the dishes."

Sandy smiled. "I'm sure you will. Come on - let's hurry and get started."

Sandy and Remiel rushed to the smokehouse while the other six brothers faded away into the thick forest.

The sun struggled to show its light from behind the dark clouds that filled the sky as Gabriel led the group into the forest.

Uriel walked with Raphael, who wandered around looking for new plants. Zerachiel slipped in and out of the shadows of the trees as they passed. Michael kept an eye on the group as they walked into the forest. He kept track of how far they had gone to ensure they returned home that same day before nightfall.

Michael called his brothers to stop as soon as they had gotten far enough away from the camp that Sandy wouldn't hear them. The group gathered around Michael.

"Brothers, the last few days, I noticed the forest does not feel normal."

Zerachiel stepped out of a shadow. "I have noticed it too, Michael. Something evil is in the air."

The brothers paid close attention to the conversation. Michael continued. "Gabriel has seen far off in the distance a flickering light at night. He had gone to investigate it some two nights ago, and upon investigation, he found out that the battle that King Black must be in is in the Kingdom of the White Rose. A fiery glow emanates from that direction all night long." The brothers looked at one another thinking of Sandy first, and then what this might mean. "We have come out today not to look for supplies, but for me to tell you not to say anything to the princess."

"The princess would be sad," Raphael said.

Michael turned to Raphael. "Yes, she would be. And this is why we will not give her more to worry about for now. Do we all agree?"

The brothers nodded.

"One more thing!" Michael said.

"The trees, the dark trees with the red markings on them - I have noticed more of them spread out farther than I have ever seen before. They stop the path of information in the forest. They are the accursed trees of old."

Michael faced the group. "It would seem as if there might be some danger coming. The princess's life is at stake. We must protect her with our lives if that is what comes."

Uriel held up his flaming sword. "Come what may!"

Raguel punched his fist in the air. "Come what may!"

***

The sun was high in the sky as Eve and her companions moved to speak with the Great Tree. They moved at a steady pace, not stopping day or night. Along the way, birds told Eve of an increase in number of the dark trees marked with the red markings of the evil ones. As they moved through a clearing, they got to a dark patch in the forest. They paused, concerned, as the shroud of evil began to consume the few patches of sun light that were able to break through.. All they could see was darkness.

Knowing they had no choice, Eve moved into the forest. All around, decaying animals filled the forest and dying trees bowed their heads. Knowing she had heard of this place before, she tried hard to remember, but she couldn't. As she struggled to remember, the group pressed forward through the dead trees and animals.

After a while, Eve noticed what she had hoped not to see. In the distance, a large dark tree without branches stood with a large letter N marked in the middle of its trunk. Understanding why the forest was so dark, Eve warned her group to be careful.

"Stay together and don't get entangled, or we might never leave this place."

The group moved carefully through the dense and dark forest. A scream followed by the snapping of wood arose from the back of the group. Eve turned around and saw vines from a seemingly dead tree, wrapping around one of the trees in her group and breaking its branches.

"It's the marked tree," Eve yelled. "It's got control of the trees around it and it's trying to stop us. Save him before he is torn apart."

As the group tried to pull their friend to safety, he was snapped into nothing more than a pile of firewood. Eve and her companions shook in fear. Eve, knowing they must move quickly or else they wouldn't make it through the forest, commanded her group to move. "We must go now! Move, move, move!"

The trees moved as fast as they could, but not fast enough for the swift-moving vines of the evil tree. One by one, Eve's companions were torn into pieces.

If those that are left can just get out of this dark forest, they will live, she thought. The beast only has control over that which is inside the darkness. "Get to the light!" Eve screamed to her friends.

The closer they got to the light, the more likely it seemed they wouldn't make it out. Eve could feel the vines so close they tickled her leaves. Diving for the light, Eve and the last survivor of her group landed outside of the dark forest. The vines that had been trying to catch them and destroy them halted in their pursuit. Eve gathered herself and stood on her roots, then helped her final companion up. The two looked at each other with a look of relief yet pain from the loss they had just suffered.

"We must move on - if we don't, then the lives of our companions will have been in vain."

Eve looked her companion in the eyes.

"We have to be strong for the sake of all of Moria."

Eve smiled at her, comforting her. She turned around and move forward. As they took their first steps, a vine wrapped around the roots of Eve's last friend tightened and pulled her back into the forest. It lifted her off the ground and pulled her back into the darkness. Eve turned around and tried to catch her friend, but it was too late. The loud crunch echoed through the forest and the last of Eve's companions died. Eve, remembering her last words, spoke out loud. "If I don't move forward, you will have died in vain."

Eve stood and moved away from the dark forest.

***

Back at the giants' camp, Sandy and Remiel stood in the living room of the giants' house.

"This needs work," Sandy said as she paced back and forth, glancing at the scattered bits of dust and clothing all over the room.

Remiel stood near and watched. "I thought we were going to prepare dinner?" Remiel said, worried.

Sandy was preoccupied with thoughts of how to organize the house. She moved around, making signs of lifting, pulling, and adjusting with her hands. Remiel, afraid of what might come next, tried sneaking out of the house.

"No, no, no." Sandy waved her finger in the air. "You're not going anywhere. You're the only one here who can move half of this stuff. Remiel, I want to surprise your brothers when they get home."

Remiel rubbed his hands, excited about the surprise.

"OK, Sandy. What do you need me to do?"

Moving furniture and trash out of the house got Remiel tired. He sat outside, panting, while Sandy tied a piece of cloth around her nose and mouth and made herself a broom using palm fronds.

Sandy swept the whole house, humming to herself. A dust cloud rose as she swept with so much energy. When she finished sweeping, she came out covered in dust. Remiel lay on the ground, snoring. "Remiel! Remiel, wake up!"

Slowly, Remiel woke up and sat up. "Sandy, are we done yet?"

Sandy removed the fabric from her face and dusted her dress. "Not yet. We have to mop now."

Remiel looked at Sandy, confused. "OK. What does this mop mean and what do you need me to do?"

"It's easy. All we need to do is fill a bucket with water and some of that bubble soap that Raphael made. Then we clean the floors with it and let it dry."

Remiel smiled, thinking it would be fun. "I will go right now to get the water."

Remiel jumped to his feet and dashed to the river to get water. This time, he was careful not to pour too much soap inside the bucket. He held the bucket near the waterfall and made bubbles inside the bucket. He rushed back to meet Sandy, who was holding a mop she'd made with a stick and a piece of rag.

Remiel looked at the mop. "Sandy, don't I need that too?"

"You mean the mop? Well, if you can make one, you can use it."

Remiel walked to a nearby tree and snapped off a straight branch. Looking around, he found an old robe which he tore into long strips. He tied the long strips to the tree branch.

"Great job, Remiel, now you have yourself a nice weapon."

Remiel frowned, confused. "You can't fight a war with these, can you?"

Sandy chuckled. "No, Remiel. What I mean is, with the mops we are going to kick out all the dust and dirt from the house."

"I get it now," Remiel said, smiling.

With Sandy's guidance, Remiel poured some of the soapy water onto the floor. Sandy showed him how to mop and tried to make it easy and fun. She knew they would finish the job faster if Remiel found the chore fun-filled. "See how the floor color changes?"

Remiel looked on in fascination as the black floor turned bright red.

"I see it, Sandy. I can see the floor!"

Remiel jumped in, whisking his mop around the floor. He mopped with gusto, eager to make the entire floor shine bright red. Sandy smiled, amazed at how fast he was working. Moving from one room to the other, he cleaned the entire house in a short time. After mopping, he moved from room to room, making sure he hadn't missed any spots. Sandy ensured he mopped his footprints as he left each room. Remiel stood back, admiring the clean floors. The floor shimmered in the sunlight shining through the door and windows.

Sandy turned to Remiel. "You did a great job!"

Remiel giggled, happy about the compliment.

Back in the forest, Raphael was busy gathering herbs while the rest sat together talking.

"Something is wrong in the Kingdom of the White Rose," Michael said. "You feel it as well?"

"Yes," Gabriel said. "I have felt it as well."

"The King would not be away from his daughter this long unless there was really some huge problem," Michael said. "Things must be far worse than we imagined."

Uriel nodded. "True."

"Gabriel," Michael called, "could you get close to the palace to see what you can? You're the tallest."

"This I will do, brother," Gabriel said. "Tonight, we should send Zerachiel to spy out that bright glow. He will be hard to see."

"You are right," Michael said. "It is high time we looked for answers."

Gabriel got up and marched into the forest. Michael turned to the others. "Let us return home now. Before it gets too late."

Back home, Sandy and Remiel slept on a patch of grass between the house and the river. After dusting the furniture and washing some clothes and taking them back in, they were exhausted. Zerachiel was the first giant to arrive home. He leaped from tree to tree and jumped down to the house. Stepping into the house, he noticed something was different but couldn't put his finger on what it was. He sniffed in the heavy smell of flowers that filled the house. He looked down and was shocked to see the bright red floor.

"So, what do you think? Clean, huh?"

Zerachiel turned around and looked down at a smiling Sandy.

Zerachiel smiled back. "You have brought a peace to what was once a storm, young princess."

He glanced around the now spotless and orderly house. Remiel jumped in. "What do you think? Doesn't it look great? It's all shinning and we organized all of your stuff and —"

Sandy put her finger to her lips. "Shush!"

Remiel covered his mouth with both hands. Just then, the rest of the giants returned. Gabriel was absent. As they approached the front door, Zerachiel stood aside, eager to see his brothers' reactions. One by one, the giants said hi to Sandy and walked into the house.

A loud yell shook the house. Sandy rolled her eyes as she knew the only one it could be. She smiled at Zerachiel. "I'll handle this."

Sandy walked down the corridor and saw Raphael bouncing on his bed. Further down, she saw Michael standing in a doorway. Raguel was rolling on the ground, laughing.

"Why!" Uriel yelled. "This is my stuff. Who touched my stuff? I'm going to kill 'em."

"Uriel," Michael said, "will you calm down? I'm sure you will find it."

Raguel was still laughing on the floor as Sandy walked to Uriel's doorway. "He thinks somebody would take that stupid doll from him. Hahahaha."

Raguel kept laughing and rolling on the floor. Sandy walked over and tugged on Michael's robe. "He is upset, right?"

Michael smiled and knelt before Sandy. "I thank you, Princess. You have done a wonderful job."

Sandy smiled. "I can't take all the credit, Michael. I couldn't have gotten it all done without Remiel." Sandy looked back over at Uriel, who was still busy creating a ruckus. "What is he so upset about?"

"Uriel is very sensitive with his things. He has always had a doll that he is attached to and—"

"I know it was you, Princess," Uriel said. "You got our trust and now you've taken him!" Uriel jumped and rushed to Sandy's side. "First off, it is not a doll. He is the Rain King. The most powerful warrior to have ever lived. He was so powerful and awesome, he lived atop a mountain that was made of the skulls of his enemies."

"Umm, if you mean that pile of chicken bones," Sandy said. "You know, I'm sure he was magnificent as a warrior, but the pile of bird bones you had him sitting on top of just didn't do him justice the way you thought it did. Have you looked at your bed yet?"

Uriel squinted and glanced around the room. He looked at his neatly made bed. There, on top of his pillow, sat the Rain King.

"Do you feel better now, Uriel? I didn't get rid of any of your stuff. I just made it neat, rather than having it all over the place. Oh, and if your Rain King needs his mountain of bird enemies, it's outside." Sandy stormed out of the room.

Uriel hugged the Rain King. Michael nudged him. "You need to apologize to Sandy. Go and tell her you're sorry for not appreciating her cleaning."

Uriel put his head down, feeling bad. He walked over to Sandy. "I am sorry, Princess. I did not mean to hurt your feelings. Thanks for cleaning up the house."

"Thank you, Uriel. Just remember to keep your room clean and you'll have more room to have the Rain King conquer."

Uriel's eyes lit up. "You are right, Princess!"

Sandy turned towards the front door. "I have to get something on the grill." Stepping out of the front door, she met Zerachiel who was holding up some fish he had cleaned.

"Sandy, I am ready for that lesson you promised me."

Sandy smiled and bowed before Zerachiel. "For sure Zerachiel, shall we get started?"

Sandy and Zerachiel walked to the makeshift outdoor kitchen, while the rest of the brothers minus Gabriel looked around the clean house. When Zerachiel placed the fish on a table, Sandy saw that the fish was ugly. "Uhmm, Zerachiel. What type of fish is this anyway?"

"Princess, don't judge from the outward appearance. This is a beast fish. Bad to look at, but very good to eat."

Sandy smirked. "Yeah, it's very bad to look at."

Sandy looked around to see what she should use for this meal. As she glanced around, she saw a large plant nearby with large leaves similar to that of a banana leaf. The idea was set in Sandy's mind now.

"Zerachiel, today's lesson will be one that is very simple to follow. Could you grab some of the leaves on that tree, please?"

Zerachiel cut the leaves and brought them to her. "First, we will clean everything, washing it with a bit of water to get rid of dirt. Then we'll season it."

Zerachiel picked Sandy up and placed her on his shoulder, then he followed her directions for cooking. He took the vegetables, the fish and leaves to the river to wash.

After washing, he waited for directions. "What's next, please?"

"Ok, it's time to season everything and put it over some fire."

With Sandy's guidance, he placed the leaves on the table and sprinkled them with some salt and pepper along with some cooking oil. He lay each fish on its leaf and added a sprinkle of lemon juice. After that, he added a portion of the mixed vegetables to each fish and rolled them up in the leaves. He covered the hot coals with leaves, placed the fish on the coals, and covered them up with more leaves.

As he'd finished, he sat and zoned out. Sandy tapped his shoulder. "Zerachiel, are you alright?"

Zerachiel looked around and then onto his shoulder. "I'm sorry, Princess. I just remembered something from when I was much younger." He stared into the dark forest. "I remember when our mother used to make dinner. I used to stand and watch as she prepared the meal. The smell of tonight's meal has brought me back to that memory. Oh, how beautiful our mother was."

A single tear fell from his face. His eyes and skin darkened.

Sandy, still on his shoulder, whispered into his ear. "It's not a bad thing to miss your mother. I miss mine. Always. But we remember those things that made them special and that's soothing."

Zerachiel sniffed. "You know, she kept us all in line and organized, like you do."

Zerachiel set Sandy down on the ground and stood before her.

"Princess, on behalf of my brothers and I, as the remnant of the giant tribe of Moria, I thank you for your help and your understanding. For a long time, we have lived in seclusion. Our main goal is to find home."

Sandy looked up at the towering Zerachiel. "I'm sure you will find your people. As for home, I think you seven already have that."

Zerachiel and Sandy looked around as the brothers cracked jokes and laughed at one another. Zerachiel smiled.

"Wise princess, I think you are right."

Sandy instructed Zerachiel to watch the food while she checked on his brothers. She sneaked behind the house and into the forest. She sat on a log of wood and wept. "Mom, I know you told me to be strong. I'm trying hard but I miss you. I know you're in a better place now, and I know at this moment you led me to my new friends, the giants. I haven't really had a lot of time to think because everything is going so fast, but I think that prince you said would find me has already found me. But now, I'm not sure I will ever see him again. Oh, and I miss him. I know this isn't like me at all. We have only been around each other a couple of times, but it's like I've known him forever. I'm afraid of what's going on with Daddy. I just need a hug right now."

"Princess."

Sandy jumped to her feet and turned around. It was Gabriel.

"Princess, I can give you a hug if you don't mind." Gabriel knelt and spread his arms wide. Overwhelmed, Sandy ran into Gabriel's arms.

"It's OK, little princess. This too shall pass. I have heard of this Prince Shamma. I know his father very well."

Sandy lifted her head from Gabriel's neck. "You know Shamma?"

"Oh yes, Princess. He is a valiant warrior. I'm sure that if he and your father are together, they are fine."

Sandy's heart beat faster. "I sure hope that I can see them both soon."

"I'm sure things will be different very soon, Princess."

"Thank you, Gabriel. Sometimes a girl just needs a listening ear."

Gabriel chuckled. "We all do, Princess. Besides, you have done a lot for us here. Anytime you need a listening ear, just let me know."

Sandy slapped her forehead. "Oh my, I almost forgot dinner! Let's go. It should be ready by now."

Gabriel and Sandy hurried towards the cooking food. The smell of grilled fish and vegetables filled the camp. Sandy glanced at the house but didn't see anybody. The giants were seated in a circle, waiting for her and Gabriel to join them. Zerachiel stood unwrapping each fish and served his brothers. When he served her, the wonderful aroma filled her nose.

"Well, Zerachiel, it's ready. You have done a very good job for your first time cooking."

He bowed. "Thank you, Princess."

Sandy, eager to taste the food, stretched her hand out. Michael coughed. "We must say grace first."

Sandy smiled, happy that they had remembered. Michael

stood up. "Everyone, please bow your heads. Heavenly Father, we come to you this evening in thanks, knowing that this meal we are about to consume speaks of you. We pray to you, thanking you for all you have done and given to us. The new friend and the old memories. Knowing that whatever problems we might be faced with, you are with us. Heavenly Father, we know that it could only have been you that has set in motion the current events that have taken place. And that it will only be you who will see us through it. We thank you for this meal of fellowship we are about to consume. We thank you for our new friend and sister, as well as the family and home you have given us. Amen."

As others ate, Zerachiel waited until Sandy had her first bite.

Sandy's eyes lit up. "This is amazing. I can't tell you when last I had fish that tasted this good." Zerachiel blushed.

Remiel, who sat close to Sandy, recounted how he'd taken his brothers round the house. "Sandy, they loved what we did with the house. I took them from room to room and showed them how we moved everything and what we did to make it all work." Remiel shoved a big piece of fish in his mouth. Sandy smiled. She glanced around, watching the giants devour their meals.

Raphael finished first. "Thank you for the dinner, Princess and Zerachiel." He bolted off to his lab. Sandy, confused, turned to Uriel. "Why is he in such a hurry? Does he have a date or something?"

"He is working on something he won't tell any of us about."

"Yeah," Raguel said. "Last time he got like this he made an elixir that made all of the bugs leave us alone. That was great!"

They all laughed. "We have learned not to interfere with his work," Remiel said with his mouth full of food.

Sandy clapped her hands, excited. "Ooh, I can't wait to see what he comes up with this time."

After dinner, everyone ambled to their resting places with their tummies filled. Sandy ate over one third of a fish. Quite a feat! While all made preparations for their night, Michael sat next to Sandy to thank her for all she had done.

"Once again you have proven to be a blessing to us. My brothers and I thank you, Princess." Sandy smiled and shrugged off the compliment as she noticed deeper thoughts behind Michaels eyes. "It's no big deal; my momma always said you don't stay with folks and not bring anything to the table."

Michael smiled and then responded. "Your mother was a wise woman. I can't help but remember our mother after a meal like this. This was the type of meal that my mother would have made for our feast of the warrior. It is our custom that when a young one becomes of age and accomplishes feats in battle, they are now a warrior, and are celebrated with a feast and traditional dance of my people."

Sandy smiled at the thought of the giants dancing. "That sounds cool, but that must sound like an earthquake." Michaels eyes lit up at the thought and memory. "Yes, young princess, it does make an earthquake. It is said that the dancers make the drum rhythm with their feet and hands with force to warn the world that a new warrior has been born. They make battle cries and chant the name of the warrior to allow their future enemies to know of their character before they ever meet."

Sandy was mesmerized by the thought. "That must have been a wonderful day when you had your feast of the warrior." Michaels eyes lost the spark they'd had a moment ago. "Unfortunately, Princess, my brothers and I never received the feast of the warrior. We were separated from our family before proper age was met."

Sandy felt the disappointment in Michael's voice. "Well

then, for as long as I am here there will be a feast every night, because you look like warriors to me."

Michael smiled in appreciation of Sandy's care. "Thank you, Princess, that means a lot." Michael stood and walked away, while Sandy looked on with a concerned gaze. Meanwhile Remiel had fallen asleep right near the fire. Zerachiel cleaned up and saved the leftovers, and Raphael was still in his lab. Raguel sat on one of the rocks near the waterfall. Uriel lay on a patch of grass near the river. Michael and Gabriel went indoors to discuss plans. Uriel, looking back over towards Sandy as he lay in the grass, called to her, "Hey there, Princess. You should go and ask Raguel to tell you a story."

Remiel woke up when he heard the word "story". "Yeah, a story!" he said. "Raguel is a great storyteller. He always has a story."

Sandy approached Raguel. Sandy looked up at the high place where Raguel sat. "Hey, there. Do you mind if I sit with you for a while?"

"Sure, little princess. I welcome you to the best view in the camp."

Raguel put his huge hand down and lifted Sandy up to where he was seated. He sat back in his white overalls and cleaned his teeth with a tree branch.

"So, what is it you want to know, girl?"

Sandy looked at him, confused. "What do you mean?"

"I mean they had to have told you I'm the one with all of the stories, that's why they call me the storyteller."

"Ok storyteller, tell me about how things were back before you all lost your family."

"So, you want me to go back, huh?"

"Well, let's see. Where do I start?" He looked up into the

stars. "Little princess, you just get yourself comfortable and close your eyes. I want you to envision this. It's almost like a dream to us, so it will make sense to have you see it as one."

Sandy lay back up against Raguel and closed her eyes as her mind wandered into the past.

"Long ago our people, the giants, ruled what was the western plains of Moria. Things were peaceful for our people back then as we had no enemies. The forest was alive then as it is now; it would open itself up to us as centuries would go by, showing us new sources of food and great discoveries. The great temple of Enoch being one of them, a temple our ancestors helped a great man of old to construct. It's lost now. You see, this forest will make way to something new, but lock away the old. Our people and the humans coexisted for a time and there was no war between our people. Our father had seen that man needed our help to grow and populate, so he offered it. We gave to them instruments for fixing things, and medicines. All sorts of understanding as to how to build and survive in this forest. Our people say at one point we might have given man too much. We gave to man the understanding of the forest. And when their numbers were many, they went in search of the new gifts that the forest had to offer. Hoping to find some unknown treasure, man found something. Like with all unknown, you have to take the good with the bad. Man found something very bad. Our father knew something was wrong. You see, the elders had a feel for the forest; almost like they could hear its heartbeat. The very moment man found that path, our father howled. Knowing something was wrong, the giant clans fortified themselves, bracing for attack. What came was more than we could understand at the time.

"It was man who stumbled across the evil ones of the forest. This is a dark evil that wanted nothing more than to control everything. Like a disease, it infected some of the trees first, causing dark pockets to form in the deep parts of the forest. We let our guard down because the elders figured that if the dark patches of forest were deep in the forest, there was no need to worry. But they were wrong, and things got even worse. The evil ones grew in number quickly.

"We had not seen their putrid faces until one night, they attacked a nearby clan with their army of trolls. The devastation they caused was great. That same night, the dark army attacked our uncle's village. We, the giants, could overpower this enemy at first. The humans were not strong enough nor ready for numbers they had to deal with. Village by village, humans were slaughtered who lived away from the kingdoms. Your grandfather came to our father and pleaded for help, along with the other rulers of the kingdoms. The giants would not stand by and watch as the humans were driven to extinction.

"But on the Eve of The Human Festival, the Nefarians had another plan. They attacked our camp without us being warned. It was an ambush. This was when our mother hid us in the wood. As the story goes and what the trees have told us, that night our father's forces were overwhelmed. We decimated the dark armies so much in their attack that when your grandfather's army, as well as whomever was left from the rest of the kingdoms, were attacked at his palace, they won the war and destroyed what was left of the evil."

Sandy opened her now teary eyes. "But there is still hope, Raguel. You all have got to have hope that the forest has protected your family. If you just keep looking, they have to be out there somewhere."

Raguel looked down at Sandy as he rubbed her hair with his finger. "Yes, young princess, it is possible. And hope we do have.

But where in this ever-changing forest, we just don't know."

They looked out into the deep and dark forest. In the house, Michael and Gabriel spoke in hushed voices.

"Did you find anything, Gabriel?" Michael asked.

"Yes, and it's not good. King Black's palace is no longer his. There is something very sinister and dark in the forest now. It reminds me of the time when the elders first felt the evil enter the forest."

Michael leaned back, rubbing his chin in thought. "Yes, this would explain the dark patches in the forest. I'm afraid the evil wasn't terminated completely. It has come back and now it wants what it couldn't have before. Everything!"

Gabriel sighed. "We need to tell the rest of our brothers. If there is going to be a war for the freedom of Moria, we must protect Sandy."

Michael nodded. "You are right. As soon as she is asleep, we will meet."

The two brothers waited for Sandy to sleep.

Sandy, lying against Raguel, fell asleep. Zerachiel tapped his brother and shushed him. He motioned for him to carry her near the fire. Raguel placed Sandy next to the fire, and turned around and faced his brothers who sat nearby. Michael motioned for him to join them. To ensure Sandy didn't hear their conversation, Remiel sat close to her while the other brothers sat with their backs facing her.

"Brothers, Gabriel has confirmed my fear."

"What?" Uriel asked.

"The evil of the forest has returned. We aren't sure how, or when, it came back. But we know it has taken over King Black's palace."

Remiel stared at Sandy, who slept peacefully. Zerachiel nodded. "I've seen dark patches spreading through the forest."

"Yes," Michael said, "it's in search of Sandy and trying to stop the communication that takes place in the forest. We must assume that those lights we see afar at night are those of an ongoing battle. No doubt a distraction so that the evil could take over the palace. King Black's armies must all be over in the fight."

Uriel raised his sword. "We should go and fight with them."

Raguel stood. "Yes, we should help restore peace."

Raphael sighed. Remiel jumped up. "We have to protect her. We have to protect the princess! Don't you see that the evil is looking for her? That's why the dark patches keep popping up. Not just to stop the communication, but to try and find out where she is."

Gabriel stood. "He is right, Michael. Eve said that she was going to speak with the Great Tree when she left, right?"

"Then we stay here for the time being," Michael said. "We pay close attention to the forest and what we feel. We wait to hear word from Eve. But if she doesn't show up in the next few days, we are going to move. It's only a matter of time before the evil finds us here."

That night the giants slept surrounding Sandy with their weapons in their hands.

Chapter 13

THE MIRROR

Back in the palace of Moria, the evil queen stood inside her chambers before her mirror.

"Mirror, mirror on the wall,

I stand before you, more powerful than before.

I seek to find that which I lost at night,

 The one thing left that I wish to smite.

Sandy Black, the princess, where might she be?

 Tell me this, and happy I'll be."

 The mirror shook vigorously before responding.

"My queen indeed,

 You have a need,

 To acquire the child in question.

But the power to see, relies in all three,

To find that which is missing."

 Realizing the need for the other witches, the queen dashed off to find them.

Underneath the palace, Chef Tasty hurried along the secret walkways with Lilly trying to catch up with him. "So many things to do," he whispered. "So little time. Hurry, my sweet."

They rushed down a narrow corridor into a dark room with small oil lamps. Chef Tasty lit one of the lamps.

"Lilly my sweet, go to the other side of the room and light the other lamp for me, won't you?"

After lighting the small lamps, the room shone brighter. Lilly scanned the room and found a table with weapons in the middle of the room. And on a stand nearby was a set of armor, very similar to that worn by the King's army. Chef Tasty removed his chef's hat and put on the breastplate.

Lilly scratched her head. "Why does it feel like I have been here before, Father?"

The chef laughed.

"Because, my daughter, this is where I hid you during the war of old. You were very young. I couldn't risk you being harmed if we lost the battle. So, I asked the King for a safe place to hide you and your mother. And since I was the commander of his personal guards, he gave me favor. That was so long ago, and now it seems history is repeating itself." Chef Tasty teared up as he reminisced about days gone past.

Chef Tasty sat near the table with his apron on along with the upper portion of his armor. "This is a bit too snug. I guess I was in much better shape before I was the chef; damn sweet tooth."

Still observing the room, Lilly glanced at her father. "I do remember being so very worried about you that day."

Chef smiled at Lilly. "I'm so glad that you are no longer confused by that evil queen. I have and always will love you, child."

The two embraced one another.

"Come, child," Chef Tasty said, "we need to move quickly; time is of the essence."

"Yes. We must help David. There is no telling what that sick little man is doing to him right now."

Chef Tasty placed a curved sword in Lilly's hands. "Do you

remember how I taught you to use this?"

Lilly grasped the sword in her hand and examined it for a moment. Then she twirled it like a sword woman. "I think I remember enough."

Chef Tasty smiled. "That's my girl. Let's move!"

They rushed out of the secret armory room. As they hurried down another narrow walkway, Chef turned to Lilly.

"You go on ahead to David - I have one more thing to take care of. Don't worry; some of my people should already be there waiting for you."

Lilly nodded and the two went their separate ways.

The queen searched for her mother and grandmother, as well as Lilly. She asked the maids working for Lilly if they had seen her. One of them told her she last saw her going into the kitchen with Chef Tasty.

The queen stormed around the palace, cursing Lilly under her breath. She found her mother and grandmother sitting on a bench in the garden. She rushed to them, and the two ugly witches jumped to their feet.

"What is it, child?" The older witch asked.

The queen bowed her head. "It is time for us to become one."

Her mother smiled. "Yes, it is time for us three to become one in power and might. It is high time we found that child that vexes you so, and blot her name from all the land for what her family has done to ours."

The two older witches cackled to themselves as the queen walked close behind them on their way to her chambers.

Down the secret walkway, Chef stopped in front of the almost empty dragon stables. Glancing around for any unwanted guests, Chef Tasty hurried over to Ballah, David's dragon. Chef

Tasty opened the door to the lair and Ballah growled.

"It's time, Ballah." He unlocked the chains that bound the dragon. Chef Tasty pulled a large piece of meat out of a bag he was carrying. "Time to eat!" He threw the meat with both hands into the air. Ballah flew out of the dark cavern, gobbled up the meat and landed on his legs. Spreading his wings, Ballah bowed.

"Thank you, Chef. I must go now before things get any worse for my master David. You should leave too; I can hear another patrol coming this way."

Chef nodded as Ballah flew into the air and dashed down back towards the ground. He blasted the ground with flames from his nostrils. He flew into the hole created and disappeared.

Back in the queen's chambers, the three witches huddled in front of the mirror.

The queen chanted,

"Mirror, mirror on the wall,

We three stand before you now,

That our power may flow this night,

So we may see the end with sight,

Tell me now the things I wish."

The mirror glowed hot as the two older witches chanted a strange song in low tones. A flowing waterfall and large house appeared on the mirror. Sandy walked out of the house with Remiel.

The queen's grandmother smiled. "Hmm. Protecting the princess is an old adversary."

The queen's mother cackled. "Yes, yes Mother. She was wise to hide with the giants."

"This is why our powers were needed to find her."

The queen said. "I would never have envisioned the giants being friendly to anyone. I will crush them with her."

The group laughed and planned Sandy's destruction.

Outside the dungeon, Lilly met two of Chef Tasty's male cooks. "I am here to help."

The two of them smiled at one another and spoke in unison. "Chef Tasty said you would come to help. We sure could use you right now." They pointed at the dungeon's door. Lilly pressed her head against the glass on the door. Inside, she could see Dr. Cain arranging his tools and whistling to himself.

"We need to get his attention, but if you hadn't noticed we are both men. I'm sure it would be much easier to get the attention of a thousand-year-old man, locked up in prison for the past three hundred years, with your good looks over our own. We are rather nice to look at, but this situation may call for someone with your toolset."

They smiled at Lilly as she blushed.

"Well, I do think I can make him pay attention to something other than David for a moment or two. So what is the plan after I get his attention? What should I be waiting for?" Lilly wondered as she put her weapons down. Just as she asked the question, Chef Tasty hurried towards them.

"Don't worry your pretty little head, my sweet. I have a little pick-me-up to give to David. The twins will deal with the doctor, and a ride has already been arranged for David after we are done."

Lilly glanced at her father after assessing the situation. "Shall we?"

In the dungeon David lay battered on the floor, almost dead. Doctor Cain whistled to himself as he scanned through his tools for what to use next. A tool fell from his hand when someone knocked the door. Cursing under his breath about being disturbed, he opened the door and gaped at the pretty lady before him.

Lilly's hair cascaded down her shoulders. She flipped her hair and batted her eyelashes. "Excuse me, Doctor Cain," she said in a soft voice. She walked in and turned around while he followed her, so that his back faced the door. "The queen doesn't know I am here. But I couldn't resist. I am a fan of your work and I also think you're such a handsome man. When I heard that you were available to talk to, I had to come see you for myself."

For a moment, he was confused as he was stuck between having fun torturing David or having fun with the beautiful lady before him, and drool fell from his mouth. As he pondered on what to do, the twins and Chef Tasty tiptoed into the room. Wasting no time, Lilly put her arms around him and the twins hit him thrice on the head with hardened bread clubs. As the doctor fell to the ground, unconscious, Lilly looked at the three in amazement. "Bread sticks?"

They shrugged. "What? It would be difficult to run around the palace with real swords drawn the entire day, don't you think?"

Chef Tasty lifted David onto his lap and opened a bottle with some sort of tonic.

"Here, my friend. This will get you back to your normal self."

The chef emptied the tonic down David's throat. David shook as the tonic flowed into his body. The twins locked Doctor Cain in one of the empty cells. David, now awake, stood on his feet as if nothing had ever happened to him.

"Thank you, Chef Tasty. What has transpired so far? I see your beautiful daughter has come to her senses."

Lilly clasped her hands, apologizing to David. "David, I am very sorry for not helping you before."

"Oh, don't worry, Lilly. Your father and I both had faith that your heart would lead you back to the righteous path."

The twins guarding the door whistled. "Chef, we must hurry - something is happening in the palace. We must leave at once."

Chef Tasty turned to David. "I have unlocked Ballah. He knows what to do."

David flexed his arms. "Good. I must get to the King and tell him all that has happened here. You get out of here and prepare what troops you may have. I shall return as fast as I can to help."

The chef ushered the twins and Lilly out of the dungeon through another secret walkway. The queen's soldiers ran into the dungeon and pointed their swords at David. He remained calm as drums rolled in a rhythm signifying David's escape. Guards rushed to his position and gates and doors started closing to stop him leaving. The queen arrived, walking through doorways and gates as they closed behind her to keep the area secure through all of the commotion. She walked in and was astonished to see David in such good condition.

As the chef, the twins, and Lilly worked their way down the secret walkway out of the dungeon, they could hear the commotion on the other side of the walls. The queen's soldiers ran into the dungeon and pointed their swords at David. The queen addressed the situation with hubris.

"Well, I thought you would be dead by now, but I can see you have been helped. No worries; I can deal with you myself."

She waved her hands, ready to cast a spell. The earth vibrated and the queen staggered, looking around for something to hold onto. With sand and stones falling from the ceiling, David smiled. "You know, evil queen, my brother will not be happy when he returns."

The queen stood, confused. "Your brother? You don't have any brother. I guess you aren't as well as you look."

A loud roar rang through the dungeon and the floor shook much more violently than before. Flames burst out from the floor and the queen and soldiers cried out as they ran to take cover. David ran to the far side of the cell as the walls around him fell, exposing the outside. David jumped out and the queen ran over to the edge, hoping to see his dead body on the rocks below. She screamed when she saw David on Ballah. David yelled at the queen. "Yes, you do know my brother, the one whose anger will be unquenchable when he returns for your head. You know him as King Black."

The dragon spat a flame over what was left of the dungeon, causing the soldiers and the queen to flee. Looking back, they saw David and Ballah high in the sky. The queen stamped her foot in disgust and stormed back into her chambers.

"What is wrong, my child?" the queen's mother asked as she walked over to her daughter.

"That David has escaped!" the queen said. "All this time he has been the King's brother and I never knew it."

The queen's grandmother called her over to the mirror. "Come hither, my sweet." The three witches stood in front of the mirror where an image of Sandy was displayed. "My dear, there is no need to fret over that which is lost. For now, our gaze should fall upon the prize that will bring down the House of the Black Rose forever."

"You are right, Grandmother. I should not worry about David, no matter who he has surfaced to be. If to his brother he goes, he does so at his peril. They will not survive the trolls."

The queen's grandmother and mother huddled close to the queen. "Yes my, sweet," her mother said. "Let us make haste to destroy this little one."

The three witches cackled as they stared at Sandy's image in the mirror.

Chapter 14
ESCAPE

Deep in the forest of Moria, Eve hurried to the edge of the kingdom to meet the Great Tree. This part of the forest was much older than the rest of Moria. It was full of elder trees that had been around since the beginning of time. Tired of the dealings with man and beast, the trees no longer spoke as they put themselves into a state of eternal sleep.

Birds sang and monkeys jumped from tree to tree, following Eve as she made her way down the path to her destination. The climate was perfect; not too warm or cold. A mist fell from the sky, and the plants and animals drank as it fell over them. There were no rivers, lakes or streams, just the mist that fell daily to give this patch of forest what it needed. Eve, stressed from her long and frightening journey, was filled with a sense of joy and a peace that she couldn't understand.

***

Inside the palace of King Black, everything had come to a halt. The queen's head of security, Minotaur, searched for those who had helped David escape. The queen, her mother and grandmother were in the queen's chambers, holding hands and chanting near the mirror. Sandy's image was on the mirror.

"We three unite,

We come together to set things right.

To evoke our power and show our might,

We call out of the shadows a beast tonight.

A terrible beast full of fury and pain,

To destroy the girl that lives with them,

Erase her path, blot out her name,

Give way to us three to rise again."

A gust of wind blew through the room, capturing their words and carrying them into the deep, dark forest. It was day but as the wind blew, darkness engulfed the land of Moria.

At the giants' camp, Zerachiel hopped down from a tree. Troubled, he turned to the rest of his brothers who were sitting near the fire with Sandy.

"Brothers," he said. "Something is not right. I looked out towards the palace of King Black, and I see darkness coming our way."

As the giants listened to Zerachiel, a gust of wind blew heavily through the forest and into the camp. The echo of the witches' chant rang in the wind. All the giants jumped onto their feet. Horrified, Raguel turned to Michael. "Isn't that the language of the evil ones?"

Remiel placed his arm around Sandy, who was unsure of what was happening. Uriel's flaming sword glowed red hot as the darkness engulfed the camp. Michael glanced around and could only see his brothers illuminated by the small fire. "Yes, Raguel," Michael said. "It's the language of those that our father fought."

Sandy tugged Remiel's hand. "Remiel!" Sandy asked, scared. "What is going on? Why is it so dark, and who's talking?"

"It's the evil ones," Remiel said, his eyes watching out for danger. "They have cast some sort of spell. Don't worry, Sandy. I won't let anything happen to you."

The brothers stood in a circle with Sandy and Remiel in the middle. As they stood, ready, with their weapons in their hands, they heard trees crack, snap and crash on the ground in the distance. The sound rushed closer, and the brothers turned to the direction of the sound. Raphael roared and bolted in the direction of the sound with his brothers slowly following him. Michael turned to Remiel. "Stay close to the fire with the princess, Remiel."

He nodded, focusing on the surroundings, with Sandy close to him. A scream of pain rang in the air. Raphael stopped and looked up at a very large, dark entity. As tall as Gabriel and with the body of a gorilla and the head of a bull, the towering beast screamed as if tormented. Chains hung from his neck, arms and legs. Uriel glowered at the beast. "Nisrock!" Uriel screamed.

The beast thrashed about with his chains. "Brothers, Uriel is right," Michael said. "This is the beast of fable. The Nisrock. Said to be a demonic beast made by the evil ones a millennium ago. Because of its unnatural conception and the torment suffered from the evil ones, he was driven mad. Full of pain and anger, controlled by those who made him."

Uriel lifted his flaming sword into the air. "He was sent here for a reason. Shall we entertain?"

The brothers positioned themselves around the huge beast. Raphael held up a shield as the Nisrock attacked him with his chains. Zerachiel jumped on the giant trees, looking for a vantage point from which to use his great bow. Raguel and Uriel both ran in to distract the beast. Approaching the beast with high speed, Uriel twirled his flaming sword and Raguel raised his enormous hammer. The Nisrock knocked Raphael to the ground with his chains. Raphael stayed covered with his shield as Uriel jumped past the beast and slashed its arm. The beast didn't react as his arm fell to the ground. Raguel slammed his giant hammer on the beast's leg. Not reacting to the pain, the Nisrock used its available arm to entangle both brothers in his chains. Screaming, the beast picked up his arm and put it back in place. Its deformed leg reverted back to normal. Raguel and Uriel looked on in amazement as they worked their way out of the chains.

"Raguel, did you see that?" Uriel laughed. "This thing heals itself!"

Raguel pried himself loose from the chains. "Unbelievable!"

Zerachiel yelled down to his brothers from a high tree, "The Nisrock doesn't feel pain and has healing properties. The only way to kill him is to separate his head from his body, and bind him with those chains."

Michael rolled his eyes. "Zerachiel, you should have let us know that before we attacked it."

Zerachiel shot an arrow into the eye of the beast, causing it to be distracted and giving his brothers time to escape the chains. "Hey, I figured Uriel knew since he was the one who figured out what this thing was to begin with."

Remiel and Sandy stood back, watching the brothers fight the dark beast. Raphael, Raguel, and Uriel surrounded the Nisrock. Gabriel yelled out to them. "Brothers, back away from him. I'll deal with this. Be ready when I tell you."

Gabriel charged at the beast. The two large figures crashed into one another like two trains. Gabriel wrestled with the beast, kicking its legs out from under him and holding it to the ground. "Now! Zerachiel, his hands."

Two arrows flew out of the sky and pinned the hands of the giant beast to the forest ground.

"Move now Gabriel! Move!" Michael screamed as he

jumped high in the sky with his spear pointing downwards. Gabriel turned to see his brother diving down towards the chest of the beast. He rolled off it as Michael plunged his spear through the Nisrock, making it look like a frog in science class. The brothers stood around as the beast screamed. Uriel raised his sword and cut off the beast's head. Raguel and Gabriel bound its body with the chains, while Remiel joined his brothers next to the Nisrock with Sandy on his shoulder.

Sandy covered her nose in disgust. "It sure stinks and it's extra ugly too."

"Princess," Michael said, "there will be things that will smell much worse and look uglier in the future. This beast was sent to kill you. And this means that the evil queen has gained the power of her ancestors, and can now call upon the darkness to do her bidding. I am glad you handled this situation with courage; you will need more of it before all is finished."

Gabriel lifted the Nisrock's body up onto his shoulder and carried it to the river with its body still twitching. Uriel had the head on the end of his sword. He glowered at it as he walked behind Gabriel. "You really thought you were going to come into this camp and destroy us? Not only do you smell bad and are ugly, but you are really stupid too."

Gabriel threw the body into the rushing water of the river and the gloom and darkness that had surrounded them vanished. Raguel tapped Uriel. "Hey, bro. You should probably stop before he answers you."

Uriel smiled at Raguel and then glowered at the Nisrock's face with its tongue hanging from its mouth. "That would be entertaining." He threw the head into the river and they watched it dissolve.

Sandy scratched her head. "What's up with that? If water

does that to it, how come you guys didn't just push him into the water?"

Remiel looked down at his little friend. "Sandy, evil returns to the darkness of the shadows or the deep when it has no more power in it. We cut it off from the one controlling it, so its power source is no more. Now it returns to the deep, dark place from which it came."

Sandy looked around. "This is just great. I can't wait for what might come next," she stated in an uneasy tone of voice.

Michael turned to his brothers. "We must prepare to defend ourselves. We are no longer onlookers in this battle. Warriors we are; we cannot lose."

During the disposal of the Nisrock, Raphael had run over to his workstation to get some of his medicine. He now arrived back in the middle of camp where his brothers discussed what preparation must be done. Raphael walked around his brothers and handed each of them a blue pill. Zerachiel looked down at the palm of his hand and back at Raphael. "Brother, what does this one do?"

Raphael smiled. "Just trust me, Zerachiel. It's something new."

The brothers glanced at one another and then each one swallowed the pills. Instantly, cuts, injuries and stress vanished. The last effect of the pill was the most noticeable. As they sat around the fire feeling relaxed and fresh, small, needle-like barbs fell from their skin. Not understanding what had happened Gabriel, who had more of the barbs, asked Raphael what was happening. Raphael raised his glasses. "Brother Gabriel, I went to my books of old and found out that the Nisrock, when faced with death releases these barbs. You can't and won't feel them, but after three days the toxins in them will kill you. I made this pill to fight multiple symptoms and clear us of the enemy's toxic barbs." He smiled at Sandy, who hadn't got a pill. "Don't worry, Princess. I haven't forgotten you." Out of his pocket, he pulled a small bottle of blue powder. "Princess, get some water to drink."

Remiel helped Sandy get a cup of water and Raphael poured the powder into it. Sandy drank the water and barbs fell out of her skin. Everyone thanked Raphael, praising him for his intelligence. Michael stood. "Brothers, I fear much more darkness will befall us. We must hold firm. For our sake, and for that of our friend, Princess Sandy Black."

To avoid being seen, David flew high above the forest. He looked down and saw the darkness that had engulfed the land of Moria. Worried about Sandy's whereabouts, he shut his eyes for a moment and prayed for her safety. While praying, he heard the terrible scream of the Nisrock before the giants defeated him. He prayed for the King's safety too. Only the King could put an end to the evil ravaging the land. "Hold on, Sandy. Hold on a little bit longer. Brother, I am on my way."

Back in the palace in the queen's chambers, the three witches waited to hear if the beast had been successful. All three stood before the mirror as the queen asked the outcome of the evil they'd sent.

"Mirror, mirror on the wall,

Tell us now and don't take long.

The beast we sent from dark to light,

Show us now how he has won the fight."

The mirror shook and shone with different colors before it showed a replay of the Nisrock being killed and thrown into the river. The queen's eager anticipation of victory turned to utter disgust and rage. "Why won't she just die?" She banged a table with her fist and flung some jewelry through a window. She turned to her mother and grandmother. "We will have to send something viler than before. Those giants are protecting her; they shall die as well. Tonight, while they sleep, they'll have a real nightmare." The queen cackled. Her mother and grandmother looked at one another and then to the queen, who was staring into the mirror with the image of a safe Sandy with the giants.

***

The daylight faded into night in the forest of Moria. The tension was high in the giants' camp as the giants anticipated another attack. The brothers took strategic positions to see in all directions and to keep the princess as safe as possible. Michael sat near the fire with his spear in hand and armor on. Zerachiel was in his normal position in the trees, and Raphael studied the toxins inside the barbs from the Nisrock in his lab. Raguel and Uriel kept watch at either side of the camp. Remiel and Sandy sat inside the house, while Gabriel sat outside with Michael. Sandy fell asleep near Remiel, who had his arm around her. Soon, Remiel fell asleep, and the rest of the brothers did too.

The wind blew and the faint sound of some foul tongue floated like a whisper in the wind. The camp lay silent as all the giants and Sandy were deep in sleep. Small voices and laughing filled the camp. Out from the river came forth tiny humanoid creatures. They were a foot tall and they had greenish-black skin with pot bellies and very long arms. Some flew on the backs of birds and landed on the top of the house. Inside the house, Sandy woke up to the sound of what seemed like raindrops. She listened for a moment and then drifted off to sleep. Zerachiel opened his eyes slowly. On seeing the creatures, he gasped. *"Oglo!"*

The Oglos were a small race of evil fairy people who, for the right price, would do anything. They lived in the darkest recesses of the forest and hadn't been seen in years. Known for kidnapping children and elderly people, their strength was in their numbers and appetite for wickedness. They had torn entire villages apart in a frenzy.

Restless, Sandy couldn't go back to sleep. It was raining but it didn't smell like rain. Neither did she hear the wind or rustling leaves. Sandy tapped Remiel. "Sandy, what's wrong? Is everything ok?"

Sandy shushed him as she listened to the tiny footsteps on top of the roof. She also heard tiny tapping on the front door and tiny voices. At this point, the Oglo had surrounded the camp. They lit small torches from the fire in the camp. Remiel and Sandy jumped to their feet, ready for whatever may come.

Zerachiel didn't want to attack them blindly, so he tried hard to remember the Oglos' weakness. He remembered a bedtime story his mother used to tell them. The Oglos were allergic to iron. The iron tip of an arrow would be more than enough to damage an Oglo. While Zerachiel reached for his arrows in the tree, the Oglo on the ground prepared to enter the house.

Not hearing their voices anymore, Sandy and Remiel stood prepared. The Oglos crashed through the window behind Sandy. Once inside, they let out a war cry and charged at Sandy and Remiel. The Oglos outside returned the loud cry, and charged at the sleeping giants. Zerachiel, noticing things had gotten worse, grabbed his arrows and shot through the fire in the pit into two of the Oglos that had been standing in line. The Oglos exploded, waking the giants up. The brothers jumped to their feet, gripping their weapons. Raguel smashed the small enemies with his huge hammer. Uriel cut through the masses of little creatures with his red-hot sword. Michael swung his spear and knocked about fifty of them to the ground. Gabriel crushed them with his giant feet.

Michael turned to look for Raphael, who was smashing the Oglo with his hands like bugs.

As Michael turned back towards the house, he remembered Sandy and Remiel. He yelled to his brothers. "To the house! This is a diversion; they are trying to get to Sandy."

Sandy screamed as the brothers hurried to the house. "Let me go, you nasty little things!" She fought from on top of a table that Remiel had put her on. The sea of Oglo overwhelmed Remiel as he kicked the Oglos away. They hung on his arms and legs and tried to climb his head. Two of the creatures stood on either side of Sandy. Sandy kicked one of them off the table and the other grabbed her as she turned to run. Sandy kept fighting but the Oglo pulled her away from Remiel, who was covered by the other Oglos. "Remiel!" Sandy screamed as she could not overpower the tiny Oglo. The Oglo pulled Sandy to the edge of the table and some other Oglos grabbed her, set to take her into the forest. The door burst open and Michael threw his iron spear through the five Oglo that held onto Sandy, pinning them to the wall. Remiel and Uriel cut through the masses of Oglos in the house. The ones Uriel cut through exploded because of the hot iron sword. Raphael cut off the Oglos' exit at the back of the house, smashing those that came that way. Zerachiel picked off the remaining Oglos outside and shot some of them into the sky as the birds picked them up to fly them away.

Michael, Uriel, and Raguel finished off those that were left inside of the house. Remiel grabbed Sandy and put her on his shoulder. Raphael came around to the front door to see if his help was needed. When all was clear, the brothers checked outside for whatever might be left. Gabriel, who had been looking for the chief of the Oglo, found him and held him prisoner in his hand while he walked over to Michael. "Brother, this is their chief - I found him trying to escape on the back of a bird. Zerachiel shot him down, and I caught him."

"Good. Let's have a talk with the Oglo chief."

The brothers walked over to the campfire and Gabriel opened his hand enough for Michael to see the Oglo chief. Michael put the head of his spear into the fire to get hot. The brothers all stood around, awaiting the information they would get out of the small beast.

"You vile little creature," Michael said. "Why are you here?"

The Oglo spat obscenities in his native fairy tongue. Michael raised his red-hot spearhead for the Oglo to see. "I know you can speak our tongue. You are a part of this forest like everything else. Speak to me now."

The Oglo's eyes widened as his face was illuminated by the glow from the hot iron spearhead. "I will answer you, giant," he said panting. "Those of the clan Nefaria. They called upon my people and made us an offer of meat. Out of the dark, we came to take her, the tender one."

The chief Oglo's gaze set upon Sandy as she stood atop Remiel's shoulder. Sandy eyed the little creature. Michael flicked the Oglo with his finger. "So, the queen sent you to kill us and steal the princess."

The Oglo looked back at Michael. "She sent us to retrieve the tender one and to tear her apart and eat her. We were only required to save her heart for the queen."

Sandy glared at the little creature, disgusted.

"Who does that? Send some little nasty folks to come cut me up and eat me? Then bring my heart back to her for what, so she can have it for dinner? I don't know how to deal with this crazy place. Where I come from, you deal with folks you have a problem with in person." Sandy shook her head in disbelief.

Michael looked back at the Oglo after Sandy's rant. "You see, you didn't succeed and now you have made the princess mad."

Michael turned to Zerachiel. "Zerachiel, let us send him to the palace with a message."

Michael looked back at the Oglo chief. "Tell the queen that the giants are protecting Sandy Black, the Princess of Moria. And that she would be wise to stay away and not waste anymore of her minions."

After Michael's statement, Gabriel grabbed an arrow that Zerachiel was holding and bound the Oglo to it. He then handed the arrow with the Oglo firmly attached to Zerachiel. Zerachiel placed the arrow in his bow and whispered some words to the Oglo. "Please keep your hands and legs inside the binding. Enjoy your flight." He then released his mighty bow, sending the Oglo chief flying through the night sky to the palace. "She should receive that message when she awakes," Zerachiel said as he put his bow back down.

"Let us rest now, as we shouldn't get another attack until much later. But we should be ready to leave in the morning, in search of a place to hide until your father can be found."

Sandy nodded. This time, they all went inside the house and slept near each other. The night had brought them two enemies to defend the princess from. What more would be in store for them as they tried to change locations?

***

As the darkness rested over Kingdom of the White Rose in the Isles of Far Off, King Black and King Ananias stood ready for another attack. The countless hordes of trolls squawked and screamed to one another as they lay in wait in the forest for an opportunity to feed upon the flesh of man. King Black's army had suppressed the trolls' plans of destruction for now, but with every passing day they grew weaker from the constant circle of fire protecting them from the trolls. During the daylight they had enough time to refortify small areas, but not enough time to rebuild the defenses of the palace. The trolls were unable to stand in the light, for it destroyed darkness. So, in that light, King Black, King Ananias, and Prince Shamma rested, trying to find a way out of this war. King Black sat back to rest many times, and could only see the face of his dear daughter wondering what was going on back in his kingdom. What she must be thinking, or feeling? He tried to reserve the thoughts of Sandy for the end of the battle. He knew all too well the torment that such thoughts brought upon a man. The kings had no choice as to what they could control, so stood fast in the hope of an end to the war, but inside they knew something was off.

It was night again and the voices of the trolls filled the night. The ring of fire illuminated the nearby forest as arrows filled the sky, flying back and forth from both sides. Catapults hurled stones, rocks, and boulders at the fires. As they passed the wall of fire they ignited. The trolls figured they could consume the kingdom with fire if they couldn't get in. So, they continued their assault, hurling incendiary devices towards the flames to explode and cause destruction. The soldiers watching inside the city tried hard to put out the fires and to help the wounded. How much longer could they hold out?

Chapter 15

SICKNESS

It was morning in the land of Moria. Sunlight shone through the clouds and into the windows of the queen's chamber. The queen was in deep meditation with her mother and grandmother when a loud scream pierced the kingdom. A commotion stirred the guards at the palace walls. A knock on the queen's door made her jump out of the trance. "Come in," she screamed. The Minotaur stepped into her room. "My queen, something fell from the sky and is asking for you. He said he has a message for you."

The queen smiled, anticipating news of Sandy's death. "I shall be there in a moment."

The Minotaur turned to leave but she stopped him. "Have you found the enemies of your queen yet; most of all the chef and Lilly?"

"Not yet, but they will be found and destroyed."

The queen walked over to the Minotaur, tracing his arms with her finger. "See that it is done with haste."

He bowed. "Very well; it shall be done." He walked out.

The queen turned to her mother and grandmother. "Shall we go out to see what message awaits us?" she said, grinning from ear to ear. The three witches made their way out to hear the news. As they approached the outside of the palace doors, a loud screaming from outside of the walls rang through the air. Seeing the Oglo's condition, the queen's excitement turned to despair. The large arrow he was fastened to stood upright as its iron tip held it firm in the ground. The arrow itself was twenty-five feet long. The Oglo was battered and poisoned from the proximity of the iron, and he saw the queen. As she came close, the Oglo spoke in the tongue of man.

"Queen, you must stop your search for the tender one." He coughed. "You must not look for this Sandy Black any longer. You have incurred the wrath of the giants that protect her."

Some servants that heard what was said were gripped with fear, for they knew the giants were not to be trifled with.

Enraged, the queen lashed out at the Oglo. "What do you mean seek her no more? I am all powerful. Those giants are but the last of an enemy from long ago. They have no power over me. Nor the numbers to make me fear them. I will show them power they have never seen before. And before I am done with them all, they will know unimaginable pain." She pressed her nose against the Oglo chief. "You have failed me, Oglo. I will deal with your people for your disgrace, and you will pay with your life."

The Oglo looked the queen straight in the eye. "You paid us to do a job. We were destroyed in battle by the most powerful creature in all of the lands, and your temper is kindled against my people?"

Behind the queen, her grandmother grabbed a sword from one of the soldiers and heated it with her hands until it became red-hot. The Oglo was still speaking to the queen. "I tell you now, evil queen. You will not last in this place. The armies of the King will put you out. And in the end, your kind will be no more as was meant to be." Before the queen could respond, her grandmother thrust the red-hot iron sword through the Oglo. "Not before your people are gone first."

The Oglo screamed in pain as he exploded. The queen's mother approached her.

"We have allowed this to go on for long enough. Let us now come together and show you how to hunt a rabbit."

Back in the queen's chambers, and with the queen calmer than she was before, the three witches held hands and chanted in front of the mirror. The mirror glowed a dark green and the chanting stopped. The queen walked over to look into the mirror, as she had never seen this color before in the mirror. The queen's grandmother nudged her daughter to speak to the queen. The queen's mother nodded, and walked over to the queen to speak with her.

"My child, it takes more than brute strength or a violent foe to bring down your enemies. You must be smarter in devising your plans. The lack of understanding has led us to this moment. Close your eyes."

The queen closed her eyes.

"Now imagine yourself as the child. What are you afraid of? What do you like?"

As the queen imagined herself to be Sandy, an image of Sandy glowed bright on the mirror. Sandy was smiling and laughing with the giants. Another image showed her cooking for the giants and cleaning the house. The queen's grandmother's eyes lit up with a sinister plan as she watched the images on the mirror.

"Have you thought of what you like?" the queen's mother asked.

"Stop, stop, there will be no need for this exercise of vision," said the queen's grandmother. "We have all that we need here." She pointed at the images on the mirror. The queen opened her eyes and focused on the images. The queen's mother smiled as she looked at Sandy's images as well.

"You see my child," the grandmother said, "the weakness of the young one is her heart of flesh. Play it as you would a harp, and at the right time crush it."

The queen's eyes darkened as she shared in the wicked smile of her mother and grandmother. Her imagination ran wild with thoughts of how to end Sandy's life. She walked to the far side of her chambers.

"I will not kill her in the way I had dreamed of before. No; death is too good for this young one. I will use that kind heart of hers to seal her fate."

She turned to the witches. "I will need your help, Mother and Grandmother. What I need to do will take considerable effort from all of us."

Both the mother and grandmother smiled with their rotten mouths wide. The grandmother comforted the queen. "My deer, our powers may not be at full strength until the darkness covers the face of all the lands, but if we must change an animal to a man, we shall make it so."

The three witches burst out into laughter. As they laughed, a dark snake slithered out of the sleeves of the queen, up her arm and around her wrist. The daylight that had shown through the window was now obstructed by dark, menacing clouds.

***

Eve moved further into the garden towards the Great Tree. The deeper she went, the greener and taller the trees of the inner garden were. The colors were more vivid than anything outside this Eden. For Moria, this was the genesis, the beginning of the forest. At one time, man and beast lived comfortably together as all of Moria was as the garden. But as man became more destructive and ventured farther away from this center of life, the Great Tree receded the borders of the garden. The garden protected itself and its knowledge by hiding away in the forest. Only the trees knew the way to its borders. And thus far it had been centuries since the Great Tree had had a visitor. Searching for answers, Eve continued forward, forgetting about the past pain and defeat, only looking forward to what she must finish that day. Along the path, a great wall of vines and trees stood as a barrier to her advancement. Intertwined and dense, it was impossible to pass. Eve stood before the massive structure, which was stretching out as far as she could see and much taller than she was. Eve stepped forward to get a closer look and tried to figure out what she could do. As she stepped forward, the sound of dozens of voices floated in the air.

"It is her. She is you, the tree, that seeks to speak with the great one. He has spoken of your arrival."

Eve stepped back to see where the voices were coming from. As she stepped away, the plants untangled themselves and separated into a walkway. Eve could identify the individual plants that had spoken, some of which had never been seen in the forest of Moria. As the wall parted, a glow so bright passed through the newly-made corridor out to Eve. Eve, not knowing what to say to the trees that bowed before her, bowed in respect and gingerly made her way down the path.

As Eve moved her way towards the light, the pathway behind her closed as she moved forward. The light intensified as she came to the end of the passageway. Stepping out into an opening, before her was paradise. Various animals ate and drank from a small lake. The sun shone bright overhead. Birds whistled and sung while they flew past Eve. And in the distance, just beyond the lake, was the Great Tree of Moria—a tall tree in the shape of a baobab tree. It stood majestic and powerful. She sighed in relief. *I have made it*! Through all the adversity she had to overcome, she was finally in the presence of the Great Tree. As she moved forward, the plants behind her became a wall once more. Eve turned and noticed she was now closed in.

"Straight and narrow is the path, and very few find it," a voice from the wall said. "You have found what you seek. Press on." Eve took a deep breath and made her way towards the Great Tree.

***

Sandy woke up to a busy camp early in the morning. All the giants were busy gathering and packing things they would need for the trip. Remiel, noticing Sandy was awake, came over to speak with her.

"Sandy, you are awake. It's good you got your rest. Michael said we are going to head north towards the Forbidden Mountains. You'll need to be ready for anything. But don't worry — you're going to be with me the whole way. Nothing is going to happen to you."

Sandy smiled and glanced around.

"You are right, Remiel. After last night's attacks, who knows? Godzilla could show up and I'm sure everything would be just fine."

Remiel smiled and nodded even though he had no idea who Godzilla was. Sandy glanced around for anything she might need to bring. "Well, it looks like I'm all packed up and ready to go."

Raphael, who was passing by, looked down and around Sandy for her bags.

"Princess, I don't see your things, maybe Raguel took them. He always hides mine."

Sandy smiled. "OK, Raphael. I'll go and ask him."

Raphael nodded and then hurried to his lab to finish packing. Michael, in full armor, walked to the front of the house.

"Brothers, remember we will be back; this is our home. Just take with you enough for a three-day journey. We will add to our supplies along the way."

The brothers dressed up in full armor, ready to go.

They all sat by the fire pit. Zerachiel distributed breakfast that he had made. Sandy smiled at him, surprised by his first cooking venture.

"This smells wonderful, Zerachiel. What is it?"

As he passed out the last of the bowls, he looked at Sandy. "It is a ritual of old from our people that upon an occasion that could be full of peril, we should eat this to give us strength and focus for the journey. In the bowl is a red wine soup, symbolizing the blood that was shed for us. And along with it, we eat a piece of manna bread. This will give us strength and might as we embark on this path." Sandy bowed her head to pray. But as she was about opening her mouth, Gabriel prayed. "Heavenly Father, Lord above, we come to You united in the fight at hand. We have counted the cost of our actions hereafter. We come to You in hope that You will see us through this time of trial. We thank You for the addition to our family in Sandy Black, and we ask that if we, as her guardians and friends, fall in protecting her from the evil at hand, You might with Your awesome power keep her in Your secret place."

Sandy burst into tears and Remiel put his arm around her. "Lord, we present ourselves to You this day as soldiers in Your army. Give us the strength to finish this battle the way Your will has written it. We will be strong, and of good courage, knowing that if we do this You will be with us."

And all of them said 'amen'. Sandy, wiping away the tears from her face, glanced around at her new family of guardians. "I love you guys."

Michael stood and knelt before Sandy, opening his arms wide. "Young princess, we love you too."

Sandy ran into his arms and he hugged her. Remiel, followed by the rest of his brothers, all shared in a group hug that swallowed Sandy up. Uriel looked over his shoulder. "Raphael, get back man. You are drooling on me."

Raguel burst into laughter. Raphael backed away, wiping his mouth.

"I'm sorry, Uriel. I was so comfortable, sorry."

The group laughed and then finished up the meal before leaving for the forbidden mountains - an inhospitable land for most, but a location even more isolated than where they currently lived.

The clink of the giants' armor and supplies echoed as they trekked forward in the dreary afternoon. Sandy sat atop Remiel's shoulder as the giants' long strides would be too fast a pace for her to keep up with. The sights and sounds of the forest had changed since the brothers had last ventured this far. Even though it was daytime, there were large dark patches with no life in parts of the forest they passed. Zerachiel, with his bow over his shoulder, leaped from tree to tree. His tall, thin, shadow-like figure scouted ahead of the group, while Gabriel walked behind. Sandy was safe in the middle of the group sitting on top of Remiel. A few hours into their journey, the group stopped for a moment to rest. Remiel put Sandy down so she could stretch. Michael spoke with Zerachiel about the journey. Uriel and Raguel stood on guard. Raphael glanced around for anything that might be useful, and Gabriel came in last with news for Michael. He walked over to Michael and Zerachiel as they spoke.

"There is a family behind in trouble. They were headed in our direction, but it seems they have been attacked by one of the dark trees."

Michael felt uneasy. *I don't like how it feels, but I know that in these troubled times, nothing is going to make sense. Well, I would rather do good and find out there is trouble than not do anything and wish I should have done good.* Michael called his brothers to come near.

"Hurry, we must do something! Gabriel has brought it to my attention that a family of travelers has been caught in a trap. We are going to help. But if at any time danger presents itself, Remiel, you take the princess back to this spot we are at now."

"Don't worry," Uriel said, "we destroyed the last set of beasts. We can deal with whatever it might be." Uriel twirled his sword and Raguel twirled his hammer. Away from their original path, the brothers rushed to the aid of the endangered travelers.

The brothers approached a calm and deadly quiet scene. Zerachiel stood ready with his bow at the top of a towering tree. The rest of the brothers made their way to a fallen covered wagon on its side, while Remiel stayed back with Sandy. Michael approached with Raguel and Uriel on either side. Raphael and Gabriel circled around so that they had all angles covered. They looked into the wreckage and saw the motionless bodies of a family. As Michael moved closer, Zerachiel shot two arrows past him into the dark tree nearby. Michael didn't flinch as he checked the family for signs of life. Raguel and Uriel looked up at Zerachiel.

"What was that for? Did you see something we didn't?"

"The tree was set to attack, and I was the only one that saw it," Zerachiel said.

Raguel and Uriel looked at one another, disappointed that

they didn't get to do anything. "Brother," Uriel said, "we can still chop this big stump down."

Raguel smiled. "You do have a good idea." The two of them attacked the tree, chopping and smashing it into firewood. Gabriel looked around in case of attack from another direction as well did Raphael. Remiel smiled as he watched his brothers destroy the dark tree. He placed Sandy on the ground, feeling confident that the threat had passed.

Michael, checking over the bodies of the man woman and teenage children, couldn't determine if they were alive or dead. He called Raphael to check on them. Raphael ran over quickly. As Sandy and Remiel stood a distance away, the sound of a crying child could be heard close by. Closer to the ground, Sandy heard the crying and glanced around to find its origin. Remiel was fully concentrating on his brothers and felt no threat was present. As Sandy scanned the environment, she saw a small boy hiding behind some bushes. Assuming it was his family in the wagon, Sandy ran over to help.

"It's OK. You can come out; everything is safe now."

Remiel was still watching his brothers as Raphael inspected the family. He examined them and found underneath the common clothing the man was wearing, a garment worn by the priests of Moria. Michael saw this right away and yelled at his brothers. "Get back! It's a trap!"

Sandy was kneeling with her arms out as the little boy ran out from behind the bushes into her arms. Remiel turned to look for Sandy who had been next to him but who was now about twenty feet away. All the giants were too far from Sandy and watched in horror as the young boy, who was now in Sandy's arms, revealed his true nature. The boy looked six or seven until he lifted his head up and smiled at Remiel before turning into a large Basilisk. Or, as he was known in the dark time, the King of all serpents. Remiel dashed to separate Sandy from the creature, but it was too late. Sandy fell to the ground almost paralyzed, as the Basilisk made a strange hissing sound and slithered quickly away after biting her..

***

As Eve approached the Great Tree, the animals gathered around her and created a pathway for her to follow. Eve cowered in his presence. His trunk was enormous and his branches, it seemed to Eve, could hide all of Moria under his leaves if he wished.

"Eve, I have awaited your presence for a very long time. I know what you seek. And I have answers to your questions."

Eve stood in awe of his wisdom and knowledge. Sandy crossed Eve's mind and before she could utter a word, the Great Tree spoke. "Ahh, yes. The child, Princess Sandy Black. At this very moment she is in the darkest place she and her companions could have imagined."

Eve's heart dropped and she feared the worst, and blamed it on the giants. "I knew I shouldn't have trusted them."

"Ooh, you think that the giants allowed this thing to come to pass?" the Great Tree said. "You will be well learned that the giants consider Sandy as a family member. Their pain surpasses yours. The evil queen and her mothers are behind this."

Eve was confused. "But how did the queen find her?"

"You thought she wouldn't find her with them. Understand, my child, there is a destiny far greater than you can comprehend. Even as we speak, they fight for the young princess's life as if she were one of their own. Look into the water, and see what I see."

As Eve focused on the image being shown to her, Sandy fell

to the ground after the bite. Remiel now between Sandy and the fleeing Basilisk, looking down at her. Then, in a fit of rage, reached out and grabbed the snake before it could escape. Michael and all the other brothers made their way to Sandy. Remiel grabbed the tail of the giant serpent and in an uncontrolled fit of rage, he twirled it continually, smashing its head into trees. The snake disintegrated and he flung it away. Uriel placed his hand on Remiel's shoulder. Remiel turned with tears in his eyes as he looked down at Sandy on the ground, motionless. Raphael attended to her, trying to find something he could do. Raguel and Uriel tried to calm Remiel down. Gabriel, Zerachiel and Michael looked on helplessly as Raphael looked for answers. Finally, he found the puncture marks on her shoulder. Some of the venom was still sitting on the skin. Raphael smelled it and his head dropped when he recognized the smell of the poison.

"The venom of the Basilisk that bit her is that of a nightmare. Only this one you never awake from."

Remiel pushed past his brothers, knelt down next to Sandy and cried. "I'm sorry, Sandy. I'm very sorry. I said I would protect you." Remiel reached out and held Sandy in his arms as he wept. The brothers' heads fell as they mourned for Sandy. Michael, with teary eyes, put his hand on Raphael's shoulder.

"How can we make her better?"

Raphael looked up at his brother as tears fell down his face.

"My brother, of all the knowledge I have and all of the cures that I have learned, this venom is the only one I know I have no answer for. The Basilisk is an ancient creature; I didn't even think they existed anymore. I have only read stories of them."

Gabriel walked over to Michael as he spoke with Raphael. "He has no medicine because she is neither dead nor alive. She is just awake. It would seem as though the queen wanted Sandy to see everything fall apart around her, and not be able to do anything about it."

Raphael looked up at Michael.

"He is right. She is in a state where inside she is alive. But outside she is dead. She can hear us and see us, but can't move or communicate anything."

Zerachiel, concerned for what might be sent to destroy them next, warned Michael, "Brother, we are in a state of shock and mourning but we must keep moving. If there is going to be a chance that we can find a cure for this dark ailment, we must protect ourselves and Sandy."

Michael stood. "Brothers, we have sworn an oath - to protect the princess. As she is neither alive nor dead we are bound by this oath. We must move on, to preserve ourselves as well as Sandy. She can't get better if we don't find a way to fix this."

Remiel stood with Sandy in his arms. "We must fix this. If we don't, we have failed."

Raphael stood. "Brothers, I must tell you one more thing before we place ourselves in another bad position. Sandy, in her present state, only has seven days to live. After that her body will give out due to the venom completing its work."

Michael sighed deeply. Then Raphael, after digging through his bag in a frenzy, found something that could help.

"I've found it!"

The brothers turned to see what they hoped was a cure. Raphael opened his hand to reveal a seed.

"This is a seed of a large flower plant that can help us. The only place I know of that could help us right now is in the renewing waters of Moria. Our problem is that we are more than three days' away from the palace, and we would have to fight our way into a palace where only the King knows the passage to the pools." He lifted the seed. "This flower will make it possible for us to take longer and we can leave Sandy here."

Remiel reacted. "What do you mean leave her here?" Remiel jumped on his feet. "We can't leave her alone, not now!"

Raphael finished what he has to say.

"If we put her into the bulb that this plant produces, it would create a bond with her. Feeding her and giving her water, while it lives off the carbon dioxide she breathes out. This will slow down the advancement of the venom in her body."

Michael looked hopeful. "It will give us enough time to reach King Black and bring him back to save Sandy."

"We left our home expecting battle. Now we must go into one to get the help we need to save one who we love."

Zerachiel, Raguel and Uriel all answered at once. "Let us go then!"

Michael looked at Gabriel. "I will not sleep until the King is reunited with his daughter."

Now the brothers waited on one more answer from Remiel who was holding Sandy in his arms still. "Brothers, I love you dearly, but I am hurt to my soul. I will not leave my friend alone. The six of you are enough to get the King here. I have sworn to protect Sandy. I will not leave her."

The brothers were quiet as they had always fought as one and looked after each other. Michael responded.

"Brother, you are the youngest of the seven. With me as the eldest, I have looked out for you almost at times as if you were my son. This decision you are making is one of a true warrior. Though it pains me to leave you alone, I know that your heart is ready. Come what may."

During the rest of the conversation, Raphael prepared the flower pod. He had planted it and sprinkled on it some fairy dust he's found after the Oglos attacked them. A large stem rose out of the ground. From the stem grew a large, translucent bulb. Raphael called to Remiel.

"It is ready!" Raphael called to Remiel. "Come quickly, it must bond with her now."

Remiel placed Sandy inside the large open bulb. It closed moments after Sandy was placed inside. Raphael looked at his brothers. "It is finished."

Michael removed a chain from his neck. The chain had the crest of their father's house inscribed on it. "Remiel, I give this to you that you may remember who we are as giants. Keep Sandy safe, and we shall return for you both in two days."

The brothers saluted Remiel. "Come what may!"

Remiel watched as his brothers faded into the forest to the Kingdom of the White Rose in the Isles of Far Off to find King Black and stop the war.

***

Eve looked away from the water. "No, not the princess! How am I to believe all I have seen will come out to be good in the end?"

The Great Tree spoke. "As I have said before, there is a destiny that must be fulfilled in us all. You see, a great destiny awaits these seven as they continue on this path. One that will reveal their past and their future. Sometimes the obstacles on the road are just that; obstacles. Placed there for you to climb over so that you can get to the end. Without training, a soldier can't be a great soldier. Without nurturing, a child will not be a good child. If the animals of the forest did not have to contend with one another for food, they would just get fat and die. Be at peace, my child, for all that has happened will come around in the end."

Eve's mind was still racing after all she had just seen. She couldn't stop thinking about Sandy and the giants, and King Black and what would become of Moria.

"But great and wise one, if Sandy's flame burns out it will most assuredly destroy the King. And along with the King will fall the kingdom."

The Great Tree chuckled as his branches shook and leaves rattled.

"Oh, you do have much to learn, young Eve. I invite you to stay with me here, where it is safe, and you will see what I see."

Eve humbly accepted the invite. "I leave with you one more bit of knowledge before we rest. Take no thought for tomorrow, for today has enough worries of its own. Worry not for those things you are concerned with for the future. You have seen what has transpired today, and the tides of destiny have come in. Let them wash the filth of this day away, before you start the bath water for tomorrow."

Eve bowed before the Great Tree, then planted herself near the lake to rest for a moment.

***

In the Kingdom of the White Rose in the Isles of Far Off, David descended below the clouds. The once brimming and beautiful land, full of green hillsides and long rivers and island cities surrounding the peninsula, now had the look of death all around. The grass had withered away and the green forests that surrounded the palace had turned black, the islands depleted, and small boats had broken and washed up ashore after trying to give aide from the start. As David got even closer to what used to be the high palace walls, he saw rubble instead. Beyond that was a dark burnt ring filled with ash and black glass around the entire palace, placed there by the efforts of King Black's army. At night, they would resume this barrier of fire. David circled over the wreckage that was left of the palace. The army of the two kings spotted David and flashed him to land near to their position. As David descended, the forest sprang to life with the trolls instantly. As the first group of dragons began spewing fire around the palace, some of the trolls were incinerated instantly. David landed to an audience of King Black, King Ananias, and Prince Shamma. David dismounted and was greeted by King Black with a big hug.

"I have been concerned for you. Please tell me. Where is Sandy?"

Tears rolled down from David's eyes. "Brother, it is most urgent that we speak. There is much to tell you."

King Ananias and his son Shamma look at one another in confusion after hearing David call the King "brother". King Black, knowing something was very wrong, turned to King Ananias. "Friend, I ask to use your chambers for this sensitive information I must hear. You are welcome to join us as some of this information must pertain to you and our present situation."

King Ananias placed his hand on King Black's shoulder. "My friend, come let us hear the words of David."

King Black cut him off. "My brother. From this point on, there will be no secrets I will hold."

King Ananias nodded in understanding. The two kings, David, and Prince Shamma made their way to the King's chambers to hear what had happened in Moria.

Chapter 16

AWARE

Somewhere west of the Kingdom of the White Rose in the Isles of Far Off, the giants moved with blinding speed through the forest. Onward like a pack of ravenous wolves they ran with a goal in mind, and all focused on what was at stake. With the moonlight at their backs, and the glow of the flaming wall up ahead to keep their path, the brothers made haste. Remiel alone sat, holding the translucent pod in his arms, staring at Sandy while he sat. At every crack or whistle, Remiel was aware that danger could come at any moment. Off in the distance, the snapping of some twigs alerted him to the presence of something. As Remiel looked up, his eyes glowed red with anger. Six sets of yellow eyes popped up and then blinked in the darkness. The animals growled. Remiel, standing his ground, growled as a ferocious warning. A low rumble was heard as the growl intensified, shaking the nearby trees. Then Remiel roared like a lion and the pack of forest animals fled into the forest. Remiel would not be moved. He would protect Sandy no matter what. Come what may.

***

The two kings along with Prince Shamma and David entered into King Ananias's chambers. After the door was locked behind them, the men all sat. David stood before both kings and the prince and bowed before them.

"I apologize for not greeting you upon my arrival King, and Prince."

King Ananias cut him off. "Under our current situation, what is important is the knowledge you have for your King." He paused for a second. "I mean your brother, and of the whereabouts of the princess."

David sat. King Black sat anxiously. David looked at the three men.

"My brother, I can only tell you of what I know to be true. On the night you left for battle and left me with the charge of protecting Sandy, you also told me to keep an eye on the queen. As I followed your wishes, I came across the queen's chambers while she was speaking of evil she planned to do. I then went to your library to find anything that could explain what I had heard. And there I found it. The followers of Nefaria have returned. Evil is in the palace."

King Black's eyes widened as he thought of all that happened the last time the evil ones attacked. He jumped on his feet.

"Where is Sandy?"

David sighed. "I rushed her out of the palace, but before we got out some of the queen's men came after us. All I could do was stop them from getting to her. I sealed the walkway we had taken and was separated from her as she escaped outside of the palace. I was taken captive and tortured by the queen and Dr. Cain. I know she is in the forest somewhere alive, because the queen kept looking for her. She has taken over everything. Chef Tasty is the only one left we can trust inside. He and his daughter Lilly helped me escape."

King Black paced back and forth. King Ananias and his son

Shamma glanced at one another with concern. King Black faced the wall.

"So this entire war was a diversion? Meant to get me away from the palace so she could take over. But what is her connection to that accursed tribe of Nefaria the evil one? They are a foul and putrid people, who can't go anywhere without being noticed."

David interjects.

"Brother, she is one of them. I'm not sure how. But she has two elders of her kind with her."

King Ananias stood. "My friend and great King of Moria, remember the past. Remember that this foe used sorcery. Some sort of spell must have been cast over the queen, so as not to show her true form. We already know well of the darkness they have summoned from the depths of the entire world, bringing forth the trolls that haven't been seen since the last great war. If they can bring this evil out, what more might they have been able to?" King Black interjected, "Yes, I know, I know, but there had to be something I missed. My little girl is out there alone."

David placed his hand on his brother's shoulder. "We will find her."

King Black turned and David saw a certain fierceness in his brother's eyes. "Yes, I will find her. I will find Sandy no matter where she may be now. And the queen and her helpers I will deal with severely."

King Black gazed out of a window into the fire-lit forest. The two kings were flanked by David and Prince Shamma and the group now made their way out of the room towards their high position to oversee the battle. King Black was trying to figure out what more they could do to turn the tide of this battle. "There must be something we haven't thought of."

King Ananias responded, "There must be; I just hope it decides to come to us now."

As they look over the battlefield, scanning the forest for any sign of weakness, the arrows and flaming boulders that flew through the sky were as plentiful as ever.

***

Just outside the borders of the Kingdom of the White Rose in the Isles of Far Off, the giants moved at an astonishing pace through the dark forest. Zerachiel leapt from tree to tree while the rest of his brothers ran at what seemed like the speed of light. As they drew ever closer to the battle, the glow of the fire wall pushed through the dark of the forest. The eyes of the giants glowed with the only source of light shining in the distance. The forest around them seemed to come alive as they slowed down. Two arrows shot through the darkness and out from a nearby tree fell two trolls. Michael and his other brothers stood over the two lifeless bodies.

"I could smell them for the last five miles," Uriel said.

Michael looked around after Uriel's statement. He located all his brothers and noticed the forest around them was covered in trolls, with scores of them coming up out of holes in the ground. Zerachiel whistled and the five brothers on the forest floor tucked and rolled in five different directions. As they rolled away, a large group of trolls landed near them after jumping out of a tree. Arrows fell from above like rain, destroying the group of attacking trolls. Michael stood on his feet. "We are very close now, brothers. Let us go and end this battle and bring back the king." The brothers branched out towards the kingdom in five directions. Zerachiel moved up a hill to the tallest tree nearby and perched himself there. From his vantage point, he could see the battlefield. A few of the trolls tried attacking him on the tree. He took them out with his bow and then focused his attention on his brothers' movements.

At the palace, King Black, David, Shamma, and King Ananias all looked over the battlefield looking for answers. Prince Shamma noticed something different. As he looked towards the west side of the tree line, he saw a group of trolls running back into the forest. He stared intently trying to find out what they might be planning. He kept looking, as things didn't seem to add up. He turned to his father.

"Father, look over there at the tree line - the trolls on that side seem to be distracted by something. I have been watching them for a while now and they keep flooding into the forest."

King Ananias looked into the issue his son spoke of. He turned to King Black and David.

"What do you suppose is causing this?"

As all of the men focused their gaze onto the small section of the forest, they held their breath, hoping the enemy hadn't found another way to them or some new monstrous trick.

King Black turned to King Ananias. "There is not a passage into your palace from that side of the forest, is there?"

King Ananias, still focused on the retreating trolls, thought for a moment. "No, there is no entrance, and besides - I have ordered all other entrances closed since you have arrived."

The giants decimated the hordes of trolls flowing into the forest. Each brother in his own area destroyed any enemy that came close. Each brother found the opening in the earth that the trolls were using to flood the forest and attack from. One by one they marked each opening they found with a large bolder. Zerachiel shot leftover trolls from above.

Michael, sensing that they had done enough to draw attention to themselves, barked orders. "Push! In your line push, make way to the middle of them."

The brothers pushed forward in their own paths, running and smashing the trolls as they made their way to the center of the battlefield. The trolls were no longer focused on the palace but on the new threat from the forest. As the kings watched on, they could now see five distinct lines being formed in the hordes of trolls. King Black stepped forward to get a better look at what was making its way through the trolls. His eyes lit up. "It is the giants!"

King Ananias and Prince Shamma were confused, knowing the giants to be loners and unwilling to help.

"They have returned to that which was their place of old," David said. "Partners with man in the defense of this land."

They looked on as the five brothers tore through the forest, destroying the trolls in their path. Zerachiel shot out masses of arrows from his bow in a single shot, taking out about twenty or thirty trolls at once. Michael twirled his spear like a propeller, rotating it around himself and sending trolls flying through the sky. Raguel swung his giant hammer, smashing all that came before him. Uriel slashed dozens of trolls with his flaming sword, keeping count out loud as he killed them. "372, I'm on a roll now!"

Raguel, on Uriel's right, played the counting game with him. "That last five don't count. I hit them your way. Besides, they were dead before you sliced them."

Raphael ran through them like a truck through grass, picking some up and smashing them together. Throwing some into groups of others, he created a sense of distress among the trolls the farther he moved. Gabriel kicked through the trolls as if he was playing soccer, stepping on them and smashing them as he moved. All the brothers in their full armor moved closer and closer to the center of the battle.

As the giants got nearer to the palace, the hordes of trolls changed their focus to the new threat. Trying to seize the opportunity, King Black ordered some of his dragon flyers to stop torching the walls and begin attacking the trolls with fire.

"This is a bold move, King Black," King Ananias said. "If the trolls notice we have weakened our defense, they might attack us."

"We must do whatever we can with the opportunities we get," King Black said. "This war must end tonight. My daughter's life depends upon it."

King Ananias nodded. Prince Shamma mounted his dragon. "If this is going to end tonight, then you can be certain I'm going to have something to do with it."

Prince Shamma jumped on his dragon and flew to the back of the palace. Working in tandem with the giants' frontal assault, the dragon flyers spewed fire over the front lines of the troll's army and then turned to the rear ranks. Finally, the giants made it to the center of the battle, forming a circle amongst themselves and causing mass destruction.

The trolls, trying to regroup and attack, sent in more stone Golems. Zerachiel, seeing them far off, sent a cluster of arrows their way. The solid rock figures fell to the ground but soon got back up and continued forward; the arrows could only knock them down and cause minor damage. As they moved towards his brothers, Zerachiel whistled to get their attention. Gabriel glanced around and saw Zerachiel directing his attention towards the new enemy. Gabriel and Michael turned to face the golems.

Realizing they had a short time before dawn, Michael shouted to his brothers, "We must kill them all before the dawn. Or they will scatter and go back into the deep."

"Brother, I have an idea," Gabriel shouted at Michael. "But

we have to destroy them first."

Michael and Gabriel smashed the Golems until they were all brittle and slower. Michael checked the horizon and saw the small amounts of light off in the distance. He waved his arms to Zerachiel, giving him the signal to shoot the Golems again. Zerachiel shot a larger cluster of arrows this time, hitting the Golems in their brittle states and breaking them into bits. Michael then motioned for his brothers to move back towards the openings they'd marked in the earth where the trolls were coming from. As the brothers arrived at each location fighting off the hundreds of trolls around them, they all at the same time jumped and smashed the ground, causing an earthquake of incredible power. The shaking caused the tunnels underground to open up, and all of the trolls that had been underground were now outside and visible. The brothers now had to keep them contained.

King Black, knowing that the night was coming to an end, sent a message to Prince Shamma to keep the trolls inside the field of battle and not let them escape into the forest before daylight. As the dragon army circled about spewing fire on the perimeter, King Black could see they weren't fast enough to enclose them. Zerachiel whistled to Michael and Gabriel, notifying them to move on. Michael motioned to Raguel, Uriel and Raphael to close the perimeter for the King while Gabriel rushed to the top of the palace. Before the first ray of sunlight reached him, Gabriel took off his shield and positioned it to reflect the light down to Michael. Michael caught the rays with his shield and sent them to Zerachiel in the tree, who in turn positioned his shield and sent the light off to his three brothers at the far end of the field. The light reflected and covered all the exits. Trolls, allergic to sunlight, scampered about looking for a way to escape. Some even jumped into the flames. The light trapped the trolls until the sun rose fully. The trolls sizzled in the daylight and burst into lumps of rancid meat. The battle of the Kingdom of the White Rose was finally over.

Cheers erupted from the armies of King Black and King Ananias. Gabriel jumped down from the wall and gathered with the rest of his brothers, and the two kings landed before them atop their dragons. The kings dismounted and King Anannais stepped forward. "On behalf of the remnant of the Kingdom of the Isles of Far off I, King Ananias, thank you and extend my hand of friendship and gratitude."

Michael stepped forward. "As the eldest of the last tribe of giants, we accept your friendship and gratitude. Though our reason for coming to your aid has to do with King Black, and the state of his daughter."

King Black's eyes watered but he didn't shed a tear. Prince Shamma's face fell.

Michael turned to King Black. "Great King Black, it is with much sorrow that we come to you this day. Some time ago now, your daughter was brought to us by a Wajenzi named Eve. She told us the queen was after the princess's life so we took her in and protected her, believing the queen would never find her. As time passed, she gained our trust and friendship. To us, she is a sister, and this is why it is so hard to bring you this news."

The other giants bowed their heads as Michael continued. "A few days ago, we made plans to leave our camp due to the increased efforts of the queen to destroy the princess. After we set off, we came across another trap, more cunning than the previous two the queen had sent. Sandy, being soft-hearted, reached out to help what seemed to be a small child. We tried to help this child's family because we thought they were in danger. The seemingly small child transformed into a Basilisk and bit Sandy. She is at the moment in an unanimated state."

Streams of tears rolled down the giants' faces. Enraged, King Black held back his tears. With tears falling from his eyes, Michael knelt before the King. "King Black, we come to you in the hope of renewing that great covenant made between our people and yours that we might be redeemed in getting Sandy to the renewing waters of Moria. This is a task only you can do. We will help take back your palace and defend Sandy to the death."

King Black sighed and controlled his emotions before speaking. "Where is my daughter now?"

"She has been placed in the pod of a certain flowering plant that grows in the forest," Michael said.

Wiping tears from his face, Raphael stepped forward and bowed before the King.

"Great King, I am Raphael. I have a vast knowledge of the medicines and plants of this forest. After Sandy was bitten, the poison left her in an unanimated state. She can sense what is going on around her, but she can't interact with anything. Knowing that the venom kills after seven days, I placed her inside the pod of a certain plant that grows in this forest. It will slow down the venom and nourish her body."

With renewed hope, King Black asked. "Where is she now? You must take me to her!"

Gabriel then responded.

"Great King, one of our brothers, Remiel, is with her now. Nothing will harm her where she is. The important thing is to get the palace under your control. We can't bring Sandy there until after the queen is dead or gone. The pod she sleeps in must stay connected to its vine to keep her nourished. She is safer in the forest with Remiel than anywhere else."

David placed his hand on King Black's shoulder. "Brother,

they have shown their true nature and have come to our aid. I trust them. Sandy has been safe with them up until this point."

King Black nodded and turned to Michael. "To the palace we go." To King Ananias he said, "I must take flight; my daughter is still alive. I will leave with you a portion of my army, to watch over you and make sure nothing will happen in our absence."

King Ananias nodded. "My friend, we will be fine. You go and save your daughter, and destroy the evil once and for all."

Prince Shamma stood behind his father, eager to speak. "I will send with you my son," King Ananias said.

Shamma bowed before King Black in respect. King Black nodded. "The help you send with me I accept, my old friend. For I know his heart is with my Sandy as well."

David mounted Ballah. "Brother, we must go now."

The King turned to the giants. "It's going to be a day's flight back to the palace. How will you make it there on time?"

Michael smiled. "Don't worry yourself, King Black. We have given you our word; we will beat you there." King Black mounted his dragon. With David on his right side and Prince Shamma on his left, they whisked off.

***

As the sun shone a few rays through the dark clouds Remiel sat under a tree, cradling the pod. Within minutes, he nodded off.

A low growl of rage constantly hummed from deep within him, acting as a warning to any creature that would want to come near them. Since his brothers left, he hadn't moved nor eaten. Food was the last thing on his mind. The only thing on his mind was keeping Sandy safe.

Chapter 17

PANIC

Inside the palace soldiers tore through walls and knocked over doors, searching for Chef Tasty and Lilly. Chef Tasty and his group ran through the labyrinth of tunnels, huffing and puffing. Upon arriving at another corridor, Chef Tasty had a tough time remembering which way to go. "I'm so old; so long ago it was I last was down here."

He looked down one narrow corridor that crossed another. Glowing rocks lit the way of each corridor. Lilly and the twins stood behind the chef as he tried to remember which way to go. All around them, they could hear the footsteps of soldiers. "We don't want to go the wrong way now, do we? One of these halls leads to another secret room. The other three lead to more corridors. Hmmmm." Chef Tasty grabbed an apple out of his bag. He bit into it and examined it in delight. "Hmmm, this would have made a wonderful pie." He threw the apple down the hall and arrows shot out from either side. The floor opened up to reveal a great pit. "Well, I sure am glad I remembered where to stop. We can't go that way; we don't have a royal seal."

Lilly and the twins waited in discomfort, scared they'd be caught. Chef Tasty's fist pumped with excitement.

"That's it! I remember now. To the right ain't right, and to the left is what's left. We go to the left."

Lilly and the twins stood still as Chef Tasty dashed in the new direction. He paused and turned around. "What are you waiting for?"

Lilly looked at her father. "You saw what happened to the apple!"

Chef Tasty chuckled. "Don't worry, my darling, we don't have a royal seal to get into some of the passageways, but I can remember most of the directions from walking through these passages with King Black. Be ready; we may have to fight soon."

The twins and Lilly glanced at one another and dashed after Chef Tasty.

The queen sat in the garden amongst the plants, which had all withered and were all but dead. The sunflowers that had spoken against her were gone. She sat with her mother, relaxing and sipping tea.

"Why won't Grandmother come away from the mirror? We can only see so much at a time. Besides, that little brat should be wishing she was dead now. And her father should be dead soon too."

"Silence, young one," the queen's mother said. "You seem to have allowed your beauty to overrule your mind. What has happened to all that your grandmother and I taught you over the years? Why is it so easy for you to lose focus? The battle is not over yet, and these humans are more resilient than you can understand. I was there when our people wielded enough power to challenge the Great Tree. I remember when the giants were destroyed. I remember because I was there, and your grandmother was there. Don't think for one moment that this is over."

One of the servants walked up to them and bowed. "My queen, your grandmother has requested that both of you return to your chambers immediately."

The queen and her mother glanced at one another.

As the queen and her mother strolled into the room, the queen's grandmother paced back and forth with her hands to her face. She stopped and removed her hands from her hideous face.

"King Black has defeated the trolls; the giants have united with him and they are on their way to the palace!"

The queen's face turned pale as her mother dashed to the mirror. The queen stood frozen, wishing it was a dream. The queen's mother spoke to the mirror,

"Mirror, mirror on the wall,

Knowing much and seeing all,

Show us truth of what may come,

Show us the King, and if he's won."

The mirror quaked, glowed, and showed images of King Black on his way to the palace.

"I'll tell you the truth, because I cannot lie.

The darkness you loosed has been destroyed by the light.

An alliance now formed will separate you from the future,

Unless it can be halted in its approach.

Turn back from your plans of domination and power,

Turn back from your plans right now; this very hour.

If you don't heed my warning surely you will pass,

Pass on from this life, straight into death."

The queen's mother, with a concerned look on her face, thought to herself what to do next. The queen, now enraged, rushed over to the mirror.

"Mirror, mirror on the wall,

What of our power, can we stop them all?"

The mirror showed an image of Sandy in the forest.

"A beautiful queen you are indeed.

But this power you seek, it will not be.

The power that is, and that which will be,

Has already passed over this three's company.

You have sought to destroy what you didn't make,

Now it would seem that this path will lead you to your fate."

The queen's grandmother, now upset over the response from the mirror, responded.

"No. I will not allow this to end like this. We have waited far too long. We have waited patiently in the shadows of the forest for our rightful time to seize power. I will not listen to this advice from the mirror. Yes, it has been an oracle to us for centuries; a seer. But the King is still not here yet, and has no power over us. We will stand together and use our power to its fullest. We will stop the King and his armies. By the power of Nefaria, we will succeed."

The queen commanded her army to stop searching for Chef Tasty and prepare for battle. Drums thumped commands in rhythms. All the prisoners, including women and children, were bound and positioned on the front lines. This the queen did to stop King Black from attacking.

Chef Tasty stopped, and the others bumped into him. "What is it?" Lilly asked. "Why did you stop?" Chef shushed them and they all went quiet. From the floor above, the footsteps had stopped; instead of coming closer they were moving away from their position.

"Did you hear that?" Chef asked.

"Something has happened; feel the rhythm of the drums. For them to stop looking for us, it must be something big." Chef continued to listen and feel the rhythm of the drums. He responded with a smile on his face to what he has deciphered from the beat. "Oh, its big alright, the King is on his way; come on." Chef Tasty led the others to a small room. Inside the room, Chef Tasty knocked on one of the bricks in the wall. A part of the ceiling opened and a ladder came down. Lilly and the twins looked at one another, amazed.

On climbing up, the group found themselves in the kitchen. Chef Tasty climbed up a ladder to a circular set of windows high up in the middle of the kitchen. He instructed the twins to cover the doors. Lilly looked up, waiting for what her father might see. Chef Tasty scanned the environment and he saw the queen's guards hurrying to prepare for battle. At the palace gates, soldiers hurriedly put on their armor. In front, the prisoners were lumped together forming a shield. Chef Tasty chuckled to himself; his heart filled with joy. He knew it was confirmed that King Black and David would soon be arriving. He climbed down the ladder to share the news.

"It is now time to take back what has been stolen. We will strike soon, freeing as many of the residents of Moria that we can. The King is on his way."

Lilly and the twins' eyes lit up. "How do you know this?" Lilly asked. "How do you know for sure that King Black is coming?"

"Because, my love, the only thing that could have taken the attention off what the queen sees as a threat in the house would be a bigger threat from outside. So, my dear, the King has got to be on his way; there is no other reason to shut down the palace in preparation for what looks like a battle and stop the search for us. We will sit here for the moment and wait. We will wait until just as the King is in the distance - only then will we be able to fragment her troops like we want to and make the King's fight easier."

Inside the queen's chambers and in front of the mirror, the

three witches stood hand-in-hand, chanting. The image of King Black approaching the palace flashed upon the mirror. The three continued chanting in their native tongue.

***

The giants stopped running when they heard voices in the wind. Gabriel turned to Michael. "It's a foul tongue."

As he spoke, a howling blast of wind swept through the forest. It was so loud, the giants couldn't hear each other. The bright sky turned dark, and twigs and leaves swirled in the air.

Still flying, King Black observed the sky and the wind. He groaned. "Witches!"

As they flew high above the forest floor, the wind blew in their faces. High in the sky before them, the image of the three witches appeared in the clouds. The queen smiled. "King Black, you will not make it back to the palace," she bellowed. "You will die like your daughter." The queen cackled and her eyes glowed and lightning flashed in the sky. King Black, unshaken by the appearance of the witches, struggled to lift his sword. The wind made it difficult but with all his strength, he lifted his sword and pointed it forward to usher his troops onward. The loud cry of his army and their dragons filled the sky and swallowed the howling of the wind. The giants below heard the cry and raced towards the palace. As the witches chanted, all manner of disasters showed up. Hurricane force winds swept through the forest, a tornado swept by uprooting swathes of forest, boulder-sized hail fell from the sky, earthquakes shook the forest floor and split large fissures into the ground below. Due to all of the wind and hail, some of the King's men fell from their dragons. As they were blown off, the dragons flew to pursue and save their riders.

King Black and Prince Shamma dodged the obstacles with

great skill. The giants below moved with such force and determination that nothing slowed them.

Deep in the forest, far behind the King and his brothers, Remiel sat with Sandy. When he heard the foul tongue and saw the sky change, he gripped Sandy and braced himself. The wind rushed past him, blowing leaves, sand and twigs in his face. A large hailstone fell over them and he shielded Sandy with his body. More hailstones fell on him, and he growled in pain. A tornado swept past, swirling trees, animals and rocks all around. Next, Remiel heard a rumble in the distance. The rumble grew louder as a massive earthquake shook the forest. Remiel jumped to his feet with the plant and Sandy in his hand. A tear in the forest floor split and ran its way between Remiel's legs. He tried to maintain his balance, but it was useless. Remiel slipped down into the newly-formed trench. He looked around for something to hold onto as he couldn't separate Sandy from the plant. As he began to slip and fall, he placed Sandy in a hole inside the canyon formed by the earthquake. Remiel fell farther down, digging his hands deep into the walls of the canyon. Sandy, no longer protected by Remiel, lay in the pod still attached to the plant that had helped preserve her. The stem was pulled to its limit and time was running out. Remiel held onto the wall, trying to keep himself from falling farther down and away from Sandy. Knowing he must get back to Sandy before anymore of the forest floor gave way, he dug into the side of the wall looking for another place to grab. As he reached for another place to hold, the wall on his right side crumbled away. Remiel slid further as he struggled to hold on and not slide into the abyss below. He looked up at Sandy with tears in his eyes. He reached out again and the wall on his left side crumbled. Remiel fell with the crumbling dirt out of view of Sandy. He reached out for her as he fell, with eyes full of tears.

After he had fallen so far that he couldn't see Sandy anymore, his descent stopped as he landed on a large rock that protruded from the sides of the trench. The ground around him was still unstable and could deteriorate at any time. Every time Remiel moved it seemed like the rock began to slip from its position, so he stood still. Frustrated and scared of not getting back to Sandy on time, Remiel had to calm himself to figure out what to do to get back to his friend.

Chapter 18
DADDY'S HOME

After receiving signals from King Black, Prince Shamma flew away with a small group of dragon flyers in the opposite direction. David and King Black, along with over seven hundred thousand dragon flyers, pressed onward towards the palace. Dodging lightning and the strong winds, King Black and his troops remained focused and unshakeable. Not far behind, the giants raced, leaping over gullies and hills. They had one thing in mind - to save their friend, Sandy.

***

The queen's chamber glowed green from the overexertion of their magical powers. Tired, they stopped chanting and opened their eyes. The queen sat on a chair, panting, while her mother leaned on a wall and rubbed her head.

"This fight will not be won this way," the queen's grandmother said, pacing the chamber. "Daughters! The time has come for us to prove ourselves worthy to our ancestors. This King's focus is much greater than I had hoped, and our powers are not strong enough to extend so far away."

The queen's grandmother rushed to the door. "Come, come

my daughters. We must prepare for the arrival of the King."

The three witches hurried to the front of the palace. The citizens of Moria were huddled together like bags of potatoes at the entrance. The queen smiled when she saw the manmade barrier. "If the palace is what King Black wants back, we will make him crush his own people first."

She laughed as the other witches cast spells around the palace, creating pillars of fire and lightning storms. The prisoners inside the metal cells screamed as the ground quaked and the skies became black. Smoke filled the air as the pillars of fire engulfed nearby carriages and wooden objects.

Watching through the high window in the kitchen, Chef Tasty saw soldiers marching. Chef turned to Lilly and the twins. "It is now; we must move!"

The chef rushed down, ran to a cabinet and pulled out a case of juju berries. Lilly scanned over the contents of the case. "What do we need these for?"

"Just crush the berries in your hands and cover yourselves with the juice. Make sure to cover every inch of yourselves."

The twins and Lilly exchanged surprised looks. "I know that the juju berry has healing properties," Lilly said, "but none of us are injured, and doesn't it work faster if we drink the juice?"

Chef Tasty smiled. "You children haven't read of the battle that happened here an age ago. Not only do juju berries heal you from wounds and protect you from ones you might sustain in battle. Bugs hate the stuff, and one of the main attacks these witches will end up using is swarms of bugs."

Chef Tasty shuddered. "Trust me; some of these nasty bugs carry diseases. Why do you think the witches look so nasty? Well, at least they always did until this queen showed up. They embody death and disease; their bodies are constantly dying.

They are tied to death and darkness like a decaying corpse. Trust me; just cover yourselves."

Satisfied with the explanation, Lilly and the twins covered themselves with the juju berry juice. Chef Tasty covered himself too. The group carried large containers of the juice and rushed out of the kitchen.

***

Eve awoke from her sleep, refreshed and in bloom. Peace flooded her as she turned around, absorbing the beauty on every side. Her mind then shifted back to Sandy. Fearing she had been asleep for too long, she began uprooting herself. As she made haste, the Great Tree's voice echoed inside her. "Be still Eve! Be still! You have not missed this coming of age, so let your heart be joyful and your mind be still."

Comforted by the Great Tree's voice, she turned to face him. His leaves were bright green and his fruits were ripe. "Come and see things as I see them," he said, smiling at Eve. "Set your gaze into the water and watch as the future becomes the present."

Eve looked down into the water as she did before. Her eyes were opened to all that was happening at the palace in Moria. She could see King Black and all his army, as well as the giants getting close to the palace. The dark sky over the palace glowed orange from the pillars of flame. She saw the captives screaming for help as they stood shackled to one another. She saw Sandy in the pod and Remiel fighting his way up the hill to her. The sights before her were troubling and the future looked dark. Again, the still, small voice spoke to her like a calming breeze. "Be still, Eve! Be still! Watch as the future becomes the present."

Eve was comforted once again and she kept her gaze on the water, watching the events unfolding.

Close to the palace, King Black saw the orange and yellow

glow of fire. The three witches stood on the same balcony, chanting with their hands raised. As King Black got closer, he saw the captives placed in front of the palace like a barrier. He signaled to David and the troops to stop.

"Hello, mighty King Black," the queen called with a voice so loud that it cut through the wind. "You are just in time to see the renovations I have done. It wasn't meant to be a surprise; I was hoping you would be dead by now. Kind of like your daughter." She cackled.

King Black composed himself even though a storm was brewing inside him. "The end for you and your kind is near. You will come to know this soon."

The queen smirked. "Well, let's see what an upset King can do. Do be careful; as you can see, the citizens of Moria are our shields."

As King Black and his army dived, the queen's commander, the Minotaur, ordered the archers to fire.

Inside the palace, Chef Tasty and his group moved towards the side exit of the palace. They encountered six soldiers and Chef Tasty shouted instructions to Lilly and the twins. They nodded and stacked the containers of juju berry juice on the floor. Then the twins fanned out to the right and left. Lilly ran straight at the soldiers with her sword held high while Chef Tasty pulled out apples from his bag. As the soldiers charged, the twins rushed in from both sides, dispatching the two soldiers closest to them. Lilly slid between the legs of one of the attackers. Chef Tasty threw the apples, smashing them on the heads of the remaining soldiers, disorienting them and making them easy work for the twins and Lilly. Chef Tasty smiled. "Great job, children! Now I don't feel so bad about wasting those delicious apples. I could have made them into a yummy pie with a side of heavy whipped frozen sweet cream!"

Lilly chuckled. "Poppa, I love it when you speak in recipes."

The group grabbed the jugs of juice and ran off towards the battle.

Outside, the dark sky was alive with light, like glitter thrown over a dark wall. The queen's army fired burning stones and arrows into the air. The witches raised their hands, shut their eyes and chanted and started a brewing storm, while a large dark mass rose behind them. Two soldiers who guarded the entrance of the balcony screamed. Covered with bugs, they jumped over the sides of the balcony. The witches stopped chanting and opened their eyes. The queen leaned over and, when she saw their dead bodies, she smiled. "A swarm of pestilence shall drown their pride."

"As it was so long ago, it is now," her grandmother said. "We now must finish what was left undone in that age past. We will right the wrong for Nefaria's sake. Man will fall to the swarm of death."

The three witches cackled as they directed the swarms of bugs in different directions.

The giants stopped under trees on the way to the palace unseen. Arriving first, Zerachiel perched atop a tree and surveyed the battle scene. On getting there, Michael signaled to Zerachiel to notify King Black of their arrival. Using his shield, Zerachiel sent the King a flash of light. Targeting some of the swarms of bugs, Zerachiel lit the tip of one of his enormous arrows with friction from his hands and released the arrow into the swarm. The bugs burst into ashes and settled on the captives below. The giants stepped out of the cover of the forest, thereby making themselves known. The captives noticed and were afraid, not knowing the giants had come to aid them. King Black ordered his men to strike. Dragons and men dodged the arrows and boulders, whisking through the night sky at them. The giants spread out and leapt onto the battlefield. The witches snarled at their arrival.

Chef Tasty and his small group reached the eastern door of the palace. The twins cracked the door and observed the environment for a perfect time to move. Bursting from the sky, the dragon army attacked with a storm of fire, turning the arrows and boulders into ashes and rubble. The trial of fire had begun. The witches focused their attack on the captives. The giants noticed, and fought their way towards the large cells holding them. Seeing that all eyes were on the giants, Chef Tasty and his group rushed towards the captives. King Black's men landed and dismounted to fight hand-to-hand as their dragons spewed flames all over the queen's forces, incinerating man and beast alike.

Chef Tasty and his small unit ran onto the front lawn of the palace which was barricaded and fortified for the fight. Just beyond the barricades were the captives, all locked together and kept in place by a makeshift prison cell that wrapped itself around the front of the palace. Lilly looked up at the balcony that the witches stood atop of and saw the dark mass of bugs floating close to their location.

"We have got to get to them before this next wave does, or many will perish," Lilly said.

Chef Tasty didn't reply as he focused on their timing. The twins lay down their containers of juice and engaged in a sword fight with a couple of soldiers. The twins killed them off and winked at each other. Chef Tasty yelled out instructions over the loud crashes and sounds of battle. "Prepare yourselves! We must make it to the people before the bugs do. Make sure your containers are ready. As soon as we get there, cover as many of them as you can in the juice. If we all do the same, we should be able to minimize those that get infected by this evil. Ready?"

The group all looked at one another one last time knowing what they must do. They nodded.

"Now!" Chef Tasty yelled and they all charged towards the Morian captives. They dodged exploding arrows, flames, and soldiers as they hurried towards the captives. From the western wall, Michael saw Chef Tasty and his group rushing forward. He cleared off an area of soldiers from atop the wall with his spear and peered closely to see where the small group was running to or from. He makes a motioned to Zerachiel who turned and focused on Chef Tasty and his group. He then grabbed ten arrows and placed them in his bow. With one mighty pull, he fired the arrows to clear the path for the chef. All at once an area that was heavily guarded was cleared as the guards sailed away after the arrows struck them.

With their path cleared, the group increased their pace. The swarm of bugs was very close behind them and not far from getting to the cells. Chef Tasty instructed his team to climb atop the cells and pour out the juice over the prisoners. As they covered the prisoners, the buzzing of the bugs grew louder as they inched closer. Lilly looked back at the buzzing cloud of pestilence and at her father. "We won't make it!" she yelled over the noise.

As soon as she finished speaking, Michael landed close to them with a thud, shaking the earth. Twirling his spear, he said, "Continue what you are doing I will help you complete it."

Chef Tasty motioned for his group to continue as he opened one of the jugs and poured out the contents. As Michael twirled his spear, it created a gust of wind that blew with tremendous power. The wind picked up the juice the group was pouring out and covered all the trapped Morians from head to toe. As quickly as they were covered, the swarm engulfed the prisoners, as well as Chef Tasty and his team. Michael used the twirl of his spear to keep the bugs away from him as they tried to approach. The witches looked on with pride, thinking the bugs would infect and kill the captives.

The large, dark swarm of death wrapped the captives in a buzzing, pulsating shell. The battle ceased as all the fighters, including King Black, looked on to see what would happen next. Soon, the pulsating shells of pestilence slowed their pulse and buzz. Slowly, they solidified into a solid black shell. Michael sighed, bowing his head. Chef Tasty's efforts were in vain, he thought. He heard a loud crack. Then a loud voice echoed out in song,

"Ju Ju

Ju Ju

Ju Ju berry

Juiceeeeeeee!"

Michael smiled as Chef Tasty broke out of the solid black mass. One by one, the others emerged from the shells. Soon the ground was covered with the bugs' hard shells.

"How did it work?" Michael asked, surprised. "I didn't think you would survive after they encased you all like that."

Chef Tasty chuckled. "My large friend, I would like you to know that juju berry juice is great for many things. It has healing powers and it is also the best juice for a picnic. It is a wonderful treat to drink, but to little creeping things it is most poisonous. Usually bugs fly away from the scent of it; I think you spinning that spear made them all get stuck in it."

Cheers erupted from the onlookers as the last prisoner emerged from the shell.

From his position, King Black saw victory ahead while the witches saw the beginning of their defeat. Determined to finish the battle quickly, King Black darted through the sky and straight towards the three witches. The Minotaur hurled a large spear at the King. King Black dodged the spear and as he landed, his dragon spewed fire and gulped down the large Minotaur. The freed captives armed themselves and fought back. The giants opened the sealed doors to the palace so that all could pour in. Seeing their general was no more, the queen's army surrendered.

The witches dashed inside the palace. King Black jumped down and pursued the witches. David landed and ran after his brother.

***

Remiel dug his hands into the walls of the newly-formed ravine. Careful not to tear down the wall, he pulled himself up. Slow and steady, he continued to pull himself up. Covered in dirt, he inched closer until he finally got himself to the top of the wall. Glancing at Sandy, who was still in an inanimate state in the pod, he sighed, relieved that she was still connected to the plant.

On reaching the top and climbing out of the ravine, he observed the surroundings. The forest looked different as trees were flat on the ground, dead animals lay around and old paths were no longer there. Bracing for new dangers, he knelt and lifted Sandy. The ground below him shook. He gasped. The ground was about to give way! Remiel looked around for something to hold onto to keep both of them from falling. Seeing nothing, he knew he had to move quickly. He pulled up the plant and jumped forward before the ground beneath him crumbled.

As he dashed through the forest like an angry lioness, the pod used to sustain Sandy melted away from around her.

Tears rolled down his eyes, as he wasn't sure he'd make it on time.

***

Back at the palace, King Black's army secured the perimeter of the kingdom. The queen's army were placed in the prison cells made for the captives. The darkness that had covered the skies of Moria dissolved and the fire died down, but smoke filled the air.

King Black's men secured all entrances and exits of the palace. The queen, her mother and grandmother used a hidden passageway in the queen's chambers to make an escape. King Black and David ran to the King's chambers. "The only place they could try to escape is through the royal passages," King Black stated as they entered his room. David replied, "We should be able to catch up to them through here." David removed a scarf and turned his back to the wall, and his birthmark opened the passage David had used while trying to get Sandy to safety. They grabbed torches on the wall and tiptoed down the passage. As they made their way through the passage, they noticed an opening had been created from the queen's passage to the one they were in. As they listened for footsteps, all the flames on the torches in the passageway were extinguished. Only the flames on the torches in their hands remained. They heard swift footsteps and hurried down the passage.

Down one of the dark corridors, the three witches scurried around, searching for an exit. The queen's grandmother, not at all happy at the outcome of the battle, would rather fight than flee.

"We have waited for too long now to go back into hiding," she whispered. "I will not run anymore. We are stronger than we have been in centuries with the three of us together. Yes, we must regroup, but if we destroy the King before we retreat, we will be able to gain more supporters faster. And then, we will take all of Moria for ourselves."

"We must not delay here!" the queen whispered. "The King will most certainly kill us for all that has happened. It would be best we go into the forest and regroup."

The queen's mother shook her head. "Child, you should know better by now. This attack was a one-way road. We had to win, or we lose everything. Now that we have been backed into a corner, this King will hunt us down no matter where we go. There is no going back. We cannot regroup until we have made a show of our power – something grand enough to evoke fear over all the land. If in this we don't succeed, death will be but a dream. For the rage of a distraught father being that of this King will send us to eternal torment. We will attack."

As the three whispered to one another, a flicker of light far down the hall caught their attention. The three froze and stared at the rays of light shining down the walkway. Each second brought the light closer and brighter. Easing their way back into the shadows, the three witches hid in the dark.

King Black and David stood at a crossroad. Before them were seven corridors.

"Hide in the dark they think they will," King Black said. "Let us light their way to their destruction."

King Black lit the corridors, sending a spark along the wall that lit each of the torches as it continued down the hall. David did the same on the other side.

"And when their dim path is lit, let this fire consume them," King Black said, enraged.

As the sparks raced down each pathway, bathing the halls in light as they traveled, the witches scurried off. King Black and David heard the footsteps. Just above them, King Black's soldiers were blocking all the exits. The shadowy figures of the three began to take shape as the last of the halls filled with light.

King Black yelled out to his soldiers, "Keep the exits secure, men! They are going to have to come through me if they want to live."

As the witches' shadowy figures became clearer, their eyes glowed a fiery red.

"There is much pain I would like to share with you." King Black raised his sword. "Come, let us meet over my blade about this matter."

The blinking red eyes moved out from the last corner of darkness into view. King Black gritted his teeth when he saw their faces.

While the queen and her mother turned to the door behind them, the queen's grandmother stepped forward to address him. "What is it you would have me do? King Black!" She steadily crept closer as she spoke, her long, tattered robe dragging across the floor as insects flew in and out of her hair. "You would have me beg you as a dog for my life and for those I hold near? You know far too well this will not be so."

King Black stepped forward. "Stop your tongue, witch! Your mouth is an open sore, and your feet run swiftly to mischief. I will not tolerate you or your kind anymore."

King Black charged with a shout. David ran up a set of stairs as his brother attacked the eldest witch. As he reached the top of the stairs, an explosion rang out and knocked down the door the soldiers were guarding. A swarm of insects flew out from the queen's mother's hair and bit the soldiers near the door. As the soldiers fell to the ground, the queen and her mother dashed into the forest. More soldiers turned up and chased them. Chef Tasty and his group fought through the flies to keep the witches from fleeing.

David ran up the stairs to the queen's chambers. He pushed the door open and dashed into the room. The mirror glowed as the image of King Black, fighting with his sword, and the old witch, fighting with her long nails, came up. Rushing towards the mirror, David unsheathed his sword and plunged it into the mirror.

The eldest witch stopped fighting as she fell to the ground, gasping for air. The queen's mother let out an earsplitting scream that resounded through Moria. The soldiers close to her sank to their knees and covered their ears in pain. The queen, in noticeable pain, staggered away into the forest away from onlookers. David retracted his sword and the screaming stopped, and a silence filled the air as everyone watched to see what would happen next. Rolling on the floor, the eldest witch laughed and bled from her mouth a black, liquid oil. King Black stood over her with his sword ready to pierce her chest if she was playing games.

As David stared at the images in the mirror, the glass shattered and blood flowed from the frame. He pulled the mirror from the wall and smashed it on the floor. The three witches screamed simultaneously, "The mirror!"

Having the source of their powers destroyed, the queen's mother's fell to the ground, weak. The soldiers surrounding the queen's mother shackled her as King Black emerged from the doorway, dragging the old witch by the hair.

***

High above the forest, Prince Shamma flew back to the palace of Moria with the small group of dragon riders. Since the battle was over and the darkness had faded away, he had a clearer view of the forest. The forest was in disarray, with uprooted trees and the grounds split open. Scanning the forest for any sign of life, he spotted something dashing through the forest. He couldn't tell what it was; all he could see was a cloud of dust spewing behind through the forest. Shamma flew a bit lower to get a good look of whatever it was. As he got closer, a giant came into view.

A feeling of dread crept over him when he remembered Sandy was in the care of one of the giants. *I hope Sandy is safe?* He wondered. Straining to keep pace with the giant, he called out, "Hello! Hello!"

Remiel, focused on getting to the palace didn't hear him. Flying closer, Prince Shamma gasped when he saw a lifeless Sandy in Remiel's arms. "Sandy!" he yelled.

Remiel looked up and saw Prince Shamma. With tears streaming down his face, he slowed down and yelled, "She will die if I don't get her to the palace soon."

Prince Shamma's heart sank. "No, she can't die!"

"I can get her there. Just show me the way!"

Prince Shamma nodded and signaled the dragon riders to fly before Remiel. Remiel increased his pace as Prince Shamma and the dragon riders directed his path. Speeding through the air, Prince Shamma had only one thing in mind – to get Sandy, his love, home.

Chapter 19

LOVE

The two captured witches were tied together and placed in front of the palace in full view of the citizens of Moria.

"All these years, you've been lying in wait for the citizens of Moria," King Black said, pacing up and down. "You've been yearning to capture the land for your own demented desire of power. I should have known that evil doesn't just go away. Because you attacked my people, my family and me, you have been found worthy of death."

The two witches cackled. King Black, enraged by their mockery, pierced the shoulder of the younger witch with his sword. She screamed as the sword sank deeper. The older witch stared blankly into space.

"The bugs of the field will by no means find any sustenance from your leftovers when I am done. For whatever is left will not be enough to fill an ant," King Black said as he pulled out his sword.

A roar from the sky echoed throughout the land. Everyone looked up and saw Prince Shamma approaching with the dragon riders. The earth shook as Remiel darted towards the palace, covered in dust. Exhausted, Remiel fell on his knees and lifted Sandy up. Prince Shamma landed near him, jumped off his dragon and rushed to see Sandy. The other giants were by Remiel's side in seconds with lots of questions. King Black hurried to Remiel who carried Sandy in his arms. Tears flowed from King Black's eyes when he saw his daughter's pale face. He turned to David.

"Bring the witches with us. The water will judge them."

The old witch yelled in protest.

After ordering soldiers to secure the witches for transport, David sent two soldiers to the queen's chambers to retrieve the pieces of the mirror. Prince Shamma stood next to King Black in a daze as he stared at the still body of the woman he loved. "We should hurry, great King."

King Black nodded and smiled. "No need to worry, young prince. I can hear her laugh as I hold her. She is not dead; she's just at rest. Soon, you will see what I already know to be true." King Black turned to Remiel. "Thank you."

Remiel nodded.

Michael walked over to Remiel and hugged him. The other brothers joined in the hug.

"You have done a good thing, brother," Michael said. "You have made your family proud and grown into the warrior I knew you would become."

The group embraced again and then everyone followed King Black to his secret entrance that led into the underground spring of the living waters of Moria. On getting to the opening in the side of a mountain, King Black turned around and opened the entrance with his birthmark. A large slab of rock began to move, revealing a corridor with a blueish glow emanating from the end of it. The King then gave directions. "Chef Tasty, guard the entrance. David, you and Prince Shamma should bring the evil ones with us."

David handed the mirror's pieces to Michael and, along with Prince Shamma, he forced the witches to their feet. King Black turned to Michael. "My friends, I ask that you come with us as well." Michael and his brothers bowed before King Black. King Black then turned to the people. "On this day, you will see what keeps our land. You will bear witness to that which is true and has been before the foundations of the world. The tree, that is life, has placed in this land his water. His living essence that sustains us will prove its power once more. I will enter into the most holy place and return not alone. Stay your hearts and your minds on what is good, and all things are possible with he who is for us."

All of the citizens and soldiers of Moria began singing in one low voice. King Black, David, Prince Shamma and the giants walked into the mountain and down a walkway towards the blue glow. The sound of thousands of voices outside resonated through the mountain. The blueish glow lit their path as they walked farther and farther down a dirt corridor. As they continued walking, the source of light began to appear. In front of them, a stream of water traveled from inside the mountain down to a large pool below. The pool emitted a bluish glow.

Finally, they arrived at the pool. A tree root sat in the middle of the pool, with flowers and other plants growing out of it. Grass grew around the rocky shores of the great pool. As they walked along the rocky bank of the water, the witches howled like wolves. Prince Shamma was startled by the howling. "Don't be startled, young prince," David said. "These are the sounds of the agony they know is to come. The closer to the water they get, the more violent their response." They pointed their swords at the witches' throats as they moved. The witches struggled, trying to bite and scratch David and Prince Shamma. The giants moved closer, ready to intervene if the witches proved difficult.

King Black walked into the shallow part of the water. When the water got to his waist, he turned around. "David, keep them on the bank and make sure they can see what happens." David nodded as King Black smiled at the witches.

"This will be a display for you as well, evil ones."

The witches stood silently as David and Shamma pressed their swords firmly against the throats of the witches, making it impossible for them to talk.

King Black bowed his head.

"Oh great and powerful Lord, I come to You with great joy in my heart. Knowing that this love of mine you have blessed me with, is truly yours. I return her to You in the hope that You might return her back to me. Knowing that if it be Your will, Your power might be shown here this day. Through water she was born, and in this water, Your living water, she might be born again. Great tree of Moria, the one that restores all things, restore this daughter you have entrusted to me. For I will not fail in protecting her again; I promise with all that I am."

King Black kissed Sandy and lowered her into the water. Everyone looked on as tears fell from the King's eyes. Waiting for what seemed like hours, Remiel dropped on his knees, fearing the worst. Prince Shamma and David bowed their heads.

Like a volcanic eruption, water spouted up from the middle of the pool. King Black opened his eyes to look down at Sandy as she lay under the water. Her eyes opened and focused on her father's face. King Black's eyes lit up. "My Sandy! My Sandy!" He lifted her from the water.

The others jumped for joy and hugged each other while the two witches gazed in awe. Sandy hugged her father and cried.

"Daddy! I've missed you so much. I was scared I would never see you again. I didn't know what to do."

King Black smiled and smelled her hair. "I know! I know, my love. I promise I will never leave you again." King Black walked to the edge of the pool and David helped Sandy down.

Sandy hugged him. "David! Thank goodness you are OK. I remember you sending me to the forest and then the walls fell on you. I thought you were dead."

David laughed. "I was worried about you too."

Over his shoulder, Sandy focused on what she had assumed was part of the walls behind them. The seven giants stood, smiling. "Remiel!" She ran towards Remiel and he lifted her in his arms.

"Sandy! Sandy!" Remiel called as tears of joy rolled down from his eyes. "My friend, you are well now. And you remember who I am."

Sandy's arms went round his neck as far as they could. "Oh, Remiel. How could I ever forget you? Day and night you were with me. And that horrible earthquake! I was so afraid for you."

The rest of the giants came over to hug her. As she hugged Gabriel, who was the last in line, she saw a familiar face behind him. Prince Shamma. He was still holding onto the witches. They locked eyes for a brief moment and Michael, seeing the chemistry between them, grabbed the witches, encasing their bodies in his palms. Prince Shamma nodded his thanks.

Prince Shamma ran towards Sandy; Sandy ran towards him too. They hugged and kissed. Uriel covered Remiel's eyes, Raphael blushed as Zerachiel put his arms around him and the other brothers whistled and clapped. David turned to King Black, wondering if the display of emotion was OK. King Black read his mind and shrugged.

Prince Shamma stepped back and knelt before Sandy. "Sandy Black, Princess of Moria. I have never met a woman like you. Your beauty, wit, and courage are breathtaking. I have searched for a woman such as you but figured them to be as fables. Written of stories of old, not to exist any longer. I ask of you this day to do me the honor of being my wife." Sandy gasped.

David coughed to get the attention of the prince. Prince Shamma turned and David pointed at King Black. Prince Shamma, with much worry, turned to King Black who had a serious look on his face. "I apologize, great King. I have forgotten the order of things. If it would please you, I ask if I be worthy to take your daughter as my wife."

King Black smiled. "I could think of no better suitor than the cunning and brave Prince Shamma." Sandy squealed with delight and embraced Prince Shamma.

Michael got distracted and the witches tried to escape, but when they saw the shards of mirror in Gabriel's hands, they tried grabbing them. Remiel stamped his feet in front of them and they fell.

Gabriel handed the remains of the mirror to David. David thanked him and carried the mirror to King Black. "What is this tattered furniture you have with you?" King Black asked.

"This, brother, is the source of the witches' powers. With my eyes, have I seen them look into the future and ask it questions of things to come."

"You say this is the source of their power?" the King asked, looking at the now-useless mirror. The chains binding the two witches rattled as they shook with fear. "Let us see how powerful this mirror is."

King Black turned towards the water and threw the glass into the pool. The witches screamed, stretching their arms towards the water. David and Prince Shamma unsheathed their swords and forced the witches back as the pieces fell into the water.

The water bubbled at first. Then it ejected the pieces from the deep. Turning into a fountain of flame, the liquid-like flame enveloped the mirror. The witches' eyes widened as they watched the destruction of their source of power. The shards tumbled and burned as the rolling fire consumed them. Then it all vanished. The witches screamed and fell on their knees, defeated.

King Black turned to the witches. "Now, for your sentencing, I will not judge you even though I am King of this great land of Moria. One who is greater than I will judge you for what you have done. The Great Tree whose roots are planted firmly in this land will judge you himself. If your actions are deemed evil by him, you will be consumed by the living water. For no dead thing can dwell within the living water. And there is no sentence that I can give that will be harsh enough for how I see you. May you receive a righteous judgment now and forever."

Sandy was filled with disgust as she glared at the witches. Uriel and Raguel pushed the witches towards the pool.

"We can give you great riches, oh King of Moria," the witches pleaded. "We can expand your empire far greater than it is now. We can even provide you with a true heir to your throne."

Looking into their eyes, King Black laughed. "Your memories are very short, much like the rest of your lives will be. Seeing as the source of your power and abilities has been destroyed before your eyes and mine, your shallow statements must have come from a scroll of lies you had prepared for this very moment."

King Black laughed and turned to Michael.

"My friend, would you and your brothers be so kind as to assist these vermin into the water?" The witches screamed in protest. Uriel and Raguel kicked the two witches into the water.

The water turned dark as the witches sank. Then they shot out of the water, screaming in agony.

"This torment and pain you feel is only the beginning of your judgment," King Black yelled. "The Great Tree has spoken through his water of life in favor of himself. You have been found guilty of treachery and evil. The state you are in is how you will remain for all eternity. This water will wash your filth and evil from our lands. I leave you with these last words – may you never rest, and have no peace."

The water began to swirl, opening a deep dark hole in the middle of the pool. The witches were caught in the whirlpool and dragged deeper and deeper into the hole. The hole closed and the dark waters turned green. Soon after the waters were still and calm, the dark color fading away along with the green glow. The water became once again peaceful and emanating its original blueish hue.

"Daddy," Sandy called, "where's the queen?"

"She is next on my list. Let us go."

Chapter 20

THE HUNT

King Black, Princess Sandy, David, Prince Shamma and the giants emerged from the opening in the mountain. The citizens of Moria cheered when they saw the princess alive. Sandy gasped when she saw the tattered and dirty people of Moria. After greeting them, she looked around. Everything had changed. Part of the palace was almost ruined, the surrounding forest had lost most of its trees and the giants and every other person looked tired. *I'll need someone to fill me in much later,* she thought. King Black turned to David.

"Brother, it is time we took care of the final piece to this disaster."

Sandy looked confused. King Black touched her shoulder.

"My daughter, there is much we have to talk about once we return home. Until then, we go on a hunt. Are you ready to fly?"

Sandy smiled, excited. "You mean I can come with you this time?"

The King smiled back. "I told you I will not leave you again. Especially not after I just got you back."

Ithros, Ballah and the other dragons landed nearby. King Black turned to Prince Shamma. "I know I have given my blessing for my daughter's hand in marriage. But I will enjoy the company of my daughter for just a while longer." He whispered in his ear, "She rides with me."

Prince Shamma smiled and bowed.

"As you wish, my lord. I would never separate a daughter from her father."

King Black and Sandy mounted Ithros. David mounted Ballah, and Prince Shamma and the other dragon riders mounted their dragons.

"Great friend," King Black said to Michael, "if I may be so bold to ask of your help once more?"

Michael bowed. "Great King of Moria, you are now and will always be a friend of the giants. Is it to track down the witch you will require our help for?"

King Black nodded.

"Count us in," Michael said.

"Our hunting party is complete. Chef Tasty! I leave the beginning of the rebuild in your hands. I know that as long as you are here with the people there will be comfort for them, even if it is in the form of a large cake. Come to think of it, Chef, tonight there will be a celebration unlike any seen before. Use what you must to prepare a feast for the entire kingdom. Man and beast alike shall dine and dance together."

At this, Chef Tasty's eyes and smile grew wide. "Oh, my King. I will prepare a great feast for this celebration of life. You have never tasted food the likes of which I will create tonight."

King Black smiled at the thought of the night's festivities.

"I look forward to it, fine chef. For now, we have unfinished business." King Black pulled on the reins of Ithros and the dragons all took flight. Sandy held her father tight as they lifted off into the sky.

***

Exhausted and thirsty, the queen staggered through the forest. Smoke rose from her limp hair and her skin was itchy. On reaching a small pond, she fell to her knees, thankful she'd be able to quench her thirst. She cupped her hands and leaned forward.

"Aargh!" she screamed and jumped back. Crawling back to the water, she stared in horror at her reflection. Smoke rose from her limp hair. Her unbearable skin irritation had caused her to scratch and rip her skin. Half of her nose was gone, a large part of her right cheek dangled and blood streamed down her face and arms.

The source of her beauty was no more. Trying to relieve her itchy skin, she splashed water on her face. As she did, her soft, golden-brown skin turned greenish black. She now looked like her mother—a witch.

She covered her face and wept. "Mother! Where are you?"

She held her throat in shock. Her once seductive and beautiful voice was no more. It had become croaky and scary. She rose to her feet and the animals near her scampered off. She stared at the water and her grotesque figure trembled. She looked again. The water in the pond trembled. *Is it that bad?* More animals rushed by and the earth trembled. She put her ear to the ground and listened. She could hear the footsteps of giants. "King Black!" she shrieked in terror.

The giants were running like a hungry pack of wolves after their prey. She could tell they were closing in on her. She jumped to her feet and ran.

"If I can hide from you for just a while longer, I'll be able to find Mother's house; I'll be able to find the book of Nefaria!"

She scurried around, looking for the way to her mother's old house. To her dismay, she couldn't find it. The forest wasn't the same anymore. She found a burnt pathway and dashed down it. *I must get the book*, she thought. *With it, I can destroy King Black!*

***

High above the forest, the King flew with Sandy, clutching onto his armor as they scanned the forest below for the giants tracking the queen. Sandy saw Zerachiel leaping from tree to tree. "There they are, Daddy. Look!" She pointed at Zerachiel. He looked up and waved.

"Thank you, daughter," King Black said.

King Black signaled to the other dragon riders and they all changed course and followed the giants. The shadows of the dragons covered the forest floor below as they passed by. Remiel remembered the burnt path he took to the palace. He turned around, recalculated his position and bolted towards the east. His brothers noticed his change in direction and followed to see what he may have found. King Black and his men followed suit. From their vantage point, King Black and his men could see a clearing in the forest up ahead. Remiel reached the road he'd once traveled. The charred trees still smelled of smoke. He glanced back and forth, remembering the way he had come from. Looking up and seeing the King flying overhead, Remiel knew exactly where to go. He beckoned to his brothers and King Black to follow him.

The queen reached the end of the path. She stopped and glanced around. *This path looks familiar,* she thought. Dashing into the forest before her, she searched for the dirt path that led to her mother's house. She found it and hurried down the path. Excited, she didn't check to see if the giants were gaining ground on her nor did she check the sky for King Black. All she wanted was the book in her mother's house.

***

Remiel and his brothers stopped at the end of the road. The forest was too thick for the dragons to see ahead, so King Black and his men all landed. King Black, David, Sandy, Prince Shamma and the dragon riders dismounted.

Walking over to Michael, King Black unsheathed his sword. "I guess it's into the forest we go." He turned to the others. "Prepare yourselves, men; we don't know what power she might still have left in her bag of tricks."

Sandy tugged at her father's arm. "Umm, Daddy? Shouldn't I have a weapon of some sort?"

King Black looked back at Sandy and smiled. "I guess you're more ready for this than I had taken into account."

He pulled a dagger from under his armor and handed it to Sandy. "I guess you have some understanding of how to use this?"

Sandy smiled as she brandished the weapon. "Born in Moria, raised in Los Angeles. Of course I have an idea of how to use this. Now, let's go find that witch!"

Sandy turned around and saw everyone staring. "Did I say something wrong?"

As Sandy walked into the forest, her father tapped her on the shoulder.

"Your place is still behind me, my love."

A little embarrassed, she giggled. "Yes, Daddy."

The group made their way into the dense forest, looking for any trace of the queen. They heard a low rumble and Remiel stood still and checked to ensure Sandy was close. The rest of his brothers stopped and listened.

"I heard that the last time I was out here and it wasn't a good sign," Remiel told his brothers as they moved slower.

Uriel spotted some footprints in the sand going towards a dirt path. He motioned to the others to follow. Down the dirt path they went. Not too far ahead, the queen panicked because she hadn't found her mother's house yet. Feeling a rumble beneath her feet, she gasped. Zerachiel, atop a tree, spotted the queen. "There she is!"

She dashed off with King Black and the rest of the group in hot pursuit. Huffing and puffing, the queen saw a clearing ahead. *This is it*, she thought. At the edge of the clearing, she saw the giant ravine she'd made with her mother and grandmother. It was the same ravine that Remiel had fallen into. It had grown much bigger and stretched farther into the forest. Worse still, it had destroyed her mother's house. The queen stopped at the edge of the ravine as small stones close to her feet rolled down. Kneeling before the ravine, she wept. King Black and the group gained on her quickly. As they got closer, Zerachiel yelled, "There's a ravine ahead!"

A gust of wind blew and kicked up dust in the air. The queen turned around and faced them, but the dusty air hid her hideous face.

King Black walked towards her with his sword drawn chest high.

"You would dare try and take what you know to be mine? You and your evil kind deserve the fate that you will soon know."

The wind stopped blowing and her true nature was seen by all. Gasps emanated from the group and David covered his nose quickly as a breeze wafted towards him from the queen's rotting fish smell.

"So, my queen, or should I say, witch," King Black said. "We see each other for the last time."

She walked towards him with a sinister smile.

"I didn't expect to see you so soon. As you can see, I've

changed. I guess I have you to thank for that, as it was my mother and grandmother along with the power of the mirror that had kept me beautiful. Now look at what you have done."

King Black moved forward with his sword pointed at her throat. "Still your tongue, witch!"

The queen mocked him.

"Or what? You'll kill me as you've killed my family? I guess we will be even then, since I was the one who got your one true love to leave Moria in the first place. She was so protective of you." The queen cackled, "I told her she would be your undoing, causing you to lose the kingship because she was not a Morian."

The queen cackled again, delighted in the pain she had caused the King. The memory of the night the King's love left was running through his mind. Yet the King still had his sword extended towards her neck.

One morning, he was still in bed when she got up to check on baby Sandy. When she didn't return for a while, he got concerned. After searching for her inside the palace, he ran to the garden. There, the singing plants soothed Sandy when she cried. As he rushed out, expecting to see his family, all he saw was the back of his true love running away into the forest with Sandy. He tried to catch up, but by the time he got to the portal it was too late. How sad he felt that his one true love and young daughter had left him. A note lay on his bed when he returned to his chambers.

My love, it has come to my knowledge that horrible things could happen to you and to the land of Moria if I stay. I love you more than anything, and will not allow my presence to tear apart your world. It grieves me to my soul what I must do. Know that our daughter will be safe. And if anything should happen to me, I will send for you to come get her. My love for you is as the sky.

Never-ending. Goodbye, my love.

The queen's cackle brought King Black back to reality.

"Yes, my King. It was me who caused this pain in you, that I might be elevated due to my beauty. If it hadn't been for your daughter's return, I might have been able to totally complete the plan. But again, at least for my second act, I was able to destroy the next love in your life. It was with great pleasure that I sent that serpent to bite Sandy. I'm sure she saw most of what happened before it was too late to save her." She cackled in amusement.

King Black smiled at the queen as Sandy stepped out from behind him. "Oh, she thinks she's funny," Sandy said, enraged by the queen's words.

The queen's eyes nearly popped out of her head.

"The power you thought you had wasn't yours to use, witch. The waters of Moria have made Sandy's life anew, and judged the last of your kind. Now, it is time for you to be judged." The queen yelled and she charged at the King. Sandy jumped in front of her father.

"This is for my momma."

Sandy punched the queen in the face, knocking her back towards the edge of the ravine. King Black, shocked at Sandy's reaction, grabbed her so she wouldn't get too close to the edge. The ground rumbled and fire shot out from the ravine. The ground gave way under the queen's feet and she collapsed into the ravine, tumbling over and out of sight. King Black and all those with him backed away as the ground rumbled the more. Grabbing King Black and the others, the giants ran back towards the dragons. As they reached the clearing, King Black, Sandy and the others mounted their dragons and lifted off into the sky. Hovering over the ravine, no sign of the witch was found. The giants sprinted towards the palace as an earthquake rattled the forest floor. High above the forest, King Black and the other dragon riders watched the ravine collapse and become a plain.

"Well I guess from the ground she came, and back to it she has returned," King Black said.

Sandy smiled. "Good one, Dad."

They saw Wajenzi attacking one of the last dark trees in the forest. The ravine and the earthquake had sucked down most of the dark trees near Moria, and a new beginning had started in the land of Moria. New passages and places sprang up. New paths and places to explore were coming to be; a new genesis was upon them.

The birds sang again as the forest came back to life. Trees and animals sang together with the birds as King Black landed at the gates of Moria. The palace was prepared for celebration, thanks to Chef Tasty. Lilly ushered Sandy to her chambers. Chef Tasty and the twins were in the kitchen, cooking. King Black, David and Prince Shamma walked down the main corridor of the palace. King Black stopped for one moment to admire a portrait of Sandy's mother. He kissed two of his fingers and placed them on her lips. They continued down the hall as one of the manservants rushed to meet King Black.

"Sire! We need help. We don't know what to do with the doctor."

King Black was confused. "Which doctor?"

"Let me handle it," David said with a devilish grin. "You and Prince Shamma can go ahead."

Doctor Cain was tied up and surrounded by servants in the dungeon. "What will you do with me?" he asked David.

David moved closer so the doctor could see him clearly.

"Ah, it is you, who I loved playing with."

The doctor's large yellow eyes grew brighter as he took in the sight of David's face. David smiled as he walked over to the doctor's place of imprisonment.

"Yes, I do remember the games you liked to play so very well."

David glanced around the dungeon he was once held captive in and noticed some of the doctor's instruments of torture.

"Doctor Cain, you have been in this land since before the wars began. You were the very first prisoner in this dungeon. The sentence that fits your crime would be death. But knowing well the curse that was given you for your original sin, you won't get that. You have already been judged with a verdict that neither I, nor my brother, can overturn. This has now forced me to be much more creative with how I might deal with you. Especially after our recent past together; a most memorable experience, I must say."

David motioned the men with him to take the doctor to the darkest and deepest cell in Moria.

"Doctor Cain, for your crimes against the people of Moria and your allegiance with the evil witches of old, you will spend all of eternity in the deep. There you will live out time, watching your original sin continuously."

David followed behind as the men dragged Doctor Cain down a spiral staircase. On getting to the end of the stairs, the men opened an iron door and threw the doctor into a pitch-black room. The door was sealed behind him. David's voice rang out through the darkness. "Enjoy the show."

In the dark room, Doctor Cain saw a glowing mist that poured out from the walls. As he looked around, trying to make sense of what he was seeing, the mist slowly turned into drops of water upon the walls. Soon the walls were covered in water that pooled over them. As the doctor looked on in fearful anticipation, the water gave off the same blueish glow as the pool of living water. On the walls the water showed images that started to move and became a video of the doctor's life. More like a cinema, it showed a young Doctor Cain and the death of his brother. He was doomed to watch his most serious crime forever. He screamed in agony as he watched.

The palace hummed with activity as servants hurried around preparing for the night's festivities. The giants had been taken to the ballroom so they could freshen up for dinner. Prince Shamma and the King stood on the indoor balcony that looked over the entire kingdom at work.

"Everything has happened so fast," King Black said as he stared at the sky. "It seems like it was just yesterday that Sandy returned home." He turned to Prince Shamma. "I am very pleased that you will be marrying my daughter. I know she will be well taken care of. I also know she will make a beautiful queen."

The prince bowed. "Great King, I will have you know that I do not plan for the ceremony to take place until there has been sufficient time for you and Sandy to be reacquainted as is your right."

King Black, surprised by Prince Shamma's words, placed his hand on the young man's shoulder.

"Your father has taught you how to be a good man. It is time we prepared for the night's celebration."

The King motioned a servant to show the prince to a room so he could freshen up for the night.

***

Birds chirped and sang in the great garden. All the animals drank from the waters that flowed through the garden. Eve, still planted near the Great Tree of Moria, awakened from her blissful state. Within her, the still, small voice of the Great Tree spoke. "Eve, it is time you went to your friends. It is time for you to see all that is new, and tell of what you have seen here."

Eve, understanding the message and job she had to do, retracted her roots from the bank of the water. The animals gathered around to say their farewells as she turned to speak to the tree.

"I thank you, great and wonderful one, master builder. I will go to my friends and tell them of all I have seen here. And all that you have made new, that is what I will I tell them. Will I be able to come back to this place?"

"Eve, there is still much for you to do before with me you stay, my child. Now that you know me and have been in my presence, this place is now inside you. There is no need for you to feel far away for I am always near. Now, I have given you a purpose and a task to finish. Go, rejoice and sing, be merry and spread good cheer amongst all the inhabitants of the forest. The tree of life grows this place anew."

Eve bowed before the Great Tree and turned to leave. The birds flew through her branches and leaves and the other animals ran around her trunk, wishing her well as she made her way out of the garden.

***

Night had come and the palace of Moria was aglow with lights and excitement. Music and laughter filled the air. Men and women held hands and sang. Children and animals played and made joyful noises. Torches were lit and fireworks painted the sky with brilliant colors. Food of all sorts decorated every table.

A trumpet sounded and drums rolled as noise and commotion ceased. Two of the manservants announced in unison, "Great citizens of Moria, please stand and honor him who we are thankful for. King Black and Princess Sandy!"

The crowd erupted in applause as King Black and Sandy walked down a red-carpet runner, and dragons spat flames high into the sky. Sandy smiled and waved as she made her way to their table. Dressed in a long blue ball gown, her gold crown sparkled on her silky long hair. King Black was dressed in his ceremonial black armor with long flowing cape, and crown atop his head. The seven giants stood at the base of the stairs, waiting for Sandy and the King. They were dressed in fine white linen robes with their individually colored vests on. Michael wore red, Gabriel wore blue, Uriel wore yellow, Raphael wore green, Raguel wore white, Zerachiel wore purple, and Remiel wore orange. King Black and Sandy greeted each of them and the crowd cheered. They took their seats as Prince Shamma's presence was announced. He sat at the King's table too. David was already waiting for them atop a small staircase. The applause and cheering continued. Fireworks erupted as the King and Sandy stood and waved to the people. King Black stood, raising both hands, and the crowd became quiet.

King Black lifted his goblet of wine. "Great people of Moria, I salute you this night. Without you, this land may have been lost to the powers of darkness. But all of you, each and every one of you, played a role by not being deceived and following that witch. If you had not stood your ground, I fear this night would not be possible. It is to all of Moria I salute this night and say thank you for your bravery and courage."

The King raised his goblet higher and the crowd did the same. As glasses clinked, Sandy noticed some sunflowers. She peered at them and they opened their eyes. "Hey, Princess! My, how you have grown. Girl, look at you all grown! You are beautiful."

Sandy smiled as she remembered the flowers from the palace

garden. Sandy gasped, surprised.

"Yeah, you thought that witch had done something horrible to us, right? Seeing how horrible she was, we remained still like we were dead. But old Chef Tasty woke us up in the kitchen by telling us he was going to use us as a garnish if we didn't talk to him."

Chef Tasty walked up to Sandy when he saw her speaking to the flowers.

"Yes, Princess," said Chef Tasty. "I found these flowers lying still in what was left of the plants in the garden. Almost everything had been destroyed, but it seemed as though these two were in shock."

"Yeah," the flowers said, "we were in shock from that witch's ugly face."

Sandy smiled. "Well, she is gone now. I'm glad you're all right. Thank you, Chef Tasty, for helping my friends."

Chef Tasty nodded. "Don't forget to tell me how much you liked the food."

King Black continued with his speech. "People of Moria, I must confess a lie to you this night. I must right a wrong made years ago - to you and those closest to me."

The attention of all in attendance was on the King. King Black turned to David.

"Brother, will you come here please?"

David and the King stood before the people.

"Citizens of Moria, the man whom you know to be David, my most trusted servant, is not just a humble servant. The truth of his identity lies in the portal to the earth realm."

The crowd was in shock. Sandy was confused.

"David is my elder brother?"

The crowd started murmuring. "Long ago, my father came

across this doorway and fell in love with a young woman. They had a child but hid his identity by making him a common citizen. They did this because they feared the citizens of Moria would reject him. After I came of age to be King, my father brought us both together and told us the truth. Since that time David has watched over me as an elder would. Our father made us vow to keep this secret."

Sandy rose to her feet. "You mean you are the uncle I never knew I had?"

Sandy ran and embraced David.

The King continued, "He has been my most trusted friend and protector for so many years. Please forgive me for hiding this from you. From now on, David is no longer to be seen as a servant of the King, but a member of the royal family. As my brother."

The crowd went quiet and the giants rose to their feet, unsure of what might happen next. Then a voice from behind yelled out, "David Black!"

With one voice, the crowd chanted, "David Black.

David Black.

David Black."

King Black raised his brother's hand and the crowd cheered. King Black grabbed his goblet to make another toast.

"My people! To David!"

The people shouted and drank. The King raised his glass again. "To our new friends before us." King Black walked down the steps to the giants.

"I must thank you with all my heart. I extend to you the freedom to come and go as you please in my palace. Your presence is most welcome any time. For if it were not for you, my Sandy may not be with us today. I hereby appoint you watchmen over the land of Moria." The people cheered and whistled as the King placed badges with the symbol of the Kingdom of the Black Rose on it, a black rose encircled by a dragon, on the vests of each giant. King Black raised his glass one more time.

"And last of all, I make a toast to Prince Shamma, who has asked to marry the princess. I have given my blessing."

The crowd erupted into cheers again. Sandy and Prince Shamma waved to the crowd. King Black climbed up the stairs to his seat.

"My people! Eat, drink, and be merry."

The party continued with singing, laughing, dancing and games. Chef Tasty stood, watching the crowd stuff themselves with food. Lilly walked up to him and hugged him. Then she planted a kiss on his cheek. The large chef burst into laughter.

Sandy and Prince Shamma taught the giants how to dance, Raphael was busy stuffing himself with food, Raguel and Uriel were having a competition on who could eat the most. Gabriel was surrounded by about twenty women who wanted to dance with him. Remiel and Zerachiel made fools of themselves on the dancefloor with Sandy. Michael laughed as he watched his brothers have fun.

The celebration lasted all night long. Not a single person got tired or retired to bed. Everyone danced and had fun till morning.

The next morning, a drowsy Sandy yawned, ready to retire to bed. Facing the forest, something caught her attention. She rubbed her eyes. "Eve!"

Sandy ran down the steps yelling Eve's name. The giants, King Black, David and prince Shamma followed. Sandy ran into Eve's arm-like branches.

"I've missed you, Eve!"

"I've missed you too, young princess."

"I didn't know what had happened to you. Did you make it to the Great Tree?"

Eve smiled. "Yes, Princess. I was in the great garden with him. It is the most beautiful place I have ever seen. So peaceful and calm; there is no worry or doubt, fear or crying there. It is perfect in his presence. He sent me back to tell you all of it and to give the giants a gift."

"What kind of gift do you have for my friends?"

Eve turned to the giants. "Come forth so that you may see what is new. That which was lost can now be found. The desires of your collective hearts will now come out."

Eve directed the giants to look down a path that was still forming between the trees of the forest. Down the path, a camp surfaced.

As the giants looked closer, the inhabitants of the camp became visible. The giants' lost tribe, their home! Tears filled Michael's eyes as he and Gabriel walked towards the camp in disbelief. All the people were giants just like them. In the distance, an elderly woman giant with grey locked hair sat in front of a tent. She looked up and smiled. Michael couldn't believe his eyes. It was his mother! Michael became a child again as he ran up to her. She threw her arms around him and hugged him. His other brothers ran up to her as well as she embraced her children for the first time in so long.

"Momma!" they all cried out in one voice.

"Momma, we looked everywhere for you!" Michael said.

"Oh, Michael. I searched everywhere for you and your brothers. After the battle, the forest changed. We couldn't find anything in its place. Your father comforted me though. He assured me that you and Gabriel would know what to do. He said you'd make sure your brothers were safe."

The giants in the village surrounded them as they realized who they were.

"Momma," said Michael, "where is Father?"

The crowd that formed around them began to part. The Giant King Metranon, father of the seven, walked up to the tent. "I am here, my sons."

The great Giant King Metranon was old. He had a long white beard and he wore a multicolored robe and a golden crown. In his right hand was a staff.

"My sons, come to me."

He opened his enormous arms for them to come and embrace him as father once again. The people of the giant village burst into cheers. Their mother yelled out a chant in their native tongue. "Yipipaweo!!!!!" All went silent as the mass of giants moved into a circle around the brothers. Metranon raised his staff into the air and the earth started to tremble. The giants surrounding the brothers created a rhythm with one of their feet striking the ground. All at once the rhythmic group squatted down and growl as one. The rhythm to their feet continued as Metranon called out in their native tongue, "Ti Twa Tuli Tom ahwwl!!!" The brothers stood in awe as they were welcomed back to the tribe with the dance of the warrior. The coming of age ceremony of their people that they had not been able to receive in all of these years. Michael burst into tears. The rest of the brothers followed in emotion as the dance continued and the brothers struggled to keep their composure. The rhythmic rumble generated by the giants' steps was now causing a small earthquake. King Black and the people that looked on were at first concerned until Sandy calmed them, with a proud smile across her face. "Don't worry, this is their warrior ceremony." The chanting and stomping continued as rhythmic claps and slaps accompanied the melodic chant. Each brother's name was called out as the chant came to an end and the rumbling subsided. The brothers, a proud but very wet ball of emotion, stood before their people at last.

"Welcome, welcome, back to your home, Princes of Bangweulu."

The reunited royal family of the giants held one another. Through the crowd, King Black and Sandy made their way towards King Metranon.

"Great King Metranon, I rejoice at your reunion with that which was lost to you for all of this time. I also stand in awe of seeing you, as my father told me many stories of your meetings in the past. My father would be happy you are well."

Because of his age, King Metranon squinted to focus on the speaker.

"Yes, yes. I remember that voice. Very much like your father's before you; ah, a King you have become much in the vein of your father. I invite you to sit with us as we celebrate this wonderful moment."

King Black bowed at the invite. Sandy bowed too.

The two kings sat beside each other. The seven brothers took their rightful places next to their father to rule over their people. Remiel brought Sandy before his father. "Daddy, I have to introduce you to our friend, Princess Sandy Black, who has made all of this possible. If it wasn't for her, none of this would have happened."

King Metranon chuckled, seeing his youngest son had matured.

He leaned close to Sandy.

"Thank you very much, beautiful princess."

Turning to King Black, he said, "I see you have recovered a precious part of your life as well, great King of Moria."

King Metranon stood to address those in attendance. "Today, I will announce once more that the pact that has stood between man and giant for centuries will last forever!"

The seven brothers stood, bearing their weapons. King Metranon asked King Black and Sandy to step forward.

"Today, before the people of Bangweulu and those from the land of Moria, my sons and I offer our arms to you in gratitude and friendship."

All cheered and sang as the feast continued.

When it was all over, Sandy and King Black returned to the palace. Prince Shamma said goodbye to Sandy and flew home to tell his father of the news of battle, as well as his and Sandy's engagement. The giants' village was just outside the palace gates of Moria. Sandy and her father spent lots of time together. David was no longer known as the chief servant, but the brother of King Black.

As the King spent time with his daughter, David made sure things were normal at the palace. Chef Tasty sang and danced with his food, just like old times. Only this time, his background singer was his favorite of all. Lilly, his daughter, was back in the kitchen, helping her father. They sang, laughed and had fun. With evil vanquished and the threat gone, the citizens of Moria were merry. There are a lot of things to say and many more stories to tell. But you know how this ends. With a happily ever after and farewell.

The End

Deep within the forest, amongst ruins of times past, a round stone building covered in vines can be seen. Voices can be heard like whispers in the wind as leaves from the nearby tree Russell as the whispers move towards the structure. A loud cackle is heard, and the word is shouted out. Birds fly from nearby trees, and a stone door on the structure creeks open. Raise of light seep through the crack in the door and start to fill a dark room. In the center of the room is now visible a stone altar; on top of it, the dim outline of a man still enshrouded in darkness. The figure takes a deep breath as his inhalation fills the room. His hand comes into contact with the light and is dark brown skin covered in black tattoos that lead up his arm until the darkness of the room cuts off our view...

Book II
Coming Soon